DEVIL'S TRUMPET

DEVIL'S TRUMPET

TRACEY SLAUGHTER

Victoria University of Wellington Press

Victoria University of Wellington Press
PO Box 600 Wellington
New Zealand
vup.wgtn.ac.nz

First published 2021
Reprinted 2021

ISBN 9781776564170

A catalogue record is available at
the National Library of New Zealand

Published with the assistance of a grant from

ARTS COUNCIL OF NEW ZEALAND *TOI AOTEAROA*

Printed by Bluestar, Petone

For those who give me shelter:
my sons, my friends, my lover.

Contents

stations of the end   9

Stage Three   21

the receiver   27

Fisheye   38

Never Tell Your Lover That His Wife Could Be
    Having an Affair   39

I still hoped the photos would come out well   41

Cicada Motel   43

25–13   51

three rides with my sister   64

why she married your father   66

jilt back   68

holding the torch   69

eleven love stories you paint blue   79

if there is no shelter   90

some facts about her home town   140 warpaint   146

I feel there's a young girl out there suffering   160

extraction   162

ladybirds   163

devil's trumpet   170

god taught me to give up on people   175

dorm   177

What You Don't Know   179

compact   193

the deal   195

if found please return to   196

point of view   206

list of addictions in no special order   219

ministry   227

the best reasons   228

postcards are a thing of the past   230

Acknowledgements   249

stations of the end

1. All that first day she felt happy and hellbent. Lost her sorry walk, just thinking of his smell. Slipped along landings at work, thighs coupling under her skirt. Stooping to sign documents, laugh see-through as a secret.

2. He had two daughters, but she didn't think about them. They were mainstays in a photograph he sent her, sweet vague blanks. One blond, one dark, standing on a wharf, either side of the body she wanted. She could taste the logo on his shirt where his chest broadened to circle them, feel the well-known stamp heat and stretch.

3. She comes down the staircase and the last five steps give her vertigo, a spinal tipping point that makes her gasp. Her wrists tingle, quarter-inched with blood. She gets misadventures of heartbeat. Her mind feels thick and wild. She can see him, out through the shallows of the carpark, the first meet, sharpening his voice into a cell.

4. Her house feels like a penitentiary. Guilt packs extra ribs into her breath. Dinner plates skid from her hands and she kneels in the grease, making slits in the ends of her fingertips. *Takeout instead, boys.* Porcelain and vinegar. Satellites of fat. The sound of a plastic bag feasting on her blood.

5.   *I want to drink you. And mess you up. Capsize and keep you there, shuddering under me. Kiss hard, talk haunting. Own every inch of your skin. Know the torque of your collarbone, friction of your thumb. Taste jaw & scalp & ankle. Stroke the tough rise of your cock under denim. Knock out your cufflinks with my tongue. Lie in the uncut grass while you graffiti my freckles. Have your grip twist a sunlight of roots through my hair. Do not send do not send oh do not oh shit Christ get me out of this.*

6.   Hotels.com sent her emails, offering her *Secret Prices.* They said she could *Now Pay Lower Prices than Everyone Else! For a Limited Time.*

7.   Sometimes, she did think of the daughters. She knew one liked music, so she thought of her fingers on the keys, small cold utensils of sound, fingerpadding loneliness. The other one was blond, so she saw her in a gang, a loud group of smiles, all depicting the latest Maybelline. Baby-oiled summertime thighs, and pixie in-jokes, and somehow-innocent fluoro shoelaces.

8.   *Congratulations, you've qualified for even more discounts! Now your Premium Room costs 20% less!*

9.   All of her days felt en route to him. It didn't matter what she was doing. She would watch herself doing it, hearing her voice, when she finally reached him, telling him. Today I . . . whatever. And whatever. And whatever. It was just a sound to make, across the humming surface of his skin.

10. Pressed down on the whetstone of his fingers.

11. He marked her neck, a terrible stroke of bruise that soaked into layers of sinew. She panicked in the mirror, staring at its flooded purple silks. It thudded like a beacon. It bookmarked her throat, like a page he would go back to read bloodier later. She spent days fluttering, stalling her husband, turning her head. Laundered blouses she hadn't worn in aeons. Chose words carefully above flimsy collars, unchic, pussybowed. Nothing was ever said.

12. For days she dreamed about the first kiss. Would he catch her by the tailbone, jack her quick skirt, would they lumber to the wall – a cinema feat of kiss, kickstarted by a look and clattering the hot halls of some darkened house. Or would it be withheld. Heads in a soft buzz of axis that neither brushes or nuzzles, but sends volts of absent touch across their scalps. Till their mouths meet, hesitant. And perishable. Would she let it happen at all. Could she not?

13. It's the little things that break her. Like her husband calling for a grocery list. So she can hear him, the traffic in his voice, the steering, the mechanised breeze mixed with easy listening, the radio station she always used to tease him for, a lame pick of 50k stick-to-the-speed-limit hits. On his way to be thoughtful, to stop at the supermarket. To ask about things, what they're out of, to have her check the fridge. So she stands in front of it, open, staring, at its cool blue rack, at its clammy shelves, and can hardly say what they're low on, what they've used up, avocado, maybe kale, can hardly say eggs. Hopes he doesn't buy her flowers. His voice sounds like it's considering handing her some tulips, in festive sprays of plastic.

14. She's all about his musk. Obsessed with the thick block of bone that is his thumb joint, the pale corner seam (so parched, so male) of his mouth. She's about the countdown of buttons, the business of cotton getting shed, the hot cost of it all come undone. The cufflinks she wants to taunt him about, their clicky inlaid stone miscellany, because somehow they remind her of what he must have looked like dressing up as a kid. Reruns of locked office doors. Seconds when he straightens, to stare at her in ultra-silence.

15. She notices things about her boys. The way the birthmark of the oldest has faded, elongated so its ragged edges pull on his shoulder like a blurred red wing. The blunted stink of their rooms, each with its different top-note of sabotaged schoolbag, arsehole, saltwater, bare feet, cigarettes. The twitch of strawberry growth on the chin of her baby, so his grin juts prickly with softness. The sound of old stored paintings they once made her, stiff pelts of paper dyed to a crackling wash, their coasts and boats and birds and buildings losing their outlines to a dry haze that turns everything blue, their tiny cornered signatures sticks. They're so big now they can grab her in the kitchen, if there's food to be played up for, to give her steep blank hugs. The indents of their dog-eared t-shirts, the yanked hems and scuffed guts and chewed-out trim. The way the middle one has to sit in the leather sofa, learning to click his fingers, a complicated rig-up of goofy elastic flicks, trying to make his lovely skin sound tougher.

16. She buys a special pencil for the periphery of her mouth, fills in its long-lasting lie with fresh hibiscus.

17. She'll play for hours, kiss-lazed, with those cufflinks, bobbling them round in her palm while they're talking, naked, nothing but flat-out love going into their knucklebones of steel construction.

18. There was a third daughter. She was small, blue, born dead. The room she was delivered to must have been vinyl-lined and silent. There must have been a hover of wheeled machines not breathing. Tubes and dials unhooked, clicked back. Purl-stitched white wool packed into tissue, spiderweb ivory boots. Ribbons expecting family. A capsule, rented, with a sterilised seatbelt, for the ride home.

19. He sends messages, brief, blunt, knowing. Imperative. His words may as well be fingertips, working the flesh between her pelvic bone, raising thick roses of flesh, leaving her plush.

20. Then, at work, when the days have lost count of her, she sits under a rotating fan and thinks of the circles they're turning and turning in, everything stale and literal and jaded, no way out of the circuit that shifts waste air back into her worn-out mouth, which spits the same phrases, *we can't keep doing this, we have to stop, meet me now, I want you, I'm not ready to break this off, I can't I can't*, on binary sequence, so they're always at a start, or at an end, and either way, ergo, fucking ergo, it's hurting, hurting, outright hurt. She tries to stay calm amidst the smokefree working-day light, to index things, action them, audit them. But sits among the hardware, and stares along the palings of her desk, like the answer might be lying

somewhere on it, she can tap it out on the keys, test the focus of the screen and it will manifest – something curative, wise, something resolved, a pledge, something ultimate. A way forward: she would sign now in blood. But all she can feel is the fan, the yawn of it, heavy and implacable, no other options.

21. She thinks in lousy lame words like *caress*. They start to spread their dumb sugar over everything. Gaze in a sappy haze, memory sloppy with half-cooked pictures all involving softest skin. She writes things like *long* and *yearn*, stops short, thank God, at *burn*, tries to ignore *fate*. Bites her fingernails down at the thought of her meant-to-be stupidity. Her dopey idiom. A new dictionary of dizzy and squish. Makes herself write things like *prey*.

22. She would like to be a butterfly pinned to velvet, stretched out and staked down by each tiny cufflink, wrists and insteps engraved by little black bad endings.

23. The bleached crop circle the oldest one leaves on the lawn where he likes to pee out his bedroom window, a late-night jet he thinks she doesn't guess, though she can hear him through her insomnia, covert, levering open his hatch, and letting go a two-storey iridescent sizzle.

24. She can't make herself feel like a villain. But she is. Doesn't it give her these little kicks? She gets sultry, surefooted with her own wrongdoing, moving in her clothes all filmy and succulent, the pink hinge sending up bolts of electricity, so her trunk glides around, indifferent, gauzy, blissed. Yes, yes. The uncut version coursing through

her. Everything else feels so Old Testament. Watch her. Honeymooning on the thought of him, inside the true colours of her loose dress.

25. The way all three boys watch cartoons, picking their noses companionably, unperturbed by one another, tipping the skull to work in a deep finger, puffing away at their overhanging fringe, eyes glued to the anime, its primary wide-eyed dazzle, its stylised clash, testing viscosity with little dabs, digging out dry scales. Eating off an unthinking hand.

26. *You've Been Given Something Special! You're Now Eligible for 50% Less!*

27. She feels like she's walking masked through the house, an impostor. She hears her voice manufacturing sound. She worries she'll choke on some counterfeit phrase, something she's always meant, so easy, *love you too, see you later*, which now feels as hollow as the possible alibis she keeps listing, *I'm picking up X, I'm working late*, the best clichés she can spin, which sicken her to utter. Though she still updates the list.

28. Flocked cotton, white ribbons, all expecting breath. A muslin-swaddled shape they must have had to pass each other. Then pass back. He must have sat in the vinyl-lined room and wept with his wife. He must have held her blue hand.

29. Inconsolable things happen inside her chest. Spaces pull between bone, making sobs of deep vowel she has

to anchor herself to weather through. The longing turns her heartbeat to leather, a swollen thing moving with a terrible sloth, stiffening, withered in the distant ribs, then punching a vast ache back into prominence. Goodbye lasts for two days. Neither of them can stick to it.

30. Lying in sheets, blown out, dedicated to sweat, not a single thing feels regrettable. His voice, hair-raising before, is a lullaby after, a smoky brand of comfort at her temple. Their vocation is to fuck, and the world outside of anywhere they touch is a desert. Like the agony outside a prayer.

31. How can her husband not be onto her, her scent – it must be coming off her in waves, dense indecent ripples of pheromone, salty odours of loaded hunger. How is the singing in her bloodstream not audible, the flinching of her featherweight heart. Seam wet as a full mouth.

32. She doesn't belong on his wife's sage carpet, doesn't belong by her well-appointed faux-marble bench. So she doesn't touch anything. The little manuscripts of kitchen lists, birthday cards, bills, another woman's blueprint on all of them, bunched and fanned into a bowl on the countertop, envelopes smudged with her quick homely efficiency. Little blots and grittings of sauce, stuck to them in that 6pm domestic clatter, all its din and sift. A half-hearted dish of near-junk marked with warmth and tomorrows and kinship.

33. It's not like she didn't ponder it – the steps she'd have to take to make it right. Some days when he doesn't get in

touch, she doesn't mope. Sometimes she feels released, cut free, level-headed again, temporarily restored. She can think in terms of a sensible trajectory, a guarded future, a solid outlook. Then she thinks of his hands and feels all the heat of her body, wanting to get them gloved.

34. She decides, from the image of his wife, she doesn't look right – she looks added on, collateral. The wristwatch she's wearing looks too big. Her sandals are serviceable, hefty. She's waving some morsel of barbecue in her hand, there's a frilled paper plate on her lap in a skid and there's a dog lounged against her, the blear of its jaw adored and slathering. A wide loose comfortable smile. It somehow reminds her of her husband's voice when he's on a business call, saying things like 'additional security'.

35. What happens when she nears him. Everything yields. The fix of his retinas, the point-blank range of love.

36. Stationed around the walls in frames of varied beige, his life, the one he's let her into. She shouldn't be here – it's a raid, an invasion – but stares at the minutiae in the pictures, their predictable sandy backdrops, their lineup of loved ones in shorts or first-ball frocks. Cricket pitches, school halls that glitter. Such an ordinary lovely cast to hurt. What stops her the most though: the small dome of plaster, a curved white plaque on a pink satin band. Five toe-buds in a curl above the sole shells. Dust in the creases of two ghost hands.

37. The blonde must have been the one who liked piano. A long pale hair on the mahogany stool they knock. Pages

of black staves and quavers she can't read. Splashed aside with their cumbersome symphony. The thud of her arse as he jerks into her across the keys.

38. *You Deserve a Special Getaway! Make Dreams Come True! Terms and Conditions, Additional Restrictions and Blackout Dates May Apply.*

39. *I want to know the smallest things: what your pillowcase smells like. Which way you curl when you sleep. How you breathe when you're angry (I want to make you angry). Claw & climb you. Kneel & never let you out my mouth. Never let you out, your hands locked under my dress, your head in my fists as you lick me to heaven. Dig through your shadows to the places you don't want to live. Sleep beside you, along you, too hard-fucked to dream, too tender to believe it could end. Keep talking. Roll you in dumb jokes & lullaby. Pash up like kids. Shield you. Map out your vertebrae. Find my way home in your voice. Send send send.*

40. At night, with her husband, she watches intrigues where people in threatening suits say *give me the flash drive* and no one ever surrenders, so the chase goes on, across ancient bridges that detonate, and glass towers that groan and collapse, to the highrise chic of industrial apartments where light glints gently off guns and exotic models' lipstick. People in silver couture who are gaunt and vigilant hold dinner parties trading piquant quips and the cordon bleu is laced with poison and nothing is ever terminal. Accidental heroes get enlisted, and things crash apart, hearts, aisles, sidewalks, cars, in eurekas of flame. There are venomous close-ups and slow-mos of

CGI injury. And the truth comes out, it always does, the case is hacked, the espionage is foiled. And she thinks of a range of sad outcomes, where probably nothing will be set alight, no gunpowder laid or bounty offered, no car bombs or kamikazes or killshots, no microdoses of toxin stirred into unsuspecting polystyrene cups. But everything will just . . . be over, all the same. She sits by her husband and thinks of it: her world, pulled quietly sky-high, just floating apart.

41. She's surprised on the day though, when he makes a quarry of her wardrobe. She hears the noise of footfalls, and yes, it sounds focused, but not stressed. Then light through a window starts tapering. Her husband is outside, in kerosene vigil, the can dumped on the grass, gutted. She gets as close as she dares, but there's a radius around him, and she knows what's in it: knowledge. It's a low-intensity flame at first, a modest kind of melting. The colours twitch nervously, embossed. Then faceted bits of fabric rise, tongues, flagging necks. An effigy of her. He's got something from the shed he's using as an oar, netting more clothes, feeding the fire their thrash. The heat must be blistering, but he's staying in it, dipping, patient, funerary. The house behind her is slowly made of boys' heads, looking out, at the scent.

42. In the photo with his daughters on the wharf, the catch is strung behind them, a glisten chained up to a frame. Another man poses by it, triumphant. There's a smear that might signal a fin, still twitching. She cannot see its head, but she feels its unhooked mouth, its rubbery hang in the sunlight. She cannot see the eye, but she feels it

behind his daughter's head, neat and vacant and wet as an exit wound. She thinks of how they won't be able to breathe when he tells them. She thinks of how her father once took her down the back steps of her house and told her. Then threw her back.

Stage Three

I gave her cancer in the end. It seemed like the best thing. I
picked out a funeral, a finger down the column in the local:
it was all too easy. One of those prefab chapels in the next
town had overlapping services in three suites: I could just park
under the lineup of trees and take my time choosing which
one. I liked the shoes on a girl I followed to the green room,
the front all glass on a bulldozed rise where they were going
to pour a pond: they had stage-three posters in the foyer, with
pink flowers planned in the water and buddied-up ducks. The
coffin was nice and closed. Some third cousin staked out the
arch you had to file through with dead-girl flyers. In her photo
she was sipping a cocktail and didn't know she was going to
be compost. There was luck in the happy-hour lipstick and
the umbrella was a yellow one, stretched on its toothpick
half-life. You could just feel someone saying 'Cheese'. But I
shot so those programmes stayed off-camera: I picked up the
chrome and the long necks on the flowers and the hiccups in
the crowd. Front and centre there was a hunch of family in
the green velvet seats. There was a nana with pantyhose the
colour of peanut butter and cut-price flowers on a self-belted
dress that still had a drizzle of breakfast down the bust. Her
voice shook all over the hymns, which was a good clip. All the
best friends blinked off their makeup while her voice wheeled
up to God on an epileptic high: I got my close-up. It got a

lot of hits. The jack on the shoes of the girl who'd led me in kept her teeth gritted, steep at the ankle to the point she had to stagger to sing. But a quarter-hour in she caught grief like a nosebleed: her head dropped forward and rocked and her lopsided bun got loose like honey. You wouldn't have thought she'd be the one.

Something about the green made it look like a cancer funeral. I took time transplanting it. Bits of the service were like jigsaw that I'd jammed in, but no one checked. People online believe in cancer. I'd posted as her aunty, after the opening blurb that she'd lost her fight, asking her friends to vote for which pic I should use on her funeral handout. But I already knew which one would get the thumbs-up. She had a face made for selfies, the kind you can't shoot in a bad light – nothing but sun and goodness sticks. So there was a gallery of teeth ringed with ColorStay, swatches of hair tossed back from the crown and frosted tight, cheekbones curving like plasticine. She was brand Cancer. No one wanted aftershots. No one asked for close-ups of her scalped and cornered in Ward Six, the ties of her beige gown tagging the bolts of shadow in her downhill spine. But I had a back-catalogue of shots. I could zoom in on details: I did the chuck jug rinsed on the locker waiting for her next gutsy solo, I did the slouchy sack of gels pegged up to slither to the white X of tape that marked her line. I did the endless screw-tops with their apricot glow and their rattle of toxins. No one checked the meds. Grief did for the fineprint. At least, it did for a while. And I wrote her off fast. I got her in the body bag before anyone could ask for flight times. I got to the Silver Shores funeral home and tracked the sad crowd filling the green fibro suite before anyone could try clearing miles in a rental car to pay in-person tribute. I had it sussed. I remember standing in the foyer after the service and smirking with faux pain at the girl I'd followed in her smudged up-do and high-rise shoes. She was one of those women whose face isn't there until it's painted into place: her lids were half-cocked now in a run of mascara, and she was angling her cellphone screen to swab the mess. But it was beyond fixing. She sloped around a lipstick but I watched her mouth keep trembling under it. Mid-river the kohl blinked straight back off. I took a lot of her. I was impressed. Her eyes were under a solid inch of tears.

The night I first posted as her, I remember a preacher being on television. Past his toupee there was a widescreen of blue planet doing 360s in space, and there were pillars that boxed it, budget-temple style like the green room I'd later let her die in. The subtitle said he was a doctor, but he was tinted orange and wore a polka-dot tie. Things like that cancel holy out. He was on about turning points and one of the pillars had gospel flashed up so you could store the numbers for later, blips of digital scripture you could take in the dark like painkillers. I flicked over and there was a show about hoarders, tiny old ladies moving in slow-mo shivers through trenches of plastic bags. There was one headcase in a floral frock, upwards of eighty with a dwarf for a kid and the dwarf got stranded on the reef of cans, microwaves and curtain frills until I couldn't stand to watch her trying to scale the landfill with her subhuman limbs. They picked an old pan out the bank and tipped it on camera and a tongue of slime came out that felt like the image of the puke that was gluing my diaphragm. Everything inside me felt past its use-by. The garbage was neck-high. I put up her photo and that she moved around a lot and how she was a part-time temp. I joined her up where girls with other profiles like hers were tilting them at all angles, arms outstretched so the flirty cut of their jaws caught the light. I left cute captions, I hashtagged her into place. She liked peeling her boyfriend's sunburn. She liked distressing retro tees. She liked friends that mixed her playlists not even for like a birthday or anything. I nailed her dumb candy chatter, I hijacked her cover-girl pics. OMG it was so easy. By the end of the first night I was already thinking about where her tumour should be.

In the café close to the Silver Shores the sky went photonegative, a kind of dark you could not have predicted for the day: until then the funeral was backed by sun. I got the two of us – me and the grief girl – a table by the window with lime vinyl seats, and a dragnet of birds moved left with the weather behind them. In the small room her eyes were a liquid compass. A waitress scuffed over to dump a couple of offhand plates, but she didn't want what I'd ordered. She played with the strap on her discount clutch and said things about the deadgirl that she couldn't end: her throat kept glitching. Her talk was dotted lines. The scenery went so dark it stopped making sense. She stared at her shoes like she never chose their height, just woke up and found herself balancing on them. Grief made her look preloaded, but her breath smelt like the sandwich I told her she needed to chew to keep up her strength: after all she was the BFF – that meant duties, like a matron for death. Halfway to her mouth it mostly stopped for memory: losing somebody leaves a slideshow like that. You could see in her face how the images clicked. The deadgirl at New Year's, the deadgirl wagging school, the deadgirl monkeying around after lights-out on camp – all the fun lucky stuff that should never have stopped. The deadgirl broadsiding in her boyfriend's car. She felt so ripped off. Outside the place was crawling with clouds.

She was talking to me shorthand, like the language of couples. But I knew it wouldn't last. The café looked like a bunker, and she couldn't see me through sobs. I wanted to dip my finger in the tear banked up in her right eye, test it for preservatives.

The deadgirl had been a near-perfect fill-in – if they'd had the lid up I could have shot her headless. They'd probably disinfected her in the right clothes, got the satin lining to ring her in those stagy zig-zags. I could have taken her from the lapels down, hands stiff at peace around a shrinkwrapped rose, long-stem. But still there was traffic on the feed I set up. Like I said, they didn't want the aftershots. They wanted her capped in her graduation pose between the silk trees, their beds of high-end pink stone. Her squealing in the dorm when the showerblock housed a prehistoric cockroach. Her on all fours playing peek-a-boo with her sister's brat. But none of it seemed as real as the view from that café. I'd known I couldn't make her stay. The sulky waitress had done another handover of ham-frilled white, but her eyes started drying. The lemon checks on the plastic tablecloth sprawled. The whole place felt pranked by the cat on the neon fridge that kept waving a motorised paw. I went to the bathroom like I could breathe there. But I could smell lotion going cool in her shadows and the plexi-petals fading out in the mini-tub of flowers. The toilet exit told me *Open this Door Carefully. Someone May Be on the Other Side.* But I knew when I did she'd be gone. I paid and left to the waitress's blatant smile.

Red light green light the expressway back from Silver Shores was packed. I tailgated a dust-bowl van that someone had tagged the screen of: *I once saw a woman whose T-shirt read GUESS so I said "   ".* You could see the pixels of fingertips, but no answer. It seemed like hours I blinked into the gap. When I pulled home I cut the funeral to bite-size frames, and added cute catchwords. I blurbed the aunt's send-off. I looted every sweet crummy thing that gets chatted on death by people who are safe and clueless, did a remix. But I did think of her eyes marinated, the tangerine polish topping her long nails counting off the forks in the canteen, their failure to glint. And all of the photos that came out her mouth, like details that should have been taped to the coffin. I was happy with the goodbye playact by the time I hit the last key. The trashy grief came in, like after like. *#RememberHerLikeSheWas.* *#ShesInABetterPlace.* The thing is: so what. After the service, there'd been a blank book in the foyer, pen strung on with tassel, the word *remembrance* misspelled with crystal on the spine. You queue up, leave wishes, as if they count for shit. Not like I bothered with a close-up of that. The stage-three ducks went on travelling in pairs, on hazy slalom through promotional heaven. Everyone crossed the consolation sage of the carpet to squeeze each other's goosebumped arms. Nana got anchored on a vinyl bench and cat-napped, making low-oxygen moans. Her head dropped back so you could see the ruts, blue with useless hymn in the chamber of her mouth. The fluoro lights gave a couple of flicks, which made everything look like it was loading for an instant. By the time I'd shut her page down and gone outside a heavyweight wind had come up. I could lie down to watch it crossfire through all the leaves that could never hope to hold on. I'm no fan of dreams, but I knew if my eyes closed that dwarf would still be in there, rustling her walls of handmade trash with taps of stunted love. Hell isn't other people.

the receiver

By 9pm at his son's eighteenth party, he's lost in thoughts of his first girlfriend's voice. He's sitting over a glass of merlot – huh, sad joke in itself while the kids have got coolers of ice crammed with premix poisons, neon twist-tops that match the fizzy soundtrack of techno feeding back off his garage door – and he can actually feel the tremor of memory that comes with his first girlfriend talking, the breastbone thrum he used to get from lying on the floor of his bedroom listening to her down the phone. Checked out to everything but her tone, a station only he could tune to – those long afternoons he was all about her voice.

That garage of teens getting messed-up in the background now wouldn't know what he was on about – they're all permanently on their phones, but never to talk. *Why don't you just call her*, he'd said to the boy he spotted out on the driveway minutes before, tapping stress-signals into the face of his phone, trying to get hold of some girl who'd stood him up. The boy had shot him an *uh-duh* blink and gone on working the screen, his fingers top-speed, sodium-lit. But what would they know? He felt sorry for them, missing the teen bliss he'd once lived for – crashed on the carpet with the cord spiralled out to its max, receiver buzzing in the crook of his collarbone, mouths turning everything to lowdown murmurs of secret, heartrates hanging on each vocal hush. Staring up into the postered distance of his ceiling, he'd come out with daredevil things, bass blue mutters of horny sweetness he'd choke on if they were face to face, and he could read her breath, could feel that every cell in her still body listened, her skin all audience – how could these kids go without that? Those blurred kinky sentences of long-range lust, lying there helpless just at the clearing of a throat, at a phrase whose shaky static left him feeling x-rayed. These kids don't know what they're missing.

But they'd all had hardware, tonight's team of late-teens, when they walked in, him lined up by the door to get names and numbers, and notes off all the underage ones who needed parental permission to ruck a pop-top out that psychedelic ice. They held up their phones – they had direct lines back to Mum and Dad, and didn't need him checking in or jacking up lifts. *Yeah thanks*, they laughed, heading past him, *whatever*, into the rigged-out garage where the playlist was pounding. He stayed in the kitchen – from time to time now he totes out snacks, the same plastic platters of deep fries and additives that kid parties always pack, just washed down with vodka these days, the guaranteed ratio of puke at the end no different. In the kitchen he tips himself sly thirds of drink, at first in disposable cups, their synthetic stubbing his lip as he takes guilty slugs – but then he gives up and lets the burble of ageing richness colour a proper glass. An old guy's glass, full-bodied. The glass of a well-off thinking drunk.

He doesn't lean close enough to Mary to let her smell it when he takes her tray up. She looks at the bland balanced nutrients he's pureed and dobbed on her plate, and asks about the party food. He goes through the menu again: the onion dip and cardboard pizza, the skin-tight pods of red meat, the blood-clot sauce squelched into its tubs. She gives as much of a laugh as she can, a rustle on her slope of pillows. *Remember,* she starts, *remember* . . . but *no*, he says *no*. He knows where her recall is leaning: once, their son's parties were epic events, and she'd be frazzled in the icing-sugared kitchen, bashing butter mixture to lacquer, sporting an elasticated pirate hat, dizzy with pin-the-tail plans and stuffing goodie bags, crossing her eyes with low-oxygen swoons as her laughter spat off the end of renegade balloons, everything a singsong of jubilant panic, last-minute candles and jelly snakes and cellophane. He says, *no, not now, no don't*. So she lifts her good hand, makes a slow manoeuvre for the spoon, as if she'll obey and lap a mouthful. *You're right*, she nods, a tilt that pulls her eyes closed, lids traced with vessels in her thin stubbled head, *yes, let's just get through. Of course.* He tells her he'll send him up later, their boy. *Oh*, she says. *No, don't bother him. It's . . . enough.*

But it's not enough. He goes and stands awhile on the landing, listens to the beat jar the shell of the garage. The songs – well, not songs, but tracks in the worst sense – seem to him mechanised as treadmills, sirens marking the wind-up of some chanted slogan meant to be a chorus. They grind into his brainstem. He hates their processed riffs, their synthy adrenaline. He doubles back to check with Mary that she can manage the din. She gives a *no, it's fine, leave them, really*, blinks discoloured eyes. He heads back to the kitchen, a little more determined to get himself good and pissed.

Which is working out well. But it turns out that boy's up the drive again, this time out by the letterbox, holding his phone at the end of a skinny high arm, like he's guiding it through a current. Trying to flag a signal, climbing on the rockwall, raking the phone on a wilder incline, getting aggro with the air. He looks out-of-it in that way that teen boys do, sullen and breakable. He can't just leave the kid out there, lank and jumpy in the last of the light. So he scuffs up, tells him *the service here's shit on old makes. Still texting the same girl?* No answer, but the boy looks bummed out. *You could just call her? You know, the landline? Used to work for me.* The kid's scowl looks like it could turn to tears, and his fingers go hyper on the screen trying to counter it. *She your girlfriend? Bail on you or something? Wouldn't worry, mate. You know what they're like.* But he stops. It's in the kid's eyelashes, that giveaway tizz: he's blinking like mad, so he doesn't come unglued.

For fuck's sake – he's not up to dealing with that. He's hardly fit to keep someone else from the edge. So he shuffles there a couple of secs, watching the kid's antsy taps on the cell, the screen all pins and needles. Then he turns back. *Okay, look, the offer's there, you know, if you can't get through.* And he leaves the kid, wanders back. He can see a thin remnant of Mary through the upstairs window. A dilute quiver of light on her eggshell skull.

And there she is again – his first girlfriend. She'd lived in a cul-de-sac he'd cruise to, low-gear afternoons, lazy on his silver three-speed, so he'd have the sight of her, slipping to the letterbox, her flimsy dress shot to pieces with sun, and he'd pull up his ride, coasting through the last stretch on a solo pedal so he could swing a cool dismount, kick out its oily stand, and then lean in to kiss. And kiss. And kiss. All this was in slow-mo afterschool dusk, before the adults materialised, before they took the streets back over, and sat you down at tables with lists of disappointment and chores. So the kiss could go on, could be wholesale with soft wet longing and dizzy with wishful heat, and he could part-lift her in his go-getter hands and even start some hijinks with her bra and she could push at the slogan on his t-shirt and huff pleas in his neck until they were both a write-off. And the memory reminds him now of spoke-sound, his old bike in the spin of cool-down, their makeout full of the ticking music of time crisscrossed in his steel-string wheels. And even after that, he'd still want to lie down half the night, after getting past homework and mum-jobs, and corkscrew his fingers in her voice, lounge in the lull of saying near-nothing down the phone, just so the pressure of her breath was in his ear, the purrs that were her wriggling her p-j'd ribcage, the semi-puffs that were her clearing the feathers of her fringe out of her drowsing eyes.

But merlot should be good for memory. He doesn't mind if he helps himself – why thank you sir. Suppose he should check in on the eighteenth crew again before he gets too sauced. He's meant to be preventing any kids from getting dieselled – right now he gives zero shits. He interlopes, looking in from the garage door. He can't be bothered topping up their plastic banquet. The girls all wear their hair the same, in topknots that are ratty bubbles – their tanks, shifting in their half-dance of mingling chat, flick him cut-outs of inappropriate skin. That poor kid outside should have gone for one of these – it's a smorgasbord of open, easy-sussed girls, feet docked in sinister shoes, tinted to look tough, sure, but underneath it tender, needy even. Any one of these girls would take him. His son, for instance, is tied up with one blonde, a casual nuzzling going on. It makes him think of student parties back in the fall-down of derro villa flats, his own half-lit blunders with strange girls, into outbuildings where they'd stage long clinches, blurry and delinquent, hearing the floors beneath them splinter, their heavy breathing laced with southern cold and lead paint. Those brokedown houses seemed to license their boozed hookups, outbreaks of ramshackle kissing no one cared about, the welcoming suck of free-trade tongues. That's what he'd really studied at uni, while his first girlfriend waited at home – he would have fucked it for good, their future, if she ever knew. But he was a wily little bastard by then, knew how to deflect and soothe her, knew what comfort to send deep-barrelled down the phone. He knew his voice worked her, settled her, so she'd mimic it back, *forever babe, true.*

He looks at his kid. It's a noncommittal groping, the lads' talk around them still going on, his son looking bored and hard at the same time. At some point he breaks off the blonde's hold and nods at his father, smug and half-cut. *No worries old man*, he bawls out. And he waves his dad over, lurching his big warm arm, slapping his shoulder when he gets there, their gruff brand of love. *All good fulla?* he says to his dad, and of course it is, what more could any man tell him – he's eighteen, ignorant, strong as a king, the way he should be. You don't want to mess with this scene. He's a solid kid, a kid with mates and swagger and sweetly pissed girls lining up, and he's straight-up and good value, and he should be let off tonight. He won't end up untouched. His mum is wrecking a youth that was otherwise pretty fucking model, that was shaping up big-time. Let him fondle the odd random girl and knock back a few too many brews. What's the damage? You can count on that later. The damage will catch up.

Which is maybe when the thought of that sad kid, stranded outside on his cellphone, comes back in. He has got a duty. He's got more than one. He should doublecheck Mary, then hunt down that cut-off kid, see where he's skulking now. He's past trying to cover up the merlot – he loads up and weaves the hall with it, reckless, clubfooted. But the trouble with Mary's room is, it used to be his, be theirs. He's never wanted to leave it. He's never volunteered. He wanted to sleep beside her, even through this. But she wouldn't have it. She asked him, begged, *please love*, clear out. She's too far gone – there's a place in pain where there is no company, where the body's just alone in it.

That's all. He knows. Sometimes when he creeps in like this she opens her eyes like she's awake but when he looks in she is gone from her own gaze, already evaporated under her bald lids. The blips of fluorescence that monitor her bed remind him of the gameshows they used to binge on, flicking on the TV while they scrounged up dinner, countdowns of strobe in the background while the dim contestants bombed – *yeah they'd mock-cheerlead from their 5pm kitchen, let's watch some people lose. I'm sorry baby but for you the chase is over.* He steps closer. In her sleep she's a sketch of bone, superficial on the sheets – it's belief that's gone from her body, it's any faith that she'll outlast. Her breath is a baritone struggle through her chest, the air trying to navigate, failing, reaching the crease of her lips with a starved-out shrill, a low-dose end-game song. She doesn't want him beside her for this, she wants to exile him, save him from it. But what he has to back away from now is not her breathing's ugly encore – it's the pinch of freckles still on her nose-bridge, his first girlfriend superimposed, that cinnamon smidgen of memory more than he can take.

It does him in, it's the end of him. Except then he's stumbling down the hall, and even though it's remodelled by merlot, acid and elastic, and its walls lurch and swell, he hears a ruckus coming from the bathroom, a raking foil-backed sound he knows is no good. And that halts him. He's too cut to tap on the door, wait politely – he barges full-force into the room, and almost upturns the boy who's squatting on the tiles, prescription debris spread around him, a jillion ways to check out, vacuum-packed. His reaction is blindside, a jolt of pure rage.

You see your name on any of those boxes?

Nothing. The kid's all heave and blink.

Do you?

A head shake, dropping a silver sheet of pills. They're splashed out of their packets like mechanical leaves, and he's sick of their rattle, their lightweight tabs of promise, their slow-release hopelessness. He kicks a swatch across the shiny floor.

Thought you'd scull the whole shebang did you? Eh? Plenty to choose from here. Got a bit distracted by the sheer choice, did you boy? Oh yeah we stock everything.

But the kid he's picking on is only a shiver, thin-skinned in his black tee. Fuck, just look at him. He could almost laugh at the underage pain of it, all elbows and desperation.

Thought that would solve your fucking snivels. What's the count, then? Eh? How many?

I haven't even . . . started yet. The kid thumps his ears, like he'd bash out the sound of his own puny voice if he could. That's how – that's how gutless I am.

These – the man grabs down and flails a box in the kid's eyeline – are not for you.

The boy folds. There's a gulp in his torso, and his eyelids flurry. I know that. I'm sorry.

They're to help someone live. To live, you get me.

Not me die.

You got it in one. You stupid little shit.

He's crying now, he's lost it, the kid, his eyes unloading, big dumb blobs of tear.

The man drops his standover pose, sits down on the bath.

She called it off, eh?

She never . . . called it on. But I . . . can't give up.

No.

She's the first one . . .

I know. I know all about that. I know the whole story.

The kid is even more spooked by softness. But he halts a sob and looks.

My wife, the man starts. She was, you know.

He stops. The kid swallows.

I still know her number. True. I could still tell you that. You believe me? I could still tell you the phone number of my first girl.

What was it?

87 653.

Real. And it's . . . you know. For her now. Is it . . . ?

It's a countdown. That's it.

I'm sorry.

Yep. It's a fucking countdown.

Then there's nothing more there. Nothing more left. Maybe the kid feels it. All they can do is sit. Song-drone and voices come in from the garage, yelps of pissed all-purpose party noise. The kid starts to scrape up the fanned pewter packets, slot them back in their sleeves.

I'm real – I'm sorry, he says. You don't – have to stress. I'm good. I can get my shit together.

And he kneels by the jacked-open cupboard, starts shoving back the boxes.

There's a bloody party going on. Hear that. We should get your sad arse back.

Eh?

If you weren't such a sad prat you would have clocked on to the fact that my garage is packed with girls. Rack off out there now will you.

You sure?

Don't push me, kid.

So he walks the boy back to the scene of the throb, the quasi-music still jetting off the steel door, gives him a shove on the backbone for good luck. The kids are all dropped in a deeper state of party, a large-scale saturated dance going on, eyes closed, the girls re-glittered with sweat, the boys banging tone-deaf limbs, their hi-tops ungoverned, a blundering offbeat groove. He hangs back to watch – he hopes they're all off their faces with nowness, blank in the knell of that cheap music. He'd like to stay too, like to let himself go numb in that pounding zone of sound, lose his head here where nothing's terminal. But when the track cycles, the bassline bridges and slows, a blond girl raises her phone, and the room is suddenly a field of swaying hands, cells flagging a hi-fi trail of radiance. One more thing he can't cope with.

He goes back to the bathroom, the clean-up, he starts up a Jenga of overbalanced white boxes. Any way he tries to tower them, the meds slip back down, her name a pharmaceutical slump. There's too much. And in the back of the cupboard he spots a carton he could maybe turf, make room. But when he yanks it out, it's the baby monitor they used to rig up by their son's crib, stumpy pastel antennae and heart-shape dials, a robot so cute he wants to puke. He sits with it for a moment, then he thumbs the thick handsets from their polystyrene sockets. The batteries are dud – he pads out to the living room, scavenges the double As from the TV remote. All the channels he needs are in his hands. He doesn't think as he heads back to Mary, as he props one up on the medical slalom of her locker. He carries his back to the kitchen. He doesn't think for outright seconds, everything he knows disbanded. He's an idiot, holding this sappy walkie-talkie, this lovesick transistor like he could dial something back between them. He snaps it on, the receiver, lo to hi, and the pain is analogue, moves him to a hunch. Thank God there's not a screen – but he's watching her anyway. He is watching her, his first-ever girlfriend, bending down to blow candles out for her eighteenth. He is waiting to hear her voice through the wire, all presence, all ache in its teen gasps and whispers, he is waiting to hear the flicker of tongue, the husky mechanics of each cute breath and lip-roll of moistened indecision, *will you . . . you know, go with me?* But the circuit could be broken.

Fisheye

The big one's head they have to hack off to fit it in the tub. But even then the bugger won't tuck, a fin stuck out the chilly bin, scales as chunky and sunlit as the packed-out ice. They're grinning like bastards when they hump it up to the weigh-in. 'Bloody good crack at First this year boys.' They dig for it in the knock of ice, flop it down, silvery, with a crisp thud. The added head leaves good frills of blood on the tray. 'What y'reckon, eh?' 'Could be. Could take her out.' Its eye is a disc of tightened slime, yellow trim with a stud of black jelly. Specks of sky could go queasy and stretched in its lens – if you look too long. But they don't check out shit like eyes. They get into brews while the bloke makes a note of the kilos. The prizes, dumped on the pool table, will take more than a few cold ones to get to.

The backs of their necks feel near-third-degree and the grass seems like it needs anchoring. Still, they'll last, as long as Kev doesn't start up again about his wife. Out on the water he'd tried it a couple of times but the chop was too stubborn and the catch too thick and fast to give him a proper shot. The poor bloke had zero clue – you wouldn't credit it. They cast out and yanked back trails of prime, while Kev tried to whine about *intimacy*. The fish shut him down all gasp and wing. The boys grinned into buckets at their tinfoil fits, their jaws adrift in throes of wet freckle. First is a trip for two to the Islands. Let's face it: any one of them could take Kev's wife.

Never Tell Your Lover That His Wife Could Be Having an Affair

Because she's not the type, understand? Her calendars are annotated. Her daughters are booked in for play dates and dental visits and clean underwear. She tucks affirmative Post-it notes in their lunchboxes to raise their self-esteem. Her heart wears sturdy shoes. When she serves her family glossy meals she pats the base of your lover's scalp, and asks him to untie her apron before she takes her seat: carbohydrates and retro foreplay. She marks red X's in children's workbooks, or rewards the chosen with a solid track of ticks. She brings the glass box with the scaly class-pet home on weekends, and sits it on the sun-baked sideboard, so your lover can listen to the beast scrape its belly on micro-gravel while she feeds it small tendrils of meat. The pink Post-it notes say *Take Pride In You!* and there's fruit slotted in, skins rinsed of pesticides. She vacuums the footwells in her five-door hatchback. She has three categories for recycling, and on the weekends your lover can wake to the high-pressure hollows of her bumping the hose round the buckets out on their concrete drive.

So don't suggest that she backed down that driveway tonight to head to her own dirty secret. Don't hint that she smudged a see-ya-later kiss on his cheek in a shade of ulterior peach. Don't speculate that the tin-foiled cordon bleu she left him was assembled with hot-texting fingers. Whatever you do, don't slide off the body of your lover, panting, lace dampened and askew, and insinuate anything, *anything* suspect about the unexpected bonus-hour he got free to fuck you. She's off-limits, understand? Her beige life is reliable and holy. Back off – that kind of talk is deal-breaking.

Put your clothes on. Affairs are for sluts like you.

I still hoped the photos would come out well

You were wasted by the time we left for our honeymoon. I had to get behind the wheel, but first I had to pick off the bouquets of toilet roll, do what I could with the stringy quartet of tin cans. Groggy laughter jilted out of you. It was pointless handing you the map. My satin had built up sticky underarms, but I was trying to keep it civilised. Only one day a girl gets elected to be beautiful, and it takes stars stapled hard into your hair. All night I'd been sipping something lilac and acid, but my pumps kept busy dancing with everyone.

We were halfway to the hotel and everything was silver. I kerbed it, and got you as far as someone's camellias, bridling your hair. The puke-work made prisms of your eyes. We kneeled in the smell of hurl and metal letterbox. I tried to tell you hush, but the sick was barking you like a dog. You yawned out the feast we'd spent eighteen months saving for. Tipped face-first into the luxury chill of my skirt.

I thought of the silky crescendo – as a hire-team, miles behind us, floated down the marquee.

Wiry hymn of a screen door opening. The old girl who came out was planning to be coldblooded, but then she spotted the dress. Scuffed back inside in maudlin slippers and moved in her thick kitchen nets like a moth. There'd been a perfect plastic duo spiked into the top of the icing carousel. You were finishing off in my lap with a last chunky gasp. Nothing felt like champagne anymore. When she came back, she helped me spade you into your seat and passed me a damp chequered cloth.

The tin cans kept banging along like stuff not getting said.

Cicada Motel

At the Cicada Motel, the woman booked me into the runt of the rooms. The caramel carpet had flecks in it the colour of cabbage tree. The bedspread was mango. She gave me a suss look, like I'd prove fly-by-night, and handed over the 17 key, fixing her glare on the palm I held out as if I had dirt all through my heartline. *My* husband *will be here*, I said, *soon*, but she just huffed like she'd won the standoff, *if you say so*, then banged her smock out through the hole-punched mosquito screen. *Husband.* The outdoor bulb sizzled with speed-of-light insects.

I'd left first. I knew it was going to take him much longer. The Cicada Motel was just somewhere to be while I waited for him to cut strings.

In the morning the sea was not the kind I was used to, just lay there and looked stale. Miles of flat grey sand pin-pricked with animal sink-holes, where dregs of silver water clicked — that close-up came later when I walked out ankle-deep. For now I just blinked out the window, a glittery reverse game of join-the-dots. He hadn't called. I tuned in to chitchat from other rooms, the sound of footfalls scuffing bored squares, the on-holiday lingo of couples being nicer to each other because they'd paid. Above the yellow sink, the mirror wore a hairline crack and smelt of ointment. I dyed my hair a bad shade to match the room and pigment wriggled into my ears. On a far-out channel folks in a black-and-white movie were tap-dancing and beseeching. It was shit reception, a choice of either violins or prophecy, a fake-tanned pastor strutting in a rhinestone vest, pumping his arm over sins of the flesh with all the holy poison he could muster. While I was waiting I starfished on the mango bed and touched myself. My scalp bled cheap bronze into the sheets. Later I made myself a bridal veil of toilet paper, and lay down quiet in the confetti of someone else's skin. I felt at home in that fruit cocktail quilt.

He did get there three days later. By that time I'd set up Monopoly from reception, and the queen spread was a landfill of tokens, houses on my cheated streets bite-size as pills. *Do not pass go*, I looked up and told him. *Do not collect. Not a thing. Not one thing.* But 17 only had one doorway, and he filled it up with his sad bulk, his hands encumbered with junk she'd fought to keep but eventually let him have, more tubs jammed in his car boot. Something alto had happened to his voice. His *wife* had happened. I pitied him, invited him in. *How did you befall me?* he said, with a soap-opera shake of his head. I was dead level with the skin he was pushing out his clothes — I grinned at the trophy and doused my grip with spit. Later I picked hotels out his spine and told him, *winner takes all*. We lay awake and listened to everything leaking.

We hadn't exactly paid top-dollar. In the Formica-fronted drawers we turned up the usual tackle of can-openers and steelos, and handy wipe-clean bedside bibles, commandments shrunk into a font my conscience couldn't decode, ultimatums from a cut-price god. On all the cups were enamelled roses like something my grandmother once said, and brown stains left runny circular ghosts round the rims. We sat up, sucking wine out of them. I liked to say unanswerable things. Like, *are hotel flies different to house flies?* Or, *why do they play the*

*f word in songs on the radio without the k? Like just taking out
that one letter makes it okay?* He demonstrated, with cartoon
suck-suck hands. *Cos that's the bit that sounds like it,* he said.
Then blushed like he'd never played so dirty. I slapped his
fingers, then worked them inside me, laying right back in
onomatopoeia.

Then he went again. All I had behind me was a life I'd
had no problem leaving, so sitting on the bed at the Cicada
Motel I didn't waste time looking over the past. I turned the
flip-covers of the things-to-do-in-town file, clingwrapped
highlights of the shithouse district, mostly takeaway joints
– the pages were endorsed by grease, sweet-and-sour meals
consumed by people alone on the polyester quilt. The fridge
with its bony low-lit shelves cut through my sleep with a
bluebottle hum. Open, it smelt like potato peel. I blinked
into its budget light but could never get hungry enough
to go out. If I did I'd just have to walk back staring into
other people's units, dioramas in a long sad row. I'd do little
rituals of housekeeping, though somehow I couldn't leave my
handprints on anything. There were the guttural sounds of
couples in other rooms taking an ordinary fuck. I'd squat on
the grey plastic O to piss and early on I could smile – in my
pants there was still a cooling stripe of his brine. To me that
eddy was holy. I was at his beck and call.

The day I met him, I'd walked straight to the mall on my
lunch hour and bought myself a trim black suitcase with a
telescope handle. I knew what was happening – the gold zips
were thick and the trunk could fold my life into it whole.
On my next lunch hour I took it back – I wanted to go after
him empty-handed. I did a bad tailgate tracing him home and
backed under a jacaranda. I could see him cleaning the plate
his wife placed in front of him, back to me, too square not to

feel me looking, through French doors. The Datsun ticked in a fall of neon feathers. I could see him rinse dishes with his teen, a sulky helper in the TV strobe. Pollen warped the screen. He never once looked out, like I was zilch. By the time he walked over and got in it was dark and I was blistered by hours at the steering wheel. Finger by finger he picked away my left hand. He looked at the words on my singlet, which were so tall and white they could still be read: *Oh Lord I Have Sinned. I haven't*, he said, head-down with repentance. But I just peeled the shirt off and made sure he did.

So he came to the motel, but had to keep on going back. I should understand. It was complicated. There were logistics to leaving. And I did get it – I'd just fuck him extra hard before he left. The fringed quilt at the Cicada felt like fiberglass, and static would net all the nicks in his hard hands. I scrubbed his grip round my breast, working-class electricity, and muttered *please don't go* again. Two kids had moved into 16 and they hated each other, were outside playing tag in pink until someone wept. He said there was still so much to sort. I unlassoed him from my legs and tried to think of his wife's wellbeing. But if I said I remember one iota of compassion for her I'd be lying. At three while he was faking sleep I'd watched the silver twitch along his eyelids. I'd kissed him until our late-night whispering turned bloodshot. He felt like my birthright. When he wouldn't talk to me I went outside and played hopscotch with the bitchy girls from 16, leaping the pink chalk squares with nine-year-old kicks. In my tight shorts and topknot I looked like a princess – at least to them I did. Before he left again I bribed a View-Master off one of those kids, and fed in the notched discs as he backed out the drive, worked the spring-loaded technicolour trigger. My eyes crossed with sick fans of Disney happy-ends.

I didn't lie waiting in a slutty getup all day, some bra held together by lace and evil thoughts – but the woman at reception eyeballed me like I did, like she knew the type. And I qualified. Reception was hung with anti-fly ribbons like a melting vinyl rainbow – when you walked through it took minutes for your collarbone to shake off their sticky ricochet. The door jamb shaved my jandal, made me do a little skip up to the desk, rubbery pirouette. I needed more long-term things: an iron, a hairdryer, more of her ultra-life milk in dinky domes. And I wanted to swap games. I wanted Operation, to tweeze out the Adam's apple, pluck the funny bone. I wanted to win cash scratching out his melted heart, to not hear the buzzer going off in his face. The woman handed his flat box over with a warning that it was intact, she'd counted the bones, and pointed down the main road to the Four Square if I planned to be a longer stayer. She was staple-gunning frills of tinsel to the counter with a line of clunks. I'd forgotten a day as bad as Xmas was coming. But when I got down to the Four Square I couldn't miss it – the checkout girl was wearing a halo, a fairy-lit number-eight hoop spliced to her head band, with more wire strapped to her smock for shonky wings. She shed white feathers in the yellow bag as she packed it with the tap of single-serve things, blinking greasily at me. The kettle in 17 must have had six hundred horsepower. But none of the sachets worked. The taste of other people's yesterdays stayed at the back of my tongue. The air felt like asbestos. I tugged on the drawers just to listen to the cutlery make its aim-fire sound. When I opened doors in the dark room all the hinges sang the motel's name.

He came and went. I knew there were going to be days when we weren't quite in this together. The days I had him, I'd slow down the order that I peeled off my clothes. I tried

47

my best to give him amnesia. It was all about timing. I'd use a pulpy tube of Revlon to paint myself an oversize grin. I'd line up pills like islands of my own tropical making, deadly getaways I just might take. *What they should stash in the drawer*, I said, *is a quick guide to not wanting to end yourself in small rented rooms.* I'd pretend to ring old boyfriends, undoing the spirals in the telephone cord with my fuckyou finger. He stared at me and smiled an unventilated smile. I promised him I'd stick a knife in the toaster. He let me bite him hard then thumb around the toothmarks, the dent-in freckles I'd left, a buckling ring-o'-rosie. Then I dabbled sorry with my tongue. When we walked the beach later, we brought home shells in casual fistfuls and left them on the sill like things we should give names.

The Lord had come and I was playing Guess Who when I saw the car waiting – so I just flicked down every face that looked like the wife, picked the blondes off in reverse order. Their clickety plastic capsize was satisfying. I thought it was him at first, here for Jesus after all – but when I realised I winched back the screen and shrugged, *might as well come in.*

His kid had nothing going for him, none of his dad's girth and heat. He scrubbed the heel of one sneaker over the laces of the other, fluoro and tryhard. In his hand he had a cracker, a tube of crimped green crêpe.

Sweet. You brought me a present.

He stared at the thing.

Mum cooked this big family dinner, he said.

Oh yeah.

Yeah, this whole awesome spread.

If it was so good why are you here, then?

I wanted to see if my Xmas wish had come true. And you'd just fucked right off.

You know, you could play nicer. Xmas spirit and that.

He's there. Dad's still there. I reckon he's staying.

Crosslegged on the mango bed I could make him look away. My shorts ended high and tight. Bull's-eye.

How even old are you? he said.

How old are you? You meant to be behind that wheel?

I'm learning. Dad's teaching me a lot of things.

Yeah? Coincidence. Me too.

I don't reckon. I don't reckon you know half of things.

Okay little boy. Go. What?

Then he started to cry, a big ruck of sobs. I watched for a while, then I tipped all the mugshots back up on the Guess Who board.

Wanna play?

He stared at me, using a fist to scrub his flushed face.

Okay, he said. You don't know my mother.

Or maybe you don't know your father.

Maybe. But I could always ask him. He is still at home.

Not for long, kid.

Yeah. Says you.

God knows why the Cicada Motel was a stop for any Xmas gig, but we heard a siren warp then, and a fire engine rigged with tinsel pulled into the carpark. Some half-cut local Santa climbed out with a swag of made-in-China presents, ho-ho-ho'ed round the units looking for kids. The checkout girl was his assistant, waving a hairy silver wand, still with the vortex of glitter cabled to her head, her white wings a wobbly scaffolding. I opened the door and watched the pink twins from 16 tweak open the sellotape on their lame gifts. The old girl from reception was blushing by the truck in her best ugly smock. Santa used his rented beard to lean in, snuggle her. She gave him a gurgle of her annual gin, and dished him a slap. I thought about sauntering over to the guy on the driver's side – in his flame-retardant hero gear he leaned out of the cab to scope the lettering on my tank: *My happy place is your happy place burning to the ground.* His grin was déjà vu. But I didn't move. Then the garish parade was pulling out.

And I'd like to tell you that I lived up to the look the old girl gave me before she trudged back to her lobby. A look that said, *suppose you're all right, considering.* I'd like to say I didn't turn back to the unit where the kid was still cluttering the tropical bed, trying to cope with the weight of his wet face. I'd like to say I was done with my nymph skin, that I let it split, and stepped out. The kid was still clutching his Xmas cracker. I latched on to the end and yanked. The bang made him flinch. I fucking loved the hint of gunpowder. I shook out the festive crap and tossed him the gag.

What's the joke.

You should know.

I slid on the pink paper crown.

It is raining out on the field today when I get back from the hospital, and I find myself smiling, as if I called it up. I stand at the ranchslider that squares my lounge off with the turf and watch the downpour chasing off the onlookers. There are mothers out there who've thought to bring shelters, staked out a shanty claim of plastic on the sideline, parka'd up the younger kids. They've squatted in spiny pop-up deckchairs pre-game to guarantee a prime view. Those mothers fight the longest. They're still in place when a rush of umbrellas heads off, the deluge whirling from their red and white panels. Everything club-coloured – chilly bins and snap-backs, PVC ponchos and first-aid kits – bumping in retreat along the flooded green sod. In the end it's just me and those mothers, huddled in resistance beneath their branded tarps. Watching the team still stumbling the muck, as the sky proves no one can hope to stop it.

When Ryan was a child we had to rush him to hospital. I remember the walls were lemon then, too, and the frieze was a march of ducklings, grins of goofy fuzz with gumboots on webbed feet and sky-blue plastic hats. It was raining on them, but that only made them cuter. I hated the things, galoshing around in the splash, their peach beaks smirky and dimpling. I think Ryan hated them too. He hated the whole room, and everyone in teal that entered into it, carrying wires to the bed, and liquids, and trays, and needles, and, lastly, straps. They'd plug and stick him, maintaining near-smiles, and gag his howl with clear-gloved fingers. We never had to guess his hatred. He screamed at them all, loud belts of terror, pitched from the struggle of his trunk, his blond-white hair spiked with fever, his milk teeth in fits. And it was my job to hold him down, to pin the tiny hammer of his heartbeat to the trolley, to lock down his clattering flannelette pj's with their pattern of choo-choos all jumping the track. To use my whole body if I had to, like a vice, bear down on my baby, his flailing heels and wrists. Mutter everything I could find of comfort, while his head swung side to side and bludgeoned up at me. Keep on with a babble of falsetto sweetness, crossing my heart with fake promises. Hating the ducks the whole time, their chubby parade around the walls where the squeaky-clean blobs of entertaining rain would never drop down hard enough to drown them.

Let the rain come. Last weekend, when there was another *minor incident*, I stood at the window and watched while the ambulance coasted, low-profile, through coloured margin flags. While the stretcher was manoeuvred off, swift, unobtrusive. While the game played on. And those mothers never moved. Except one. But she wasn't from the home team.

I've taken to wandering over to the back of the clubrooms on some nights that I can't sleep. Maggie sees me coming, where the spotlights smudge the mist above the field, and taps out a couple of smokes. We sit on a pair of overturned white buckets she's scrubbed out by the bar door. With the heel of my runners I fiddle with the handle, so it keeps hitting the concrete with a thin silver click. I don't know why, but I find myself falling a lot into rote motions like this, waking up with my unthinking body caught in little drones and tics. I tap and rock. It might be my own therapy – my body trying to jerk out a new mode for itself – but if it is, it's a poor joke on the exercises I watch them putting Ryan through each morning, his big frame stranded on the bed. He blinks at them when they call it training, when they cast the tiny twitches of muscle as heroic, when they chant in big explosive hoots for the vacant limb they haul through its range of movement. It's my job to make the same noise. And I do. I'm relentless, an over-age bogus cheerleader, flapping my nonstop applause. There are pinboard panels on the ceiling of the therapy room and he blinks up into them. I want to give up and stare with him, count the black array of dots, an unmoving hole-punched universe. But I don't. I'm still full of promises, I brim with them. I swear, I vow, I pledge. I set targets, forge pacts. I'll get him up on his feet again. If it's the last thing . . .

I don't have to press my body over his to block his protest. He never makes a sound. We're still in the children's wing, which would have once humiliated him. But now he doesn't care. The frieze this time is of giraffes, the long freckled glide of their spines around lanky trees, the doped, friendly glaze of their eyelashes. A patch of them skipping, dorky and cloven, meant to be adorable. I just stare through their hides to their happy bones towering, the way I watch the vertebrae of figures who gleam at home from our late-night TV, picking up nothing of the plot, tuning out the buzz of dialogue, so my husband will sigh beside me, hard, on the couch, scoffs of reproach he doesn't aim straight at me but over at the brown scrawl of curtains or down into his can of DB. But I go on staring at the bodies on the screen, the seamless way their hidden bones arrange their easy movements, their sliding thoughtless links beneath the well-lit skin. Waiting for the crack.

Maggie has known me since secondary school. She was a bitch to me back then – but I had it coming, a stuffy little priss, part Barbie doll, part religion. I'd put on lipstick, quote scripture, and girls like Maggie, with spiky fringes and homemade tats of maryjane and khaki army-surplus satchels, would have to hold themselves back from lobbing a fist at my sanctimonious pink mouth. She makes me laugh about it now, as we sit on our tubs and inhale and huff, and sometimes munch on the odd leftover courtesy meat-pie. She still has the bad ring-o'-rosie of metal stuck along her left ear's cartilage, a silver pick-and-mix – I remember when she lanced the first one, in a bathroom off C Block, where I hid in a stall and tried not to sick up as I watched her school-shirt spat with safety-pinned blood. I love the toughness of those studs now, the saggy ammunition of them trailing their curve, the grey roots tracking out her way-too-red dyed hair, the lined mocha slur of her smile. She sneers at everything. She's worked the club since she was in her twenties. A couple of weeks back when her cellphone got pinched out her ute, the boys hunted the culprit and pounded him, a lesson delivered big-time. She's an institution now. Revered. So fucking watch it, right?

Her son, too, has something wrong with him – though it wasn't the game, he was just born with it. Sometimes she has to bring him in, and she sets him up at a station in the kitchen. He likes to butter the big yellow sleeves of bread, flicking marge out the tall white boxes and striping it with a wide grin onto the slices his mum has chequer-boarded around the stainless bench. He has to study hard to close up each sticky pair, a drool of twenty-something concentration. I don't know if she just dumps the bread. No one's ever had the guts to ask. And she doesn't ask about my son, either, doesn't offer me any cheap proverbs, or trite old tags. When people do, I'm tempted to follow her example and aim for the fat goal of their smiles, take some platitudinous teeth out. We just sit and lick pixels of pie crust out our gumlines, and blow the air with tired fuckyous of smoke. And Maggie takes the piss about how uppity I used to be: 'Tight-arse little princess, but me too, eh, I could be a bit of a dick. Hāngī-pants too. Check us out now. Haha. Ah well. Is what it is.' And we'll watch the last of the tanked-up kids lacing through the carpark, the topple of trios of high-heeled girls, their tube-frocks moist with oblivious sick, and we'll wish the dumb young fuckers well in their stagger home to normality and think of our sons.

Inside the club, there's still a picture of me marrying my husband. There's a whole wall of club weddings spanned across the decades, but girls that win the captains, like I did, still rate at the top. And she's right – I am a tight-arse princess, iced into white satin, strapped into a shiny cylinder of it, so I wince each show-offy breath through the dress's boned column. I'm so goddamn delighted with myself. I've struck a trophy pose, and my husband has the shield on his blazer and stamped on his diagonal tie. He's a thick-set honey, his tousle of hair greased back, with a beautifully munted smile. He's a team player, and I'm marrying the whole team – and I don't mind, I feel like a matchfit goddess. We've even bought a section that fronts onto the club grounds, and he's going to knock us up a house right there, like we're in permanent reserve, with his own rugged number-eight hands. And I'm going to get myself knocked up, and feel my babies ruck inside me, and let my captain stroke the globe of my stomach and crack lame jokes about them kicking, coach them through my waters with his gruff game-play commands. *Be dominant* – that's his favourite one, the one he'd roar from the sidelines while our son blitzed by, a hulk of strain and froth, thudding through the cross-grain of bodies, braced around the ball, gouging forward – *Ryyyyyyy-an*, the syllable stretched like a curse on his opponents, *be dominant*.

Be dominant.

Plummeting the turf to a soundless stop. While the crowd kept bawling my baby's glory.

And later, while he lay in the rattle of the hospital, his body in the throb of the tubes and the tests and the strobes, more than one person posted the outcome to his Facebook page: *mate, we wasted 'em*. Even a mother, oblivious. *Letting you know the score! We took it out 25–13!*

They're decent, the boys. It could be the same bunch that worked over Maggie's thief, head-down over a stack of lumber in the backyard when I get home from the hospital today. They've volunteered to help with the ramp. There's a row of them, good-value kids, and a couple of dads, and the skeleton's going up quick, piles thumped in, a good frame righted in struts. The lads are trying to out-hammer each other, and one or two are going at warp speed, jerking in guffaws off the end of a nail gun, until they get yelled at, *don't arse about or I'll knock your bloody heads together*. For the most part, they've stripped off their t-shirts and wear them stuffed above their bums, so when they swag around the lawn their sweaty flags flail around. One has his tee collared back over his scalp so it girlifies him with a long blue veil. There's not a drop of sunscreen on any of them, and the ozone glints on their torsos already, a promise of third-degree.

When I pass them, their antics go quiet. The hassle, and clatter, and joshing stop. They half-drop tools, stare at their gawky hands. They don't exactly grin, but their mouths do something sweet and bungled. There's a muttering that sounds respectful. But it could just be fear.

I'm an institution too. But no one knows what to say to me.

I watch for a while out the kitchen window, their klutzy progress, their loose aim, their uncouth trunks. They swing boards round, only half hoping to miss, a mongrel ballet, slapstick, amateur. They don't skip a chance to roughhouse each other, tousles of sudden punch and passing scrags, topped off with hefty laughs. I think of my boy, their captain – of course he was their captain – who should be out there calling the shots, pulling a blokey pose, overseeing the work, mock-bawling-out their foul-ups, clocking the back of their scalps if they clash too much. Then I think of him, three, in the clobber of his dad's tool belt, taking goofy outsize stomps to keep up its leather anchor. I think of him, six, lying head to head with me on the cooled trampoline to stare up at the milky chinks of star: I think of the smell of his wonder, the black mat buzzing as he waves up the disbelieving wriggle of his hand. I think of his fontanel, the soft pulsing gap of it fronded by his cottony hair, a thrum of feathery bone I could touch my mouth to, cradling, as he fed. I take out supplies to the boys. I take out a tray of tomato sandwiches, Mountain Dew and Coppertone. I take out a handful of my son's old caps, the scent of his skull still moulded in their stiff domes. There's half a handprint of red paint daubed onto one, a mucky blotted lifeline. There's the coast of his temples, sweated in a fine grey tremor that leaks along the white of the peak. Today in the hospital he hadn't wanted anyone near him, so I'd had to wait till he slept, to edge closer on his pillow, to creep to his crewcut hair, where the stubble sticks out like his last crop of nerve endings. But here in the backyard I hold out the stains of him, all the rip-shit dents and scuffs – he was always going for broke at whatever activity he was attacking, full tilt, brute force, a mighty irrepressible blur. He was a feat of nature, my boy. A reckoning in teen male skin.

The boys don't talk to me. Bar one. Daniel's the one who's turned up most to the hospital, although my son still refuses any visits. I see him down by the letterbox, faking a standoff with a hi-top, like it's packed with stones he can't bash out. I know it's an update he wants. So I wander over, chuck him a tube of sunblock, pretend a half-hearted telling off. But he's too tender, this boy, for the sheer hulk of him, the stout block of muscle that is his jaw. The stocky throat wobbles, his eyes glaze too quick above his heavyset smile. I think of the nurse I liked best at the hospital, an elegant singsongy male who trilled at us coyly as he swished through his work, and blabbed bits of high-pitch nightshift gossip, but touched us, firm, a genuine no-bullshit touch, and sometimes even a hug, his grip a sincere grab right to his ribcage, matter-of-fact with suffering, and crooning some comfort. When Ryan wouldn't see the kid, this was the nurse who'd steered him away by the shoulderblades, propped him on a park bench outside and nodded as he snivelled, lit him a relay of smokes. But my husband has clout in this small town – they don't forget you here once you're captain – and behind the scenes he made sure no more male nurses were rostered on to Ryan's case. He told me of his victory – it was the least they could do for him, things were going to be hard enough, without the extra humiliation of . . . he couldn't bring himself to describe the scene, the handling of our boy's body, its long-term needs. He didn't see my rage. And I make sure now I don't show it to the boy by the letterbox with the too-soft eyes.

Instead I tell him of the day I first brought Ryan back from hospital, a tiny warm survivor, squashed into a car seat, sleeping off the unexplained battle of the last few days. The scrape of the instruments, the evil figures in teal, the march of the ducks. I'd parked and lifted him out of his seat, a wobble of wool and limbs and shuteye, and my husband had come to the car door to help and I'd handed him over, a see-sawed transfer of weight. But when his body left me it was sudden. I found myself on the gravel, crumpled. Wracked with deliverance, giving great gasps of spluttered prayer.

I won't know that feeling again.

There are things the boy could say to me. He could come out with some banality, the slogans they drill them in over at the club. I hear them nearly every night, shouts that echo from the field, their barks of courage, stale. But he doesn't. He takes the cap I offer out to him, and he slides it on, so his face darkens, thickened with shade. He farts his palm with sunscreen, fumbles it over his face. That's what makes his eyes red. He's a tough boy. And he is learning. I don't know if he'll be visiting Ryan again.

The rest of the boys don't say his name to me. My husband assures me, though, our son's a legend to them. Nothing will ever change that. He tells me later there's plans for the boys to line up along the drive on the day we bring him home, guard of honour. They'll do the haka for him. Kia kaha. They'll be spruced up, their thick bodies jammed in their formals, sternums huffing under blazers, throats tweaking yanked ties, awkward with clean-shaved ahems. Then the shout will fire up, and their hands will rout and clap, they'll outface, their shins will thud. It will be bloodthirsty and beautiful, a boom on the earth as their big limbs thunder out a warrior's welcome.

And I'll wheel my son past them, where we've tucked him in his contraption. Where he doesn't want to live.

There are traditions I can't stop. I know that tonight, when I hear the haka pounding the dancefloor over at the club. It's been a big game, a decider, and there's a band in: I watched

59

them unloading the van from my ranchslider earlier, a clapped-out troop of musos dragging in amps and light bars, stopping mid-packdown for a fag, a trio on the sunset blockwall in matching black tees. I know it's a zero-sleep night: if I bother to lie in my bed the bass will only detonate my chest-wall, a deep controlled bruising. And I've lived alongside club nights long enough. I can pick out every item in the soundtrack: the shrill as the hatchbacks of girls arrive, their preloaded silvery high-heeled squealing. The hoots as the old blokes, sinking their brews since mid-arvo, start pulling their stumbled boogie, weaving the girls in harmless nostalgic jolts, getting freaky with their senior hips. The lineup for the feed, the clack of plastic, shovel of chips round the steel bins, squeak of the arse-end sauce, the wrangled chops. I even know the tone of funerals, or weddings, or birthdays, the shift in decibels, the dead or alive playlists. And this: the tribute of half-cut boots thundering the wood floor. A spasm of remembrance before the band cranks up its millionth 'Sweet Home' or 'Simple Man', and they're all too plastered to stagger any further. The frieze around the walls is of themselves, as gods. There isn't a stretch where they're not mighty, ranged in their divisions, lined up in their frames, fists held hard on their wide-planted knees or squared across their chests, no mistaking the set of their jaws. Here to dominate. Season after mud-gold season. The frames rattle as their stance hounds the floor. There are traditions that aren't up to me. If they have to thump their grief against their sternums, if they have to stomp and bellow it, then so be it. Grief is not a language I understand any better.

I think what I want to sign mine is a whistle.

I think I should be allowed one. It's a whistle I want when the doctors half-explain to me, when the dash starts shrieking on his ray of machines, and they sprint into the room, and the sound of their efficiency, played against the vinyl and sterility and metal, terrifies me, their mouths moving in fast-paced clips of jargon that make every blip feel fatal. There needs to be half-time, they need to let me call it, take a breather. And it's a whistle I want when the journalist, who's been told no, hung up on many times now, tries to sneak in and steal a bedside soundbite to headline their hard-hitting exposé. When the same reporter stakes out the dayroom and catches my son's girlfriend ringed with her besties, who try to tone their giggles down to ICU levels, but who still spill details, of the backless ball dress his girlfriend won't be wearing, can't resist all its chic sequinned specs, and the night they won't be spending at the Sun Kist Inn where he'd booked *like the actual honeymoon suite, OMG, supersweet*, for their first time, clumsy and gentle, a room with a waterbed in padded crimson velour and a dozen red roses he'd pre-ordered, and *how sad*, but they'd heard it could still be, *you know, um, managed*, in the long-term, *you know*, there were ways it could be sorted, all blushing in simpers, making tragic corny bats with their lashes, little measured blinks of semi-wet tint, because it was all so (dainty sob) like *ultra saaaaaad*, while the journalist sketched down their soft-core handicapped dreams.

And it's a whistle I want, tonight, as I'm walking to the clubrooms now for my out-back toke with Maggie but she heads me off, jumpy under the spotlight, clearly aiming to stop my gaze falling on the girl who's groaning up against the wall, and it's not like it's a shock to see a girl corralled there, staggering the brickwork with a boy in control, so her head is bobbing on the end of his thrusts, and she's maybe even tipping out a little pre-mix puke mid-groping, then tripping off after, her torso a-trickle, oblivious to what's been pumped into it, except she's been anointed by one of the boys, so she can afford to zig-zag back to the hall and gabble her baptism to pals on the dancefloor, and drunkenly point to the boy who's left his mark, imprimatur on her greasy thighs, and dream maybe he'll hit her up for more, maybe even let her wear the hallowed branding of his first-fifteen jersey to school on Monday, *way romantic*, it's hardly a shock she's there, but I want a whistle when I know that it's her, it's my son's girl, straddling a hard-at-it boy, not a gentle replacement, but a rough-as-guts fuck, though the boy's grunting dopey endearments while he's blocking, and she's rambling something too, some drivel about broke hearts, cold facts, lost love, but she's already forgetting what she's lost, except all the remains that will drain from her later and the brickwork remembered on her spine in lagered bruises.

And if the boy turns I know he'll have too-soft eyes.

'It is what it is,' says Maggie beside me. And somehow that works as well as a whistle.

And what is there to do then but let Maggie lead me round to the rear mess door, and prop me against the barred screen while she fetches us a couple of quiet ones. And then let her lead me, white tubs in hand, to the mini crane-lift that they service the floodlights with. She's an institution in this place, and she's got the keys – *too right*, she eyebrows me, as if there was any fucking doubt. She bangs the yellow crate, *up ya get*, and fiddles with some mechanism over on the frog-green cab. Then she hoists her arse over the rails, and upends a tub with a hollow pop. 'There you go. Throne, ya uptight princess.' Her ragged teeth are grinning at me, pushy and gapped.

I do as she says and climb on. Maggie's tough thumb-joints jog at controls and we're aloft, a slow grinding rise above the field. It smells like rust and ascension and turf. The mist is coming out, a float of it over the green, and we drift over its illumination. The floodlights are like some sleek artillery from heaven.

'I used to do this with my boy sometimes. He was into it. There've been some choice moments.' She nods at me. 'Not much, eh. But something.' She answers herself, 'Well I reckon anyway.'

The altitude is radiant, a good place to get pissed. So we do, careful to do it mostly silent. Although I tell Maggie once, or maybe more, that the lift-tray makes me think of when Ryan was little, how he used to love to huddle in the plastic laundry basket, and beg me to launch him overhead. And how somewhere, over my baby, locked in his terrible isolation, there's a line of animals extending their lonely wet eyes to out-of-reach trees. And once, in the clubrooms, I remember him nicking off with someone's nana's wheelchair, and hooning it, on long giggling burnouts round the hall. And Maggie blows listening grooves of smoke and says nothing. I look out over the lines of the field and think of the old man who comes to mark them, who's done it for years now, a patient ploughing of the paint roller, jittery and silver on the grass, along the string lines he's measured, meticulous, pegged out, recalibrated, offside. He's religious about it, kneels on the turf, doublechecks, genuflects, before he stamps it white. When Ryan was little he'd sneak out our fenceline and follow him, poor man – stuck with a toddler, rowdy and fidgeting and nonstop nattering beside him as he yanked round his trail of paint. And everything would grow through it, burst, bloom, smudge, break, the bodies just scrape away its borders, so he'd have to come back and do it all again before the next game.

three rides with my sister

My sister's car was a powder-blue deathbox. It smelt like heavy-petting and eyeshadow, spermicidal silver sachets and leaded petrol. Her painted toenails accelerated hard, a patent heel tossed out the footwell to me – if I was lucky enough to call shotgun. She hated how the seatbelt crushed her work-of-art bust, so she'd flick off its cleat as soon as we cleared our cul-de-sac. But she ordered all the windows wound down: her mahogany hair graffitied the breeze with bad perm. Kilometres came at us wild. There were gusts of her perfume and kinky gossip. Her passengers giggled, not-quite-bad-enough girls. My sister pulled breathtaking tricks in the traffic, thriving on their squeals. She hair-pinned, gunned it, spun on the handbrake. Mostly hunted boys. Stalked man-wagons, tailed suits, revved surfers, overtook. Raced stray moonlight up the beach, the shrapnel of seashells clattering the chassis. But sometimes she just drove, aimed out our small town, nailing the centre line. Tinted mascara lit up her deathwish eyes.

+

It's hard to lift her into the car today. I relay her feet in, still icy in their ward slippers. I wind out the belt, click her safe, watching stitches. Count her chemical breaths on my jawbone. When I ask where we should head, she just blinks. The sky moves over her powder-blue scalp.

64

On the journey home from the hospital, road-workers have messed up the marker paint, so it speeds in a trail, spilling the kerb in a random white splash like a tidebreak.

Or a monitor-reading, spiked.

why she married your father

She had a job in a green smock with a zip front, stocking Four Square shelves. She'd left school with mild Arithmetic, acne under a spiral perm, and Home Economics. The shop was the only one in town so it carried everything, a blockade of brown-cloaked boxes out back where trucks beeped in. She loved the sound of gashed paper, long stripes of it ripping from her coral-coated nails. She gelled her fringe to grow out behind a barricade of clips (tortoise-shell, 25% staff discount).

She was on shelves until she earned trust. She was aiming for the till, but the boss was wary of fresh girls now: he'd just caught one embezzling. (He'd sprung her on the ladder as she pasted up *This Week's Mega Deals* and a hairband of twenties had peeked out her smock.) So it was trial-run – if she was lucky the boss'd let her work up to a bit of aisle display.

A decorative pyramid of canned baby peas.

A stapled fan of neon coupons bursting from a baked-bean stadium.

Mostly she kneeled and stacked, bummed boxes round the gritty linoleum, lined rows up, label out. She loved the sticky tempo of the pricing gun, the spiky *Specials* tags.

And then there was the cigarette racks. The weekly rep, passing her the packs to load the wire carousel, sending her the odd wink that made her stomach skid. Until this Thursday he craned down, gorgeous, let an outbreath of smoke cruise the neck of her uniform.

Has anyone ever told you you're beautiful?

Marlborough and hope looped her ponytail. She pivoted, No, on crumpling knees. Something was slipping out her zip-front heart.

He leaned lower, grinned.

No – and they're never likely to neither.

jilt back

When he didn't marry her, she realised how much dress she had left to drag behind her. A thirteen-kilo streamer of satin snagging against everything she slalomed: altar, guests, trestles, lychgate, marquee, kerb. Every few minutes it would lynch her at the hips, so she'd be pinned in frilly limbo, until she could work her fingers down the white slide to unhitch. She got tired of unbraiding herself. The world is full of nail heads, and she started to pluck herself free with a cut-throat tug. She felt less like confectionery then. She pulled the spiked ring of flotsam off her scalp. The sequins of her bodice felt like microscopic headlights. She pushed into the open, crazy-glued with extra light. She thought of places she could go: into the magic show at the casino to get her ivory bulk sawn in half, down to the overpass to let her sleek banner be gas-canned with wild have-not graffiti. Down to the river, to scrabble through the miles of white-shine for her own be-muddied thighs, to finally fuck the boy she'd loved since fifteen. She felt like she was on the true path. Under all that boning she'd had no aspirations. The white lines polished her with dark resolve now as she passed. Her dress sounded like a long hot tirade.

holding the torch

I want to know: can you still smell our memories? We slept in our togs, their rockpool scent – our bodies sucked all summer on their itchy stretch. Because I remember: we are tucked into bed top and tail, but we squiggle up, breath to breath, to mutter what feels like the whole night in our rubbery pelts. We must close our eyes eventually – but when our lids drop we are still half-talking, the story dozing off in the soft joint fumble of our tongues. We try to nudge each other, poke ourselves awake, hitch up our lashes. But the bed is too much for us – that old wire-wove, battered and deep and warm and wonky. We want to keep whispering, giggling, but our beached-out limbs get too lulled by its flocked flannelette. Do you remember giving in? Whose hair was whose as we snored and nuzzled? We both stank of dune days, sheep shit and seaweed and salt, and big hunks of sunburnt white bread. With the last of our silly chuckles, as our trunks fell slack in the bed, trickles of sand crept out of secret pockets.

The beach house was ramshackle, bulwarked with long grass. It looked to us like a giant kids' hut. It sat in an infinity of seedpods and it creaked on its nails, sun-parched till its white paint scaled and the wood beneath turned blue. Inside it was crooked and gritty and cradling, its dark core a kitchen, with a muddle of tacked-on rooms. There were faces in the boards and beams, but we just slid into our shared bed and crowed at them – nothing could scare us here. It was a summer without nightmares (or almost). Not even work could get us. Like home, the air of the place was tinted with dung: there were stock in the steep back paddock that wandered down towards the tilted out-sheds, and bobbed at our hands across low-slung thorns of wire. But they were not our job. This was not the farm. The difference was the ocean – and the hard ground the salt air had baked white, so our tough feet flaked it. We loved our feet bare, not trudging round booted, sinking. We loved the bang of them, skidding up dust as we hightailed into endless play. We'd never been on holiday, never heard of such a thing, but we arrived at that broken-down bach and it took us less than a second to split into the distance, get the knack. The sun had cooked off the need for chores. The grass was made for conspiracy, knitted into shady places to whisper and escape.

Our mothers must have felt it too. I remember the lazy mornings of our stay had the feel of a shrug, of a low voice murmuring *someday*. 'We've got time,' I remember your mother said, curled into the slump of the wingback, tossing her sandals under the table with a carefree slap that halted my mother from whatever task she was ploughing through with her usual brisk fuss. The coil of your mother in that chair: I don't think I'd ever seen anyone loaf before, but that summer her ongoing pose of lounge and mosey glazed her for me with a kind of glory. Can someone be that golden? That chair was a spring-blown hulk in faded red, but once she was drooping there, I couldn't help but worship the so-what dangle of her legs, her sultry attitude of fritter and sprawl. The most she would move was to pick at the arms of shredded brocade with an absent finger, half-close her eyes as she traced the dappled grooves. 'Ease up. You've got the time.'

At first my mother kept lumbering around at dawn, her routine too long-term to quit. But slowly I watched the sun displace it. And then my mother became another woman. My mother without irritation creased into her face, without haste twisting the seams of her clothes, without her make-do hair sweating out of its grips, without a quick-smart, get-on-with-it, not-a-second-to-waste tone in her voice, without the swat and shoo of flustered hands, the thud of preoccupied footsteps. My mother with no daylight-is-running-out swish, no huffy don't-bother-me edge. My mother with almost, nearly, nothing to do. You could waste her time here. And she loved it. The order of the house fell apart. No times, no tasks. No shoulds. The rickety washline trilled in the offshore. The black gutted woodstove stayed unlit. We ate offhand grabs of bread, or mismatched picnics, our mothers suddenly flicking the lawn with old scout blankets, upending leftovers onto our laps. We'd dash in from our games, where we were cannibals or princesses, and dive down for a swift feast that suited our wildness. Rush off guzzling worm-eaten ground-fall fruit. They must have felt the same kick, dismissed from duty, no summons to the muck, to the yards and the troughs, to the quarts and gates and offal and hosedowns. The strict parts just dissolved from our days, and our mothers' voices mellowed with them, hazy trails of singsong hello, smiled half-reminders to take care as we rushed beachwards, happy and diluted. No I've-got-a-job-for-yous, no don't-be-lates and make-sures.

Somewhere about the third day, my mother appeared in the shimmy of your mother's frock. I can see its rose print, shivery and damask, as it slithered along her flanks, the thick curve of her spine in its trickery of buttons, her ample arse blooming at the base of them. Her near-beauty came as a shock. Perhaps it did to her too. She took sudden delight in it. The bodice with its overflow of brown dewy bust. The improvised tumble of her silver-skewered hair. Her pulling a klutzy pirouette in the kitchen, then almost a leap through the door to twirl in a borrowed breezy dance out on the lawn. Skipping the toetoe, pointy-toed and electric. How all her petals jiggled as she laughed and laughed. A share-milker's wife in the boss-woman's get-up – what a lark! Then she tripped herself up.

The fathers had to come some time, we knew that. They were due, and we sometimes used our fingers to count off the dates. But we'd learned to cram lifetimes of play into our free hours, seized with story and wide-awake. We were busy. With no one to interfere, our games built for days, whole sagas of crescendo and doublecross, hearty deeds and clashes and acts of God, as many gods as we felt like pretending into being. The sky was full of their antics and falls, and us masquerading as them. And there was the clay track to rush our descent, a cutty-grass tunnel, tree roots to shin and twine, then the tideline of weed-junked sand, and crunching past that, kicking driftwood and dead fish and sticky green pods, the planed shine where shore met sea. Ankle-deep games played in its cool hiss. Corners of rockpool to fossick in with dribbly fingers, prodding at hairy tufts of light, wavy stamens that prickled away from our splashy wading, our curious bunts. The bubble of a dead sheep reeking in the creek, a woolly cloven stink bomb ready to pop. Eels to yelp at, sure they'd slimed our thighs. Mussels and pipi to slunk in big buckets, shovelling for them with deep gluey paws. Driftwood to gather – which wasn't work, because we were jumbling it up the sand for nothing, just for the clattery joy of dragging it round and slinging it into a pile, a crackle of limbs sticking every mad which way – and we were going to be allowed to light it on bonfire night. The night before we had to go. But before that: a life of paddle. A sun-flushed life. A life of fronds. A life our mothers would sometimes visit, chopping down the track with their costumes on, then ouch-ouch sprinting like hell for the water's edge. Sometimes they made the whole race holding hands. Your mother's hair was up in a tawny overkill of rolls. My mother's doughy face was stretched by the violet suckle of her pansy-trimmed swimcap. Once, I remember, she even teased yours for never dunking her face in the salt – she duckdove then arched up, spurting a mouthful in your mother's direction. Who spritzed it away with one of her posh little waves. Then gentleness, all ambling home. A life of late cocoa, tepid and mottled with skin, a life of flops into bed. Our skins still needled with juicy grasses, suits still storing specks of beach, clips of shell, pricks of stubbly weed. Even feathers. We'd fish them out, use them for a final tickle. And then the bed let us slip.

Our mothers didn't need to share a bed. But why wouldn't they want to? We thought it was bliss to be huddled to each other, humming our little tales, naughty hushed disclosures that made us pinch a belly, flap out a shin. We liked the feel of each other's disintegrating plaits, our squeaky suits and dirty toenails. We liked the clink of elbows, grubby and tranquil, the bony wrap of knees, we liked to snooze that way. We liked to trade memories, even if we'd just made them that day, to murmur them over, fresh. We liked to clip our warmth together, hinge ourselves, to sleep hooked in place. Wake scrabbling, soft, at shared limbs. And some nights our voices were joined by our mothers', through the flayed rose-papered scrim of the wall, the same kind of gentle prattle as they lay and napped, sighs dipping and little gasps whistling. Why shouldn't they? I wondered why they still bothered changing into the formality of floral nightgowns, didn't just kip in the stains and tang of their suits.

Your mother had hijacked your father's cigars, a whole carton. She broke it open on the back lawn, rummaged their musty chocolate stack. 'Time to try out his disgusting habit.' She shucked one off, made a cartoon mouth with googly eyes above. Awkwardly lit up with sputtering matches, lay back and honked in a reckless puff. Her lungs went straightaway into battle. But she still tried to out-glam her guffawing. We cackled at her till our sides hurt. But she kept on smoking, her intake getting serious. My mother quiet, watching her, said, 'So why do you put up with it?' Your mother's stare aimed at mine for a long time, before it over-blinked and slid away, skyward. 'That is the burning question,' she answered. She pretended to be all Hollywood again, shammed a film-star posture, lobbed a cigar at my mother. It hit her in the chest, and eventually my mother scooped it up, scorched the end of it smoothly, took a long, even breath. But for a while she just crouched there, and never touched it.

In the end we didn't know whose murmurs we listened to – their talking spilt our sleep. Until the night we were bumped aware by their shrieks, the rumbling as my mother drubbed at the mattress, clobbering at the flames their sleep had lit. Your mother was a goner for those cigars by then, dozed with one paring ash along the sheet, too lazy with its stub. Woke with my mother pummelling her, clouting at sparks in the horsehair for all she was worth. We fluttered the hallway to get to them. Stood with our eyes full of fire, while she flogged it out. Single-handed. A working woman. When it fizzled I waited for your mother to say something witty, to give a cheeky signal, encourage us all to bounce back into the blackened bed, do something frisky with the cinders. I could somehow see that happening, but it didn't. Your mother just stood aside, watching, like she had lockjaw.

Then the gods came in the shape of our fathers. We could never have invented them. The bach was a castaway, so your father had to park his Bedford truck far up on the roadside, its door a slam that buckled down the hill. His descent was blank-faced. He didn't pet you, didn't scrub you at the crown, ask how you were. He strode past you into the house. We hovered wary steps back from the door. His prowl made the kitchen look dollhouse tight. And both our mothers sat at the table, feigning some chore, some drill with dishes they hadn't carried out in weeks. They kept their eyes on their tools, on their fingers. His voice paced around, big chested, and his boots struck after, a thick, resounding follow-up. My mother spotted us, and skedaddled us out. We went and dawdled out by the stock, who munched along after us so we could stroke their scaly coats, sending up gnats and dust. Even the cows here were not just supply, not yield, not cuts of rib and shank. They weren't just what could be done to them, they were the thing itself, and they strayed to our palms, warm and tousled. Their wirebrush lashes were sun-tipped. We stared down into the sad brown dreams of their eyes. Your father raised his voice, until it peaked on 'reputation'. We heard the kitchen table jolt as he spoke, brought the word down on its surface like an axe.

But after his visit, we still didn't go. There'd been a pounding in the kitchen while we'd stayed outside last night, the knock of household thunder. Things flung, an oaken struggle of chair legs, the blow of an object at the door.

We'd scurried, too scared to wait for details. And then we were fetched by my mother, shoved to bed, her lips crossed with an index, a do-as-I-say hiss. We made ourselves sleep, deep and blinking and soundless. But in the morning, your father was gone. We sortied to the beach, planned to hit the water with a kick of celebration. But the sand was streaked with jellyfish. A swarm of glass bubbles with fanned blue bags, the crenulations of tentacle screwed up behind them, a scintillating blue. We knew about them. There was a legend in your family your uncle had nearly died getting stung, an off-patrol soldier who'd dived through a tropical lagoon, felt the stab of a different man o'war. We kept a tiptoed distance, turned back up the track. And when we got to the kitchen, the mark round your mother's right eye was another bluebottle, a swollen tremble of sightlessness, the pouch of its iris finned with blood. My mother dabbed it gently with a lukewarm cloth. The long sting of tears leaked from her.

But we stayed on. There was a set to our mothers' faces. Their tread in the humid rooms felt grim. My mother started fixing things, tidying, straightening again. She struck a washroom fire, and boiled a tub of clothes that she staked out, flapping. Yours rested her head on surfaces, her neck making delicate calibrations, like the globe of her mind was a dead weight. The lashes of her bloated eye were slowly unsticking. We watched its contusions when we could, like coloured smears in a rockpool, until she moaned us away. But they both tried. The beach was off limits, with its bulge of debris, its trim of glittering indigo bulbs. So our mothers tried to entertain us. Once your mother was walking they wax-papered up a packed lunch and we hiked up a nearby road. The only house on it was said to be haunted, a jagged villa with a wide frilled porch. Your mother knew the legend: an old woman perished here, locked herself away for love, solo and withering. It sounded to me like a fable she'd nicked from a book. But it was spooky, told with her grape-jam eye. And the house did give off jilted sounds. Its spires looked ladylike and supernatural. We broke in and crept around the rotted halls, putting our feet down careful round the bruises in the boards. It was dazzled with bird shit, and the curtains swung in dregs. Wings threshed as we chose our path, giving us gooseflesh. And giggles. We gasped at china tiles and fancy porticos. In the tall loft cupboard of one grand room we startled something stashed away with wide shining eyes. A ghost! My mother made a clamber on some chairs, undaunted. It was just a possum, nested and stunned in its posh wreck. It stared at us with quivering breath. Like the boxed-in bearer of a too-sad story.

I would like to say my father was different. He was, in that they didn't need to ward him off. He repeated a fair match of all the words your father had – they'd had enough of a getaway, what did they think they were playing at, by now the whole district knew what they were up to – but they sounded toned-down in his mouth, as he sipped, and issued statements, from the edge of the cup they'd planted, china-white and far too dinky, in his grip. They were comments he seemed to have borrowed, rote, from his boss. He spoke them, firm but empty, like mottos. No doubt he was on orders. He looked very tired, his Adam's apple scraped strangely clean. He didn't throw his weight. And when his dog rocketed away to the beach, and turned back up welted, belly-crawling, my father cradled its simper of black and white, and used a forearm to smudge its foaming jaw. He let it retch venom on the tightly appointed buttons of his torso, while my mother murmured sorry. I think he did have a softness for her. Although I remember in the yard once we did get back, when he was due to slaughter an animal, he shot clear through the throat of the target and downed the beast the other side of it, so the two of them staggered, their wounds unfinished, through the wet grey yard while all of us watched. A keening and dumbfounded crumple. Prolonged. A pitiful ungulate circling. My father never missed.

In those parts, a holiday was unheard of. We never had another one. So I remember: still running in the dark bowl of night, a game of catch triggered by stars. The burps we made with our lips clamped down on clues as we donkeyed round playing charades. Your mother curled in her riven chair, her habit extinguished, her faint smile leaving mauve furrows. Days we were pirates, thirsty to be out raiding, roguish and bawdy and gallant – always ready to slip off our pronouns and roar. A life of sheen, with quick soles silty. Your chalky curls where they pinged out your fishtail. My mother having us in stitches by whisking her tea leaves, pretending to pick out bogus fates from their sprinklings. Riddled with salt, your warm skin's night-night squirm. Two carcasses, hung in the shed, the sway of their ribs like a meat-roped ladder. My husband said he saw yours at the stock sales yesterday, and you were in trail alongside him, a stolid red-cheeked infant wedged on one hip, a toddler whining beyond. A life of float. The hands-clasped stroll of our mothers toeing the tide line. A bonfire of limbs never torched.

eleven love stories you paint blue

Waist deep, only your lower half in love with him, those early days. Only your knees loose and hazy with warmth when you see him, and up in the core, in the muscle, the laze of his far-off hello-smile leaves an easy thrum. But he's at a distance, safe, with fields and roads and rooms still yet to cross, cars to dance through at laidback 3pm speed. You're okay, in the presence of others, the press: what could you do? So you're just in love low along the autumn length of your legs under a thoughtless dress, a weightless old dress between breath and cloth, wearing a drizzle of long-ago flowers on blue, the kind of blossoms history is made of, petals adrift in sweet vintage ticks. Your drifty legs, with the slope of love ending in sandals full of schoolyard dust, that get you to kerbs, that get you to corners, the road-patrol kids with their wide signs slowing and halting you, that get you to a vista of trees arched low with the park cool under them in long clay ribs, your ankles aimless and soaked in leaves and shade, the falling of edges and yesterdays that old trees always speak. There's the sound of his shoes on their shovel through leaves, off-time with your longing and your blink through fresh-washed fringe and your too-loud scuff. Hello. Oh. Hi. Yeah, hi again. Half wordless, still paces apart. And only your lower half, cut across the dark grass, doped at the soles and lonely to the thighs, just getting to the place you have to go, to pick up kids, his kid, your kid, but in the hipline want is making you tense and sway with a non-committal rock. Just a hemisphere of muscles in love you can't be held accountable for. Keep eight paces, keep five, even three, between you, an easy border in the dry blond leaves and nothing bad will come. So you can't stop wanting a skinful of his fingers, so you want to hold him lodged, locked at shoulder, knucklebone, cock. So what? So what.

It's a small town edged with the rattle of blue trucks, the 3am blue that you can't dream in, the nights made of loads being towed to a distance, to songs on a station no one listens to. The shudder of all those loads makes the outline of four walls when you close your eyes, an echo of your bedroom, silver and riding that muted clatter through the night, to towns you'd throb to visit, but you're too small, you're too fixed, and no one. And how do they even hold up? – those dark linked beds, those tremors of jointed metal, when it sounds like the wheels could detonate on one stone fleck, drop the deck in a sparking slide, the steel panels unbolt and gouge the road towards you in long symphonic shivers. You expect to hear that: you lie still, wait, your house on the crossroads. When it's deep night the trucks don't brake and the far-off quake of them starts up in your thorax, rises gritty in your trunk to pinpoint your offcentre heart, shakes the house in apocalyptic gusts, then moves on, a bass note of disintegration, tracked into nowhere, the last pulse of them a telescopic flutter that leaves you little but a blue trace over your scalp. Cold with questions. Months since you met him, the residue of sound turns bluer, like a fingertip down the spine's machinery, like the quiver of a dress come undone when only you are barefoot. Half alive under lit-up eyelids you travel the noise that goes on hauling dark apart.

There's no husband in this story. He's not here because he's not real. You knew it the day you married him, the days before that, when he pulled up in his wagon, worked the horn with the heel of his hand, his talk like smoke that trailed out the window, warm, habitual, but nothing to do with you, as he took you to the same places he'd always taken you, parked in the same degree of shadows lowered by the always-there trees to edge his hands through clothes onto skin in the same slow-breathing fumbled sequence, so when he finished you could drowse watching fern-shade and letting the trickle of him fade like his thudding dull need was never there in the first place. So there's no husband in this story. There is you, there is the man, there are the passing trucks. That's all. That's all the story can hold. You know it when you get up, like the house has already set out a map of your possible steps, walk to your kitchen where you can see the crossroads, your limits laid out in four corners. You know it through your sleep like the ripple of pale walls. You know it when you reach for the edges of the story and lay your hands flat on the ways that it can't end well.

There's so much this story cannot be about – like the kids doing show-and-tell when you're rostered on for your morning of classroom help, and they clamber to the front of the room, on a slalom through knees and sneakers, a wobbly leapfrog of knocks and laughs, and they get to the spot on the carpet-square where they hold up their cut-outs of current affairs, ragged events they've snipped from the paper, their sticky fingerprints crinkled to black, and they tell, in their own mock-grownup drone, what is going on in the headline, the picture, they list who has died or been saved, but mostly they chant through the victims, they like the stories with a high body count, aware that there's big news out there, news with ammo,

81

news with blood, news with repercussions, and angles the camera revolves around in strafed red flash, news happening in x-rays in worlds where cities are dyed night-vision green and magnified homes are hit with cross-hairs that bomb them shapes no one lives to see. And even the children know this, as you squat on the pygmy plastic seats and help them star-shape foil sheets and necklace their crayoned ornaments with itchy strings, as you listen to them stumble their spelling words, their mouths on the consonants spitty and back-tracked, as you lower their wax-etched portraits into thin blue tubs so the skeleton picture sticks, as you push-pin their charts of feelings in primary colours to the hessian walls, they know that your story is nothing, that your place in this classroom doesn't count, and tomorrow you will not be listed, you will not show up, but they'll still show-and-tell and the refugees will starve at the chainlink borders, the protesters will be gassed in grey squares, the revolutions will run software with faces of the lost outlined in red glories, and they will have forgotten who you are – and so they should.

But there's no way the story can't hold his kid – though you keep yours safe off the edge of the narrative. Because you know from her face's flat ratio, its pale bulk and thick-cornered eyes, from the lovely moony colourblind smile she gives when he slots out the handle on her schoolbag, so she scampers with it like she's twitching a puppy on a leash, tugs it like it might pounce or yelp, you know you are unforgiveable. But her love for everyone is loose-mouthed, so she bestows it on you, her smile with its blob of pink tongue, its gaping glee for the air swishing leaves on her t-shirt, for the pasted treasure she tows from art therapy in crooked glue-gunned struts, for the new blue treat of her special shoes, which clump her through the autumn crunch. *Downie*, mutters your kid one day, so you have to pull him to the side of the path, to the outskirts of the story, into a sudden hunch where you hiss, red-faced, *don't you dare say that*. But don't you dare? You dare much worse. You go on daring, unspeakable want. But she likes you, and she likes to look close, her wet eyes opal under big glass rings, her fingers wombling your cheekbones, poking the paint of your lower lip, so you crouch to let her, and she tries out words, but her teeth are deaf, and barked in her throat her loud voice blots them, sluggish. She paddles your face and nods up at her daddy, gives him a big smile, rubbery and brimming. You are beyond selfish. She's as close to an angel as you will ever see.

And doesn't it happen from a distance, at first − so he's something embodied in a series of muscles through eyelash, spasmodic summer-bright blinks. The miles barely let him into focus. The road is long and barely lets him take the shape of a man. And you start to think something, but the heat drawls the road into waves . . . and you never finish the sentence. It doesn't stop you doing what you're here to do, what you're meant to do, what you always, always. You pick up your kid. You do. That's what you do. You walk to school, you hold the hand you're meant to hold, walk holding it home. It's not an afternoon with the stain of his shape. It's a bloodbeat, a flicker, less. Isn't that the way it is? And other things must happen that day − there surely must be a streak of something turning in the recalled light if you really stop and look. He wasn't that important, that crucial. There were lots of other things. Like maybe you washed down the kitchen floor, sloshing the toeprints with citrus bubbles, the sponge on its rickety plastic stem, which you lean on, fizzing the detergent from its pores, because the floor is a collage of footfalls you feel

83

on your sole-heat, your dinnertime trail round the benches tacky with a serenade of daily grit. Or maybe you planted something, clawed a neat rut in the raised bed that you'd left for seasons, maybe you pressed in a tendril of something, with ribbons of nerve-end or small crocheted leaves, maybe you moistened it, with drizzles of irregular lukewarm sputter from the parched lime hose, maybe you even rubbed your thumbs and prayed. Or maybe you wound down the wire washline and stretched out a bleached load by tight-pegged corners, reached blindfolded by sun into the tub to scrabble up the plastic clamps in their rainbow colours and thought it was a miracle you grabbed exactly the right count to pin to the very end of the wash, to the last beloved limp blue sock. There are miracles. They happen in your life. While you're standing in the dry hexagonal yard, and washing flaps at the bands of your memory, come clean of all the pieces you'd like to forget.

You want to make the story about three things. You cut home via intermediate school, and stare at the shimmer of three things and want to make them into a story and take it across town and tell it, direct and wet and illuminated, into the skin of his face. The three things are: 1) you see a dark boy kneeling by the white H of goal on the rugby field and a girl is crouching over him, elbowing her breeze-messed hair while she concentrates, guiding the warm chrome stamen of an earring in through his lobe, which is fiery with homemade holes, while he tries not to flinch by gazing at her jaw in the swing of sunlight interrupted by hair and tenderness, and when she giggles you can see it ripple with half-wanting to hurt him more. And: 2) you see a girl, and she's different but the same, and she's holding a boy's foot in her chequered lap where they perch on the low rail that is blanched log and jutting nail, and she's painting his roman sandal, dabbing a brush in a vial of Twink and stroking words along the leather where they mingle with dirt and halt at the buckle. And: 3) you see a boy and he's cartooned his fist with a face, crossed eyes and a grin round his knuckles, so when he sneaks up to the girl-he-will-not-admit-he-likes he squawks it with black-lined gobbles, poking it puppet-style into her getaway squeal for a goofy kiss. And they're all in uniform, and that makes it somehow a sweeter and a crueller blue and you want him to know – even now you should just walk there, turn back across town and tell him. Stand on his doorstep, empty-handed, say, I tried to walk a different way so I didn't see you, so I wouldn't pass you. But that didn't work and now I have three blue things and they're not a story but they're what we need to know.

And do you really want to help? – when you go to her class, you sign up as aide, and you squat by the art table helping her shingle strings with thin white corkscrews of shell, because she's been to the beach with him, and you wonder as you knot in the spiralled pieces, the bone-smooth rings where the soft-clawed animal rises to the broken lip, you wonder what he would taste like, standing in the coastal trash, the no-man's-land of black weed, where he'd wait until her head was turned and his hand would track sand across your neck, collecting a tide of tingled secrets, and his mouth would pick a dizzy second to risk a kiss fishlined with hair. But no, you do, you do want to help, so you focus. The project is for her mother – and you've seen her mother, who sometimes manages to fit in a Friday 3pm and turns up in lycra with hi-vis ticks and a bracelet of digits to tell her how many steps she's burnt, and straps the kid in a space-age trolley, an offroad aerodynamic pram, and is already running before she's cleared the grounds, dodging through other parents' scuffed-shoe lassitude, half hellos and nods of post-school laze, a slalom of goal-setting elbows and cardio intensity and bodycon tights, her kid's legs bobbing from her canvas all-weather cradle, chrome at the high-stress joints. That's her mother: targeted and beautiful, and just because she packs the kid up so quick you shouldn't think that she's ashamed, because who are you to judge. You're what's wrong with the story, not her. And the little girl wants to surprise her mother, and she flops her palms with delight at your network of shells, your threading of calcified stars so clever and clattery, and under the ceiling fan the crop of her hair is shuffled with puffs of cool and she can't even shoe-tie, you know, you've seen her with the mother, who is busy and sighs to double back and kneel down to finish her daughter's laces with quick tough yanks that won't slip this time, so you hold her wrists to guide her through loops, you splice with her bungling fall-behind fingers, and then you hold the spray up and the long links twinkle and circle and clack. In her smile her tongue lolls with pure bliss. You're what's wrong with the story. Nothing to show, less to tell.

The weather wants to help you stop – it levels the town with rain, silvers the crossroads with nowhereness. The names on the signs turn liquid, erased, headlights only heighten the blur. You back the car out, to get your boy, along a gully of flooded grass. The weather wants to help you. But the school is a gridlock, there's nowhere to park, the traffic crawling in the backwash of half-light, the windshields flushed with rhythmic glare, so you head for the pitch but as soon as you've pulled in you know it's a bad move, the wheels in the mud flux, deep. But you leave it, run in to find your kid, and race in the downrush back to the car, the rain a tumble of cold off plastic and down your spine. You can't get traction. You know it. You knew it. You get out and flail and hump at the brake lights, grunting as if you could hope to heave it, your sandals sinking into the slush in a sloppy skid. Until he sees you. And then he's directing you through rain, bending his torso to the car rim, and waving you to rev, and the bogged-in tyres are somehow delivered to grip. So what else is there then, when they're so soaked, but to offer to drive them. The weather won't stop you. And do you take them back to your place, and towel down the kids and switch on the TV, do you lead him out to the shed, where the window has been painted over, so pigment spills the grooves where you pilot his hands, an oily indigo speckling the skin where you usher him deep-breathing under your skirt, a shadowed blue where you stifle his wet touch, getting lacquered with his tongue, leaving details, like paint sucked back onto the brush, his jaw for the asking, vibrato, like the picture coming apart between your hips, and backing into the stacked-up shelves, the tins of things you could use at school, the tints and resins dripped and welded, cans of sultry colour and gloss, you could tip on the art bench and flex there, fingerpainting poison. Do you? Because that's the kind of thing you would make up.

Before you married you needed white shoes. But you couldn't find any in your hometown. So you drove to the next town, the town after that, and after that further, on a white-shoe search. It seemed to take weeks, driving solo with just the thought of white shoes trailing a sunset, your lone route stretching, steered for a horizon of possible shoes where the lineup of shop girls would shake their heads, *sorry*, and you'd have to search further still. And sometimes you thought you'd never turn homewards, the journey would just veer on and on, the next town stocking white shoes but not in your size, and the one after that selling only platinum, cream. But then you did find them. And when you found them they cost so much you rang your fiancé to ask if that was a price you could afford. And he told you he loved you so spend what you need. You almost let him in the story for a second. You almost wished he could always feel real. But when you were all put together in white and the long white day was almost done, he said, *keep on the white shoes while we do it, so we can get our money's worth.* And now sometimes when you can't sleep you unpack the white shoes from their tissue and you put them on and lie in bed like they'd float you feet-first down the distant roads they came from. You're not careful anymore what you wish for.

Where's it all going, all those loads in the blue night – who is it needs so much? Why do we? Why do we? You lie and listen to the din of the trucks, out on the brink where it thins to a muffled chime. Who is following that hydraulic odyssey?

Only you. Only you.

But how is it then you don't hear the truck that leaves the road, that takes the shoulder, and ends on the low grass slope up to your house. It is waiting when you get up in the morning, when you stand in the kitchen by the crossroads lookout, a silver hulk braked on a slant in a disbelief of light. And how can it stay there stranded, no one coming to hook it up, to claim it, to ease it steaming back down to the road? How does it? But it does. And by the afternoon, when you've called it in, you've tried to track the company, you've phoned the police, and it's still not been moved, you go out to the cab and climb up the first metal step, balance on the second. How can it not be locked? So you manoeuvre in, and slide channelled vinyl, you think about taking up the main seat, you stroke your soles along the pedals, your fingers play the bolts of the wheel. You look for clues, you look for notches. You turn the dial of the radio, waiting for love songs: there's a blue everafter of sound. The windshield has a silky fringe, which shimmies at the finest hint of direction.

if there is no shelter

remove yourself to a place of safety if possible

The last time I went to the white chairs it was raining – the kind of thin rain you barely feel. The rain meant less tourists, although some were still gathered, in their bright zippered parkas and aerodynamic soles, taking photos, their selfies awkwardly solemn. It's the wheelchair they want in the background, and the baby seat, its fabric sprayed so white it looks petrified, its hard straps like wing joints. But it's a bad angle, tough to get both in shot: the tiny capsule, on its scant-grass bed, will vanish in the legs of all the other empties – the office swivel on its five-wheeled star, the barstool, the deckchair, the white cane colonial. I don't offer to help. And no one asks. On one visit some woman had a child with her who wanted to slalom through the rows of chairs, who saw no reason not to skip up the unroped aisles and wriggle into place like a game where the music stopped. She danced over the baby seat in hot-pink gumboots, a leapfrog her mother's lurch was not in time to halt. So the woman had no choice but to weave through the queue, head down, fish the child from her clamber among seats, hissing in a language I didn't know but could still tell she was sorry in. I didn't say anything. I let her yank the child away, one-handed, kicking in its heart-print coat.

My father drives cabs full of tourists like that. He's worked cabs in this city his whole life. It's a shabby job, he knows it, and to compensate he is all class, my dad, slicked back, well-trod, soft-spoken, a gentleman behind the wheel. He gets fares full of sightseers, who slump in the backseat and vent about the urban mess they've witnessed. The so-called Rebuild Tour is like a cruise around a war zone. It's a ghetto, they tell him, a dead pool. They'd thought it was recovering; they'd thought, from the brochures, it was rallying, reconstructing, slapping high-rise life back up. He picks them up from the pop-up mall, where they've tried to contribute to the regional economy, but end by just sulking over virtuous local-ground coffee, the wind bearing down through the overpriced bunkers. They feel compassion, but also ripped off. It's like booking a luxury break in a carpark. If they've been pre-quake then their memories are boarded up, or worse, they trek round cold squares following the stars on the foldout map to find rubble and scars. They don't recognise yesterday, its landmarks crushed. The gouge through the Cathedral roof is like a hole straight through God.

My father knows this syndrome. He's seen it enough. When he first got back on the job, he couldn't find his way around the city either, though he'd driven it a lifetime of lone-man nights, endless bored circuits on near auto-pilot, the same streets always beneath him in a long-term drone. Before the quake, all routes were known. My dad was a master of shortcuts, byways. I watched him come home post-quake for a handful of days, defeated, then I called shotgun. But my navigation proved as bleak. At least we could sit together, pulled over at an oblong of no-man's under hurricane wire, and trade the names of the roads we thought we could head out on, point out the turns that might still take us somewhere we needed. I wish they'd put up the white chairs earlier. Sometimes it seems like we could pilot the streets by their lineup, plotting our course by that corner with its shining lounge of ghosts.

alert those around you

The chairs in the hotel were black. I waited for my lover, blinking on a cheap dark throne, sometimes shifting to the next if his car took too long, but always standing by the time I heard the engine reach our park, its memorised tinny diesel *grrr*. They were eighties metal arches, tubular ebony with hi-gloss legs, and padded velour that felt clammy and fingerprinted, splotched Miami chic in mauve and teal. One afternoon we fucked on one, adding to the build-up of low-lit human stains. He was due to be inside me when the quake hit. That's the way it should have been. We should have ridden out the damage on bad velvet, moaning of true love in our four-legged rut. I should have had my hands spread on black bars, watching the wet crook of everything we wanted, pumped into coupling, stooped through the spine to the grin he upturned for a dovetail kiss. We shouldn't have noticed that the world was leaking plaster, dusting our pangs with a fibrous mist, that cracks were snaking in the budget walls, stucco bouts the shorted sprinklers turned to gum, the grey carpet roaring. Our bodies should have moved as the room coughed a canopy of grit, as the hotel turned to confetti.

The hotel chairs were black, and I belonged on them.

I remember once, when he was late, I spent the wait scouring my body for flaws. I huddled in a black chair, and hunted my stripped-back skin for places I hadn't prepared enough. I wanted to be marble, I wanted to be silk, so I'd stretched myself for hours, to clean, to shave. But contorting on my chair before he came I found nicks and tiny broken veins. I found the dry buff of blued elbow skin. I found a microscopic rash in raised pinpricks. I found a single toe where a curled blond hair had evaded the razor. It obsessed me, that toe. I'd been using my fingernails in vain to tweeze when he walked in the door. And I'd forgotten it.

The room always turned over when he walked in.

If they'd found anything in the rubble, I could have identified it. I stood long enough outside his building – or the capsized hulk where the building had been. They should have come to me. I could have told any part of his body, from a follicle, a half-moon, the merest fleck. But they kept us on the margins, staked out perimeter tape to hold back grief. We're pushy, the leftovers, the ones who know the wreckage holds no hope but who still have to watch. I stood, lit to neon by floodlights and sirens. I stood in an aluminium blanket. I stood, and mumbled answers to somebody holding a clipboard who had stars on her collar. I thought of games we had versed in the cheesy motel, I thought of sheets we'd kicked off for Jenga towers, a squatting naked playoff on the woozy mattress surface, blocks thumbed out of plumb with a squeal of fluke, before we scrambled them with coming again, a shonky wooden splatter under our spines. I thought of how little I knew of him – tax bracket, allergies, IQ, blood type, place of birth – except every inch of his body, his birthmark in a smear at the nape, the zig-zag punctures of long-ago stitching on his knee, hair nesting down to his crotch in a sweet-and-sour whorl. But the woman with lapels didn't want those answers. Her pen stopped scoring on its hard-backed cleat, and she tweaked the foil blanket tighter around my chin with a tut. Then she moved on: there was no shortage of people lined up in the smoke, to stare and yell and shake. When she came back she suggested we start again. I made more sense on the fresh page. I'd realised by then I shouldn't be giving the details of my lover, but of his workmate, my husband.

don't use lifts – keep left on stairs

My husband had known, since the first quake, that the building wasn't right. But no one he talked to seemed to listen. After I'd met him in town one day for lunch, he took me in and he stood me in the stairwell, made me hush, so I could pick up the wind amplified on the rails, the outer wall's strange buzz. I didn't like it. Something odd and faint was thrumming, like a tuning fork. But I shook it off.

Most of us did.

The first quake had taught us we were blessed. So many of us woke unscratched, our houses dented, our streets hashtagged with wire, but with nothing irreversible taken. We hovered, relieved, in the clutter that had swilled from high shelves, the silky muck that slid from the tarmac, sunk our cars. We dozed back the slop of belongings, and shuddered at the blizzard of glass that had levelled the shops, and traded near-miss stories, and counted ourselves saved. The worst had hit, and most of us slept through it. Nothing seemed fatal. There were only a few, like my husband, who didn't feel delivered, who couldn't believe this state of calm. Who kept pointing out the cracks.

And he was right: as we stood in the stairwell that day, I remember there were hairline trails, thin splits that climbed the plaster, flutters of fine-tooth crumbling that met in deeper throbs. He held my palm over one of them. The pitch of something wrong shivered the surface, a hint of sound that travelled my wrist. But then his colleague lurched out onto the landing above us, took the slope down in three bold thuds, levering off the handrail to touchdown at our feet. I stared at the salvo, the muscle buttoned into blue business shirt, the slick black shoes detonating on concrete. His good-to-meet-ya grin, so casual, left me feeling concussed. *So you're Chicken Licken's wife*, he smirked. My husband punched him, a cut-it-out jab at the arm he was already aiming over, in cheeky greeting, at me. *Mrs Licken. Good to put a face.* My pulse ricocheted from his decent handshake.

And so I joined the ranks of those who no longer listened to my husband.

I should have leant in to where my husband tried to steer me, I should have pressed my temple to the stairwell wall. I should have felt it coming in scalp and eyelids. The building tried to tell us. In gooseflesh. In a minor key.

Later, after my husband was proved right, I would be stranded in a stairwell at the hospital, tracking his gurney as a straggle of volunteers tried to lever him somewhere, anywhere, to be seen, the lifts cut and crooked on their cables, and bodies pushing past to some other rushed triage, and aftershocks coming so the concrete strobed and lights dropped and peals of panic kept swelling while they jimmied him aloft.

But I couldn't see that disaster falling. The one I felt, standing there on the flight, with my hand in that grip, was the man in front of me. He was all the emergency I could breathe.

Lovers say: my world will fall apart. I'll break into tiny pieces. You have torn me down and open. We should be banned from speaking.

I live with my father in his yellow-zone one-bed, along with a driver who works with him. Jack is a crusty old darling, all eyebrows and pot gut, his kneecaps spangled with psoriasis. He lets me sneak out to his den, which is just Dad's carport tarped and boarded up, and squat on his stretcher, tap a smoke from his stash, and he doesn't let on to my dad. He runs his scaly old fingers round his grin like a zip, and gives me a mortal wink. I light up, inhale, pass it to him, and we take turns fiddling gaps into the tarp splits, wheezing smoke out of the crackling plastic. Dad knows what we get up to, of course. He makes out that some new dispatch he's catching on the half-munted TV is much more crucial, that his flustered jig around the lounge with the aerial to make the broadcast stick is life and death for a bit. Only once did he come out and sit with us, shaking his head in the chill and fug. He felt guilty for snapping at a fare he'd picked up, another foreigner who'd moaned about the state of the shops: *What do you poor souls do for retail? All this time and it's still like a bomb's gone off.* Dad couldn't take it. *Give us a chance,* he'd said. That was it. Just give us all a chance. But he shook his head in Jack's lean-to, and told me, *What I wanted to use was that word you do.* He'd never speak it, my gentleman dad. He's a churchgoer, too, a faith that has lasted the quake, none too fond of my godless vocab. So I blew out a gust and said it for him. *Give us all a fucking chance.* Jack near wobbled off his stool, made the whole night echo with his wicked chortle.

Jack likes to escort me to the portaloo, if he spots me going out at night. We shuffle on gummies, and bang our torches, and work our way round the gaps and swamps, the letterboxes and pickets that have finally tipped. You never know when the stuff that looks to have survived will fold up suddenly: paths ripple, wires shirr off, gulfs open, leaks darken brick. Sheds make a sigh, turn to metal origami. Concrete garden beds prolapse. Toppling aerials scatter birds, and washlines swing down a tailspin of wet clothes. You have to watch the edges of the world now, for the drop-off, the plummeting. That's just the way it is. *We were always in a red zone in this part of the world*, Jack says. *We just didn't bloody know it, eh.*

So Jack and me, torch-lit, scuff along slow. Lately he's been helping me at the hospital, too, calling round on the days I'm on training, the trial nights when I'm left with my husband for a stint of sole charge. *Dodging off shift for a bit*, he'll wink. *Suits me to muck in. You're a bloody good excuse.* He runs me through the steps, *caregiving eh*, like he's interested, gets me to recount the instructions that the nurses drill in. *Somebody else may as well learn the ropes*, he says. *You'll need a hand when they let him back home again.* He even helps with my husband's pan. We two-step the corridor, and when I retch he takes the weight; he never says a word about it, the sloppy indignity of sound against metal, the animal stink of our limits. If he has to, he'll help me turn it over, upend it into the beaming sink. If he has to now, in the road outside our unit, he'll even stand and wait with his torch, while I crouch in the stall for long sobs he doesn't mention. When I falter out, he'll steer me back home. If I stumble, if it lasts, he will even get down on creaky knees, offer me his brand of blokeish comfort, patting my back and saying, *good girl. Come on now. You're all right. You're a good girl.*

report any damage

I know my husband's body now, the way I once knew the lover I lost. I know the flare of red on his skin from the endless pressure of the sheeting, I know the places that ulcerate, sacrum, coccyx, heel, where the serum leaks. I know to anchor the back of his head, to pack his nape with a halo of feathers. I know to move the spoon in slow motion, dabs of soft mash, and I know when I wave it, even if his eyes are blank, I have to give it time, to wait for his lip's reflex, to watch for his tongue tip reaching out for the pulp. I know the side of his mouth that leaves a tremor of grease, and I know when I wipe it he might half-talk, or at least, his chest-wall might move with a load of vowel sounds his mouth can't shape any further. Not in a language I know, or one I deserve – because why should he ever talk to me? I know the clefts where the flannel must be thorough, the crevices I must sponge with gentle drips; I know the intricacy of shit on hair. I know the gouge that buildings leave when they are not to code, know the rare ways we crumble. I know the pigment of bedpans, and their tone in the night, the acoustic slosh of loneliness. I know how to breathe in the narrow room, its microclimate of piss and sweat. With his hospital bed and my cot, there's not even room for a chair. And that's how it should be.

unless the building has collapsed, await
instructions to evacuate

I want to tell Jack I am not a good girl. I want to tell him when he's at our kitchen table, writing a postcard to his wife in his slipshod hand, all flashy off-kilter letters, and a sloppy X to end. She fled the city when the first quake hit, and there's no chance she'll come back – *she's always been the one with sense*, Jack nods. He's stocked up on shots of the city that was, from a tourist stand they once flogged in their cabs, bolted to the seatbacks, and he sifts them out of a shoebox, one a week, like coupons for memory. *Spots we grew up in*, he tells me. *Spots we took the nippers, even spots we . . . got up to mischief.* He shoots me a devilish wink. The muddle of berry jam and Vegemite he's paddling onto chunks of bread leaves the latest message tacky, but he's happy with it. You've got to have a project, the way he sees it.

His project, most days he's not driving shifts, is to comb the suburbs hunting for junk to trawl home. There's no shortage. There's street after street lined with offcuts of furniture, cast off bric-a-brac, the abdicated slump of old mattresses homely with ground-down springs, the silver-brown watermarks of sex or birth or heat. The arms and legs of oak props and panels, the white metal faces that no longer tick, the fringed lamps shimmying like a frilly joke. Come into my parlour, where everything's dust. Tablecloths scalloped and murky with fingerprints, the tatty knots of curtain half-hooked to splintered rods. The crooked trash we used to need to live. He keeps on tugging it home. *Free to a good'un*, he'll report when he comes back towing a haul – he needs us to know he's a cut above the looters. His takings are all above board. Just another family trucked out, left it all behind. *The whole shebang. You'd hardly credit it. Sign up saying help yourself. No smiley face though.* He doesn't get smiles from us, either. We hardly have the space for it all. But we've let him wedge his lean-to with it, curio cabinets with no walls to tack them on, the copper dents of a firescreen though we don't have a hearth. A set of chipped enamel tiles sitting in a stainless tub, curlicues of crunched deco sheen. I don't know what it means, this hoarding. Perhaps he imagines he's storing up the makings of a fitted-out base so his wife will come back. *She's always been the one with sense,* he says, *but I'm the one with hope.*

So much hope that he scurries the crumbs off his polo and wobbles into his boots, determined to get to the postbox, feed his note into the slot. And I go with him, keen to block him spotting the latest leftovers piled on the berm, hitching home with more shards. He likes my company, though he half suspects I'm tagging along to thwart his fossicking. Sometimes he pulls a dopey dawdle like a toddler wowing over some new speck – you can just see him as a kid poking fingers at a flickering insect or oil spill on the pavement. I swear when he starts to dally round a junk pile, grubbing at the crisscross and fishing something free, he shoots me a cheeky-boy glance just waiting for his telling-off. He puffs happily at my stroppiness, and turfs back whatever it was he'd forked out. His grizzle never lasts. And we go on, cagey, to the box where he plants a big kiss on his latest postcard, a cheesy smack on the script before he slides it in. We can hear it flap down into dark. He gives two knocks on the side for luck.

I want to tell him that I'm not a good girl. I want to, all the slow route home. I want to as we pick through upturned chunks of footpath, as we veer and backtrack to skirt the fresh wire, to bypass the mix of taped-off buildings, some gutted, vacant, some half spliced back up. I want to when he pulls his trademark move, leapfrogs an orange cone, to prove he's still a spry bugger. And when he says, *do you good to write too, you know. You ought to be trying it. Doesn't bloody matter what. There shouldn't be a lock on that head of yours. Pick anyone to talk to. Even hubby, love. He'll hear you, I know it. You just scratch it down.* He claps his rough hands, one-two, a just-like-that diagonal. *And send it off.*

It's me that points out, then, a spiral of floor-rug that's been lugged over somebody's letterbox. His eyes light up, and he's over at the huddle, pulling out a flap to suss its condition. It's thick, baroque, its blue pile not even flooded. *When they've squared your new digs – when hubby's home with you*, Jack tells me, *this beauty'll be just the trick. Consider it a housewarming gift.* I don't say a thing, but Jack is too keyed-up to notice. So I let him roll it tight, and we do a clumsy dance lumping it home. Like the freight of a body. He's so stoked that he forgets to ask the question.

I'm not a good girl. The last thing I wrote was a letter to my husband, on the day of the quake. Telling him I was leaving him.

position yourself away from windows

It is Jack who's been working at the task of bringing my dad in from the garden. He started it sly, with a game of chairs. I'd first come across him queuing for water when the tanker was parked up three streets over, and told him about Dad in his tent, the green slump pitched out back on the unit's scrap of lawn. I thought I'd never get him in. I'd wave to him from the taped kitchen window, bait him with cups of tea, grin over the tiny gas-ring – but he wouldn't budge. It had been weeks. To make him eat I'd have to tote the meal out to a drop cloth, dig cups into the lawn. He'd try to chew and chat, for what it was worth, but would always duck back under his awning. From the house I would watch him blinking from the span of guy-ropes at bricks still pretending to stand. Some nights I crept out and crouched by his shelter, tried to hear his breath over the crunch of the northerly bivouacking the plastic.

Then Jack called in, the taxi stashed with chairs, three eyesores he shouldered round back, one by one, grinning *flaming tada!* The deckchair he shook out its scrawny concertina and motioned me over, concierge-style, to its yellow fibro slats, *for madame.* The school chair, old splintered balsa bolted onto brown legs, he jabbed down, flicking off a few rough chips. The last was too good for us, or at least it had been once, a frame of thick mahogany whorls, its soft plush polished by upper-class bums until it purred. *Do the honours,* he nodded at Dad. When the old man looked cagey he scoffed, *don't be an ungrateful bugger.* And so we perched, in a rickety trio, for our first half-silent night out back. *All you can damn well do when things are dark as this,* said Jack, *is wait for stars.* Which came out a bit bogus, as if he was taking the piss out of himself. *And there,* Jack pointed out, *there the blighters are.* And they were stuck there the next night too, when he popped in, sat another chatty vigil. *If you plan to come back tomorrow,* said Dad, *I reckon a whiskey would help them come out quicker. Too right,* laughed Jack. *That's the proper cure.*

I don't know how long it took for Dad to click on that the ring of chairs was edging closer to the house. When we found ourselves off the ex–vege patch, free of the trip-risk of the tent-pegs, he must have twigged. By the night we were east of the washline, watching its wiry shadows grate round the flat, perhaps he'd given up, faced the fact that the margin between him and the brickwork had now shrunk. The solid world was bound to catch up. Jack had moved in to the carport by then, his jerry-rigged walls going up in bright plastic flags – once I'd found out his own room was redded he had zero say. Dad watched him lash up his collection of sails and said he could take the house. *No bloody way,* Jack snorted. *That's your daughter there, not mine, mate.* Soon after, Dad appeared on the couch one evening, with his newspaper, not catching my eye. He stayed for an hour, while we half-watched some channel of shit reception – inevitable lovers in a haze of bad fate and changed minds – and he had a good old grumble at the ads. Then he bent, gave my cheek a heavy peck, before heading back out to his tent. I didn't try to stop him.

Out in his shelter, he still doesn't zip up his sleeping bag. So he's ready to run.

for emergency help dial 0 from your room

A few nights ago my father was between pickups, parked outside an office complex. He was out in a less-hit suburb, and watched from the cab as lights flickered on four storeys up. A couple had entered the space, a glass-fronted box of chrome and air-conditioning, and it was soon clear what they were doing there so late. Their clinch was a staggering tack for the desktop, the parts of their bodies they needed to meet yanked free of clothes, just clear enough. The tube of her skirt rucked up, his belt suspending the pucker of pants at his knees. He worked on her. My father would have tried hard, but there was no way to blot them from his wide screen. Her hands zig-zagging the surface of files so they flooded the carpet with a flap. His face lowered, lapping. The override of his body come down on her. My father told me none of that. He would never have breathed a detail. But just down the road there was a pub where a covers band was loading gear into their van. When they scoped the couple, they jogged to the white line, choking, zoomed in to shoot it all on their cells. It got posted online, a still frame headlined the paper. The lovers probably didn't keep their jobs. I don't know. I never followed

103

up. But I did watch their bodies, while the clip was still live, the way they battered into the cubicle as the overhead strobed, the hard intent you could see in their grip as they swerved out of clothes. I'd say they'd fucked each other plenty. They bypassed tenderness, mounted quick, barely traded a kiss. It was a choreography I knew. It was a stage I recognised.

I can't help picturing my father, pinned in his cab beneath this scene. He would have looked anywhere but into their cupping and jolting. He was shocked that they made no move to block the spot-lit view. They didn't seem to care, he reported later, shaking his head. It's not a story he wants to clip out and keep, although he got so close to it – not a headline he'll trim down and file in his scrapbook. He's been collecting stories from the quake, but he goes for the heart-warmers, the hazy testaments to overcoming. His favourite is the wedding dress they let the bride rescue from the red zone, her big day set for after the quake. He's scissored out a series of their articles, the roped-up salvage team winching down the plastic-covered glory of her gown, the open-air ceremony put together from the shellshocked, who picked flowers, traded shaken speeches, toasted love, kept trying to rise above. He's right. It is a beautiful spread.

But not these two, fucking so blind, in the open. They didn't seem to care who saw. Their flagrancy baffled him. Maybe, I wanted to say, in the context of this city, they just believed there was no point waiting. Maybe it was the act of people who know that tomorrows can cave in, that buildings can fall. Maybe it's the shaken who learn to be bold, the trapped who seize their days. But instead I let him look at me, stretch out a hand, give me a quick pat of consolation.

He was taking comfort that his daughter would never be so brazen.

The hotel ceiling was always falling. Our bodies kept knocking its glitter down, tufts of its scratchy fibre dusting our workout on the kingsize bed. I'd find its pigment when I propped my head on his chest, twitching to his heartbeat, blown free with a laugh. Once, I remember, I bayoneted a chunk on his nipple: he took the bait, and flipped me onto my back. It would sometimes be in my seams when I trekked home, a dirty sediment I'd crouch in a shadow of my bedroom to brush when my husband wasn't watching, a gritty fleck of secret like his trickle of come still cooling beneath my jeans. It was always falling. We'd slink home with its smut in the roots of our hair, as if we were a reno couple, smashing out the Artex, sanding a sharp new living-room from its seventies crust. But we weren't restoring anything. Every time we met we were dismantling something, bigger pieces of world coming down than the chintzy powder we lay in and laughed at, that we flicked as it stuck to the replayed sheets round our hips, itched through our next kiss. But you don't stop, even when you know what you're demolishing, even when you know you're kicking base-blocks out the tower. Secret by secret in the no-star room, we were pulling down each other's futures, and the gaudy glisten that chipped off the roof of our room just made us bring it down faster. In some way, I think, by the time I was waiting on the final day, I knew the world would drop.

And we'd deserve it.

And maybe I'd pay for it again, even now, to be back there, crashed into the lull after a fuck, our recklessness disjointing the clock hands, our pashing turned waxy with the build-up of whispers, semen, minibar piss. Anything to have ridden his shuddering into a drowsy layout of limbs, still panting, to have skidded from the last glaze of head, faceplanting on his chest where a pinprick of plaster waits to hurt my eye like a close-up on a galaxy. The world come too close, finally exploded.

To be lying there, fingertips browsing his torso, nuzzling his skull through scurf, the air in the cheap room meshed with the shimmery mess we were making of everything.

know the location of all exits

The last letter I ever wrote is still waiting in the red zone. The third time I went back to get it, I was mistaken for a whore.

You could draw a line down the street where we once lived. One side is flattened – and I know why they rail us off, keep us out of that downrush of brick. From the hurricane fence I can see the plunge of stone, the open floors heaved into mounds. Unhinged doors swing open over sheer drops. A tide of masonry, speared with metal. Strange rags of plaster still held upright, streaks of wall projected in ripples. Rooms prone, crushed. Others dangling. A clutch of glass still sticking in a frame, jigsawed with light. I can see that we need to be stopped from going back, combing for belongings: stone waits there in a deadly tilt. But the other side just stands there untouched. I could undo the door, retrieve the letter. It wouldn't take too many footprints. I'd promise not to dislodge anything else. I'm not looking for trinkets, for mementos, stores, clothes. There's no photos I need, no basics. I just want that letter I wrote to my husband, the day of the quake, saying I didn't love him.

That end of town was always whore central, but it's dotted with even more now. Where the blockades end, the women begin, a trail of underfed working girls, tees sketchy over ribs, hair mottled with dust. There's plenty of work to go round. It's a hi-vis city, the inner quadrant, staffed with men in hardhats, men with steel tools, tough attitudes. The girls know where the work is, gather where the utes brake, press their skin along the barricades.

Of course I could have been one of them. Nothing to tell us apart.

He baled me up when I was close. I'd made it past curfew, edged through a slit in the fence, raked my stomach in a tunnel of wire. I was nearly at the door when he yelled, a thick bark of warning. I tried bolting the last steps. I could see our red oak oblong, the eyelid of the lock. But then he was on me, grappling. He backed us out, me flapping off his grip, my elbows winging as he bumped me through the boundary fence. Once he'd dumped me clear, he bent down, took a closer look. Offered me a flat fee, his dick, which he rumbled from under his belt, like just another tool. It didn't seem too bad a deal, to earn a way back. I countered. Just minutes through the wire. My house didn't have a scratch on it. Please, I'd do anything. But he wasn't having it. Enough bodies in there as it was, he wasn't adding more. When he knew I wasn't taking his cash, he shrugged, tucked his cock back down, the bills rolled back at its side. He was a good bloke, spat into the rubble, let me walk home.

place the heel of one hand on the sternum
at the centre of the chest

It happens because you're trying to do good. This is you on outreach, mucking in for the relief effort. There is still so much to clean up – but everyone has lived, there's something thankful in the line-up of people driving their spades into the scum. And the sky is clear, if toned a bit watery, and volunteers shake each other's cruddy hands and get to know each other, side by side in the mire, roughed up, but celebratory. And children are picking up brittle things and flicking them into plastic bags, which they wheel and swing, their gumboots all fizzly in the silt – this is just playtime, sand they can pivot their sticks in and skid down, it's a good game, all this slush. They jab their plastic spades in, load up toy dozers, and they don't care what wells up, though their frazzled mums do their best to keep them out the worst gunk. They ferry off any bits of junk they can use as playthings, laughing in the sleet. But it's lain around for long enough, all this waste. And the aftershocks keep spitting it back up. The adults put their backbone into it. And no one's in charge, so there's no instructions, it's just a group of people trying to do their bit, to lend a hand. So no one minds that it's kind of feeble, the meagre scratches you can make with your spade, no technique and less muscle, dopey and off-balance with the big blade. You're giving it a go, aren't you, getting stuck in? That's what counts. But you're still sort of self-conscious. And you don't want to stop, you want to keep slogging with the rest, but you have to take a break for a sec, and you wander up the line, drag your shovel behind you, a lazy metal itch, bouncing off the odd stone. And you could call it kind of beautiful, this row of strangers, all panting but positive, and buoyed up with each other's grimy nods and raw good will. It should be a moment when you see the best in everyone – a day where you store up some image of human good, and the details you should keep in the frame are the woman rugged-up in the wheelchair over by the car boot handing out mugs of steaming tea, the old girl with Osti frock hitched into knickers battling a barrow under the treeline, the man with a newborn strapped in a doze to his chest helping shoulder a sunk stationwagon out the sleaze.

But you don't. Because that's him. That's him. That is the guy you met in the stairwell. Your husband's colleague. And then you don't see anything. Just the grit that's drizzled on the end of his curls. Just the gleam dislodged from muscle. When the spade wedges in, you can stand and watch the mud glint on his trunk. When he straightens up you can follow the eddies of fine hair that weave down into his jeans, a waistband your fingernails long to slide, sudden, low-riding. Then he catches your eye. And it's too late. Desire is an airlock. His smile rocks the whole world backwards.

close all doors behind you when you leave

Sometimes, in the early days, we used to get coupons for food left on the doorstep. Now it's all flyers for church. My dad consults them all, if I don't get to them first and trash them. One or two he's even fished out the bin, planed their wrinkles with a thick, patient hand, not glancing at me. *I liked the free food better*, I say, banging around the kitchen, while he levels their font on the Formica, stroking their promises flush. *Holy Consolations. Divine Comfort.* At least it means he's inside with me, for a bit. He's got a little sheaf, tucked up by the side of the telly, with a clip on it, messiah blue. Some nights, he slips them out, reads them over again, *Hope in a Dark Hour*, nudging up the bridge of his glasses like it will help redemption come into clearer view.

But he can't go into a church.

He just can't set foot.

Churches are heavy and tall with pain. He can't sit tight in the lines of dark pew, stare up into that glass citadel. He can't watch the ornate rafters stretch to their pinnacles while the singing shakes. He used to love the way the chapels cast back all the chants he's known since childhood, the long sculpted murmurs, but now their echoes fill his head with unholy weight. He can picture them bloodstained. The hymns are full of threat. The tapers flicker too much, God buzzes in his strongbox. My father knows we'd all dissolve like wafers.

I know he muttered prayers to the fare he was carrying in the backseat on the day of the quake. He was pinned to the steering wheel, and she was a voice from the downpour of masonry behind him. They'd been parked up, on the first ticks of the tab, then the thick stone frontage of the shops let go. His cab was crushed. But the driver's side ruched around my dad, left him a cavity, jutted him at trunk and shin, but breathing. The voice of his fare had called, and stopped. She was young, a twenty-something in a print frock she'd grabbed at the hem of to stop the breeze whipping it. He remembered her sliding into the cab with a blush, a babble of happy instructions. He'd been late, he'd apologised, tardiness was never like him. He could offer her a discount off the meter. But she squiggled her mouth, a peachy no-matter. *Happens to everyone*, she brushed it off.

And then it hit.

He didn't know what else to do but pray, my father, out loud, on dull repeat. Her noises had been high at first, a thick treble of blood. Then the vowel sounds gelled. And whistles that weren't voluntary rose from her, bricked-in moans. She forgot most words. In the beginning, he remembers, she kept telling him where she lived, as if they could still drive there, as if he could just light the buckled dash, and pull them both away from the ruin of the kerb. Then she panicked that she needed to pee. *I'm busting*, she kept saying, *please, I'm busting*. She fretted that by the time she was pulled free she'd have wet herself. *How long, I can't hold it*, she kept saying. And my father kept praying, *oh Lord, let your hand be with me, and keep me from harm. I'm busting. Oh Christ above me. I can't hold it. It's all right. You can't help it. I'm busting. Christ where I fall. Christ where I arise.*

do not pull the emergency cord

I finished the letter to my husband on the day of the quake. But I'd been trying to write it for weeks. When I couldn't find the words I would walk through the house to convince my body it was capable of leaving him. I'd watch the proof of my footprints, tacking on the rimu, tracing a slowed getaway. There were only seventeen steps from the edge of our double bed to our front door. I even trekked with a suitcase, as far as the car boot, to show my left hand the grip it would need. The push off the hip to hump it into the trunk, wedge it down on the thin black carpet among blown-out gym shoes, the pouch of tools from my father (as if I could tinker with the engine myself, pop the hood, lean over, *she's right*, and torque at pistons). I stared at the case, a brittle red relic from my mother's teens, silver-rimmed, patched with stickers, a faux-skin lining, zebra-striped, that felt like the surface of a snooker table. All my slutty little articles, balled up neatly, nested in its black-and-white pelt. I slammed the boot, and pretended I could breathe. That day my neighbour watched me, over the street, from a prim twitch of curtain. I longed to give her the finger. But instead, I stood and stared at my licence plate, as if that number would crack some crime. I went back inside, and in place of words, I inked its raised metal code on the page, a whole sheet of digits, six black figures like tracking coordinates into the distance. Then the numbers became letters, became a new sheet, excuses, facts, reasons. What I'd done. What I was carrying. What I was making myself go through with. For the longest time I couldn't write his name: it didn't seem possible to leave it there, heading the whole longhand mess, like the last bloody clue. When I wrote that last line, I sealed the envelope, and I found myself moving through the drilled route as if it would detonate. Of course, it's still standing, every step, but they won't let me back in.

I think of it tonight, as Dad calls Jack and me for a meeting, the chairs triangulated, formal, out in the yard. He's taken to holding these sessions, itemising provisions he's made sure we're stocked with, underlining *preparedness*, bullet-pointing stats and risks. He takes it deadly serious, scoring through charts with a marker, leaving thick black checks. I poke at Jack when he starts to drowse; he plumes his brows over *spare me* eyeballs and is partial to a punctuating fart in his school chair. But there'll be moments even he's struck sober. The last meeting Dad presented us both with a first-aid kit, a sturdy box with a cleated lid – he lined the contents up on the lawn, an audit of casualties, a breakdown of how to salve and stitch. In mine there were sanitary napkins nested in the gauze: he'd thought of everything.

Tonight Dad passes out maps of our unit, our yard, with every path blocked out, a walk-through of arrows barbed, emphatic in felt. He's copied them out by hand – so I can see the tremors where his wrist hit *what ifs*, where the outline's jarred by knowledge. It's cost him, to think his way through these plans. I never enter a building now without scoping the exit points. The supermarket is the worst, all the till bleeps ticking up to a void packed with metal, great vents that hum with gravity. Staves of light, and joists that press on your mind. These are contingencies he knows about. I can see it in Dad's map: what if point A plummeted, what if you fled to B and it coursed down. And we know too, as we watch him smooth his diagrams out, tap on sites of shaky safety with an index. We know about the seesaw, the splinter of angles where you brace yourself, the myth of shelter under doorframes. We know about the pitch of surfaces, handholds. Nothing is a shield. We know about glass – we know it careens at you in jerks, until your freckles are lit up, red studded. We know about the world capsizing and everyone floundering, no help, no help at all. Dad rolls out his map like it's a kind of guarantee. But we know what we've seen. We know the whole world is paper.

Still, it's something to let Dad coach us through his plan, to pick it out with our feet. We navigate round his escape routes, halt when told, Dad bullying us with a whistle. He wears it permanently now, on a cord round his neck. *Hell's teeth*, mutters Jack. *I should have bloody throttled you with that thing when you first came home with it.* But we stick to Dad's diagram, inside and out. Remember the base-boards buckling, plaster streaming from the stud. Remember when the fenceline was all claws. Jack and I play it up, do little one-twos on the exit routes Dad's charted.

We've done it before, down this path, Jack and I: a slow dance with collapse.

I think about the route through my house as I left it, the steps that I can't ever take back. I think about the blood I trailed outside, in Jack's grasp. The track of evidence. He's never said a thing. And I don't have to worry about the neighbour who saw me load my case into the boot that day: she's dead now.

if instructed to vacate the building, follow
the evacuation procedures

Today the old girl from three doors down is trailing at the end of the driveway. Her cardi is mangy and her floral nightie dangles into her gumboots. She looks at the tarmac, still forked in a wide black crack, takes two steps in her loose wellies, then shuffles back again. She is holding a birdcage, dithering.

I go out to her.

Mrs D?

Her head has a teeny rattle on her neck. The skein of her pegged hair is silver and scant. Her pearly eyes tremor in their deep tan creases.

Oh, I didn't want to bother you.

She looks up the road then, and hitches one side of her nightie, like she intends to wobble off. The bars bump her tiny shins, poking from their rubber boots. I can see a crisscross of impact in her old skin. But then she steadies herself on the letterbox, holds out the cage.

It's featherweight, the base a sun-baked lime, the spokes bowed and thin. It's trimmed with entertainments, a spangled mirror, a ribbon looping on a pecked seed bell. The newsprint lining is fresh, only punctuated lightly with shit. But the bird is dead. It's lying on its back, the tiny lemon skull on a tilt. There are delicate ridges in the skin of its sealed eyelids. Its claws curl, unbearably frail. The downy trim on its chest shifts in the faint touch of easterly. But it is gone.

You see I'm not sure, she says. I thought, he might be . . . but then, I didn't feel quite right saying. You don't want to be in the wrong, do you? Just imagine that. So I thought, if I kept him for a few more days.

I look at her.

Do you think that would be all right, she says. To keep him just a few more days. I didn't want to be bothering you. But I thought you might know.

I can hear her dentures give a soft click as her mouth trembles. She works to stop it with a lurch of her pale tongue.

She taps at the cage, her own twig fingers curled, gives a near soundless tweet.

Pretty boy.

Mrs D. I think . . . I think the kindest thing to do is . . . tuck him up. Somewhere nice.

I've got a little camphor box. On my dresser. I could keep him in there. You're right. It's very soft. He'd like it. It's got a blue Chinese lining, you know, with all those willow sort of trees.

No, I mean. I mean, yes, we could pop him in there if you liked. But then we'd have to put him . . . down in the ground somewhere. Pick a patch of sun. Or under one of your fruit trees. We'd have to . . . dig a little space. Make a bed for him. Then, you know, cover him up. Wrap him up safe, then just tuck him in. We'll make it nice. I promise.

She nods then. That's what I thought you'd say.

The sag of her cardi pockets has a gravy trim. Flannelette roses poke out the knit olive rib. There's toothpaste smudged on her collar, a daub of sky blue, and the milky top-button wobbles in the skin of her neck, loose. So I know she is crying. Just one small iota of tear though, an offwhite trickle.

He was the apple of my eye, she says. And he got through the whole thing. All the business. The shaking. And the shocks. I thought he'd be a goner, nearly every time one hit, to begin with. He used to have such a tizz. You wouldn't believe it, the palaver inside his cage. The jolly caterwauling. One night half his plumes flying out. I said, now look you little so-and-so, you've got to pipe down or you'll be starkers, the rate you're moulting. And what blinking use is a bald bird. I told him, look I'm just an old bird too, and if I can stick it out then you can. And he listened, you know. He really did. He still got all flustered – he'd do it before they were coming, have a wee tiff, so you see, I'd know, like an alarm – but then he'd simmer down. I don't know what I'll do now. How'll I know when it's happening without him to warn me.

There is a tiny opening of beak, a dot of tongue, rose-white and rigid. I stare at the jointed pale feet, their helpless crimp. The feathers are traced with thin black rills at his hood. I don't think I can do it.

But it's the old woman who gives up and clucks, a good round of boohoos, while I pat her back. Against my t-shirt I feel her repeat to herself *there there. There there.*

But where?

Ounces of soft wing and hollow bone.

> *place the other hand on top of the first*
> *and interlace your fingers*

It happens when only Jack's left with you.

You're not sure if it's the earth contracting, so you watch the pattern of the carpet slipping. Then the aftershock wanes, and the tightening's left in your womb.

He stands you up, amidst slow yanks of muscle.

The carpet is stilled now, under a thick haul of blood.

Hell's teeth, he keeps muttering. I'm no expert, but this is more than monthly, right?

But you won't say it. You're bent around the secret. You're trying not to spill. But Jack's face knows.

Is your dad in on this?

You can only twist *no*, before the next pang.

He shakes his head, stares at the carpet. The blood is real. The words aren't needed.

Right. We're heading straight to A&E then. Hear me?

But you won't. You've been camped out at the hospital for

weeks, watching the injured still red-lining. That's a place for emergency, for people like your husband. Not for you. So Jack's got no choice but to let you stagger into boots, help you steer a bloody path out. Thread the dark with a torch where you aim your joint stumbles. The tarmac's made of crack and quag. Your trunk is trying to split you open. He bundles you on, and thumps on the side of the portaloo when it's occupied.

Greater need, he bellows. *Greater need.* A young bloke flails out, pissed, into the torchlight, clutches his belt, starts up, *whatever cunt.* But when he sees the state of you, he heads for shadow.

Jack lights the cubicle, pushes you in. You try to close the door, but he stands guard, spotting you. *Good girl, there you go.* You try to talk back, but your trunk curbs and burns. Your voice is coming loose, your head pushed between your knees. *You're all right, there you go. You're all good. There you are love.* Then his voice and the pain and the light overturn. Until your baby is empty.

Then cold is echoing off the plastic, and it is such a comical scuffle, Jack trying to pull you back to rights, rigging your clothes, tapping your cheek, *stay with me, good girl,* while the whole booth rocks. He holds you jammed and pumps water one-handed at you, and your head does nothing but bounce against his palms. Everything has sobbed between your legs. So you say nothing when he braces you and works the flush. A reflex. You can't stop it. You can only stand together and listen to the blue howl, its chemical scouring. Your ribs will be hollowed, everafter, by that automated scourge.

Oh God, Jack mutters. I didn't mean. Oh, Holy Mother.

But you shake the head that lolls against him and can only whisper, Thank you.

He doesn't say another word.

I scrape a notch into the backyard soil. I can only make it shallow – *that'll do*, Mrs D squawks if I dig too thick. She makes me fuss with the dark bed, tamping the trowel to get it comfy. *I'd like to make it cosy for him.* She directs me to tuck him into the right patch of dirt, *left a bit, no over*, to whisk out any muck she doesn't like, twigs, a beetle that might pester him. I've wound him in a petticoat she fished from a drawer, buttery, with moth-coloured stains. The sunlight catches in its synthetic. We have to unroll him three times, give her one more little tickle, before she lets me put him away, a soft bump in his chiselled box. Then Mrs D fondles its eastern trees, waiting over the hole, where I hold her.

If your dad were here, he'd have a prayer, she says. He's got a lovely way with the Lord words, your dad. I don't suppose any of them have stuck, from listening?

Our Father . . . *you took away the walls of the world.*

But I do want my father. I want somebody who knows the words that end in God, that end in comfort and answers, amen. If he was here, I wouldn't stand in the background muttering, wouldn't watch him go through his little ceremonies and scoff. I'd shut up. I'd let be. I'd say a prayer, because what the hell else?

Our Lord, whose loving hand hath given us all *that we sit in the wreckage of*, bless and keep him *and don't let the earth spit him up.*

I can't get my dreams to knock the city down. When I sleep there is so much still standing. The stones climb each other's dark blocks neatly, and hold history up in a strong Gothic grid. In the CBD the walls stretch glass to the sky, their joints float, the clouds kept tight in bright high-rise panels. It all looks real. It all looks lasting and solid. Like the concrete will be under my next step. Like I'll walk through a door and there will be shelter.

Waking crushes it. You can walk out, looking for the rebuild, looking for evidence of the new. But the view along any compass point is still gilded with smash, sunk with wounds. All our street blocks chipped by God. A foliage of wire and plastered clutter, like something the Lord is ready to winch into a skip. Faces blinking out from pasteboard hovels, the air still dusted with fine-grade terror. Our houses are fibrolite and honeycombed glass, blotches of duct tape holding on hinges of tarp that keep our senses crackling, their fine spackles of movement crunching in our sleep. The earth, sounding the wrong note deep in itself, could jerk at any moment, tug our strings. Everything webbed with flight-paths of grit that keep lifting and knitting the loneliness. Hunks that still crumble. Buried things shimmying to light. It's too late, the buildings have showed their bones.

I walk past the hotel because somehow that's what you find yourself doing, adrift past what's gone. Staying. Staring. The front of it has cracked off clean. It's like the dollhouse my father built me once, the front face unhinged. They haven't bothered salvaging much. In some units it's all still installed. The bedspread the colour of flax. The IV line of the lamp cord. In the bathrooms, tiny headstones of soap.

I think of his body, on the days of our meetings, how he could barely get out of a doorframe before I'd backed him down, hijacked zips, primed the noose of his tie, pulled his laughter down on top of me.

The thing about a rented room is that you remember what happens in it – almost as if you've paid to stop time, to seal memory. You set the blinds to a different shutter-speed. The hours can't get through. You only filter now in, sun crossed with the white sheets, the weft of his skin as you slide his belt buckle clear of it. The scurfy ashtray is a chalice. Everything else dims – traffic, cicadas, promises. You take your dress off too seriously, so he scoffs, and you whack him one, *fucking behave*. The ceiling fan doesn't let anything down but heat. There's the tenor of next door's TV, the curtains – because you need curtains plus blinds, there's so much to block out, the hotelier knows it – toughened with maximum sun. You love the wistful end-of-stock wall-print, some monochrome horizon where a nice couple kiss; you love the tree of cutlery, love the misfit plastic flowers. There's a bible in the end-table, like a novel for the half-blind. You love the snagged quilt, fingernailed by so many inmates – if you lean into its fibres there's a whiff of their salt. There's the hum of the tenants on your right, pulling something equally sleazy in their chenille hideaway. There's the billow of him, kicking off all the covers, before the fabric melts to your skin. There's your follow-through lick along tendons as he cranes his head back over the ledge of the bed. You think this is bliss, and that you can have it forever.

On the misshapen pavement outside, it's gone in a blink. The smallprint of all the walls is torn out, trailing. The plaster is fleecy, shot with wires. You can stare into the hallways, where the carpet is marrow. Hatches of roof feed in the sky. There's no crescent on the sign, no neon flash of vacancy. It doesn't matter what the hotel was called – it's not named anything now except *DO NOT ENTER*, a notice handwritten on cardboard, twined to hurricane wire. We used to laugh and call it the Luminol Motel – if you sprayed it God knows what would have showed up, the walls an irradiated frieze of human splashes. It was a sick joke, our own special crime scene. We giggled like idiots, picturing spurts of DNA, unit 17 a carousel of chromosomes. I wormed up under the kingsize shroud, my hair pricking out in a nimbus of static. He just pried me wetter, not caring where we left evidence.

Now it's the building that looks like it's ready to crack its own sick joke, level more of us. The lobby end it's humpbacked, but still four storeys, with huge chunks of sky punched out of its height, so it looks on stilts, just waiting for the final wobble. If I get as close as I can to the façade I can stare through to the front reception, the light still dangling from a tactless chandelier. *Room please* – I could still ding the silver bell for attention. I could wait for service, watching the circuits of tropical fish in their tank beside the counter, their spiny fluttering fins. I could still pick up the key.

listen for official warnings

My mother used to build me huts out on the lawn. An expedition in sunlight and linen. She'd help me lug a trail of sheets out to a clearing, she'd range out deckchairs and drape around a home. I'd lie in the hollow, rayed by cushions, watching billows. I'd scold and cuddle the doll in my grip. A sky above me coated with softness. A candy-striped ceiling that couldn't hurt anyone.

Tonight I crawl in under Dad's green tarp. It's been too long now, the chill is getting permanent again, too many nights are tipped with frost. I can't see how he can last another season. From the unit I stare at the stake of his shelter, its bent scale, its slack lines, and fear it will be lethal. He's weathered too much. He's packed the thing with every precaution he can think of, wraps himself up in insulating layers. *You look like you're trekking to the effing Pole*, I tease him, use his silence to try to pressure him to decamp. But he won't hear of leaving, he swears he'll stick it out.

So I just lie with him in his lightweight vault.

He holds my hand while we listen to the wind test its ripples, the night stretch its ropes. Traffic grinds the turf beneath us. Cargo trucks shiver the ground-sheeted grass. The land's spine is down there, and ours can only listen. It still pays to listen.

I think it's time I tell you, Dad says. But then he cuts himself off.

The quiet goes on so long I bump his coat-sleeve, almost a punch at his arm's thick swaddling.

I'm too freezing to wait for a prologue, I tell him. I rub my icy shins together. Get to the point.

His voice coughs cold. It's a bark of chilled breath that stays above us.

You need to know something. Jack's notes.

Yeah.

Well, his wife.

What. Dad. Spit it out.

She. Well. It's just.

What.

They're to no one. Well, no – they're to his wife. But she isn't.

Isn't coming home? Or what?

She's gone.

Dad's voice can't offer more.

I lie there with that fact in me. All Jack's postcards go to no one. I think of him crouching over their images, his grin as he fills me in on backstory. *That day*, he tells me, *oh my, that date she was wearing a dress that could make your eyes hurt*. The careful capitals of his lettering. Bridges, blossoms, tramlines, glimpses of her moving past a clocktower, vanished in the sheen of a street. *We went for a walk and I swear the river nearly turned its track just to keep alongside her.*

Dad and I listen to a gale brush the tent wall.

I think it's better just to leave him.

Yes. We can leave him, Dad answers. I don't have the heart.

The complicated padding of his weather gear polishes the night as he shakes his head against the groundsheet. There's a dog a few doors down that must feel an aftershock toying with the end of his chain.

There are things, Dad finishes, that don't need to be brought to light.

If the wind unsettled the huts my mother built me, the sheets would only graze your face. You'd still have time to scatter out, squealing. You'd have time to bunny-hop back and save your babies. If the chairs started tilting, they'd warn you with a lightweight clatter. But their collapse would only sound like summertime.

if you are able, make your own way directly

There are days at the hospital when we always seem to be shifting him, like we've never made it out of that stairwell. We seem to have been winding his body through halls, and tests, and lights, and wires since the start. Then there are times when the stillness sets in, nights high, storeys deep.

Some nights I think it's his voice that's woken me, but when I kneel up off my stretcher his mouth holds nothing, the knowledge in his irises flattened.

We met in the slate vault of a cathedral. We'd been sightseeing, on our OE. He'd been checking me out in the loud queue into the grounds, but when we filed through the nave a hush came down, so we grabbed the straps of our packs and shivered. We both got the chill of something ancient. Up the central chamber columns of knights were laid out, stationed in their cool stone boats. We stopped at each carved body, wondered at their chainmail, their spiked crowns, the serenity of their crossed feet. Our yellow-laced boots were too weathered and downunder. I heard him exhale, and a curse come straight from home.

That's butchery. Holy fuck.

He meant the graffiti. There were ruts gouged into the engravings, the stone beds defaced with crosshatched names.

Who'd tamper with this much history. Seriously. What kind of person would stand here and do that?

I shook my head. The notches were sacrilege. And it looked no different from the lists in a toilet stall. Who'd fucked who. Knifed in granite. Who was proud about it.

They should be . . . fucking smote.

Yeah. He grinned back at me. If there's a God, he should smite them.

Sometimes, running a cloth against the dome of his ribs, I feel the same. His vacant temples. His shoulders waning, rocked from the collarbone, his nape on a yaw. His greyed crown of follicles. His abdomen chalked with breath, the scrape of the rag edging all of his helpless creases. The fastenings of his eyelashes, granular along the rim.

There is zero recognition. But sometimes his parched lips tic with lost language.

I think of the marks that I left for him, a signature I may as well have scraped into his side.

When we walked deeper that day into the chapel, the steeple was too high for me to see. I couldn't crane up, and my pack threatened to topple me. So he helped me shrug its burden, told me his name, said, *you can trust me, eh*. He offered his palm to brace my neck, let the glory at the apex lie me back on a lean. And all the stains at the zenith poured down on me.

a floor plan with FIRE EXITS highlighted is mounted
on the back of your door

It happens because you are trying to do wrong. The hotel wall turns into a windshield. Something was deadlocked under land, but now it has blown out. Your voice is exploding with it. You don't know what you're captive in, a space of glass and roar. All the lines of the hotel have fractured. There's an apocalypse of plaster.

When you can, you run out. The minibar fridge is a landmine. Your bare feet are chattering. The lift is cabled to hell. The doors that number the shouting have all bust open the faces hidden behind. The sprinklers baptise you, the carpet is barbed, a downhill of splinters. People climb out with you, wearing red tape. The tank in the foyer has been torn loose. The fish are drastic, lying there, lip-reading.

The streets are not breathing. You pass other people, frozen or stumbling, and you squint at each other and sometimes call, but all your words are smudged out by mouthfuls of shock. Sound is coming through the wrong end of the telescope. A distant siren is pinpointed inside your head. Its squeal may never leave you. Some people are hoisting what's broken, clawing their way over stacks, their feet and hair toppling, pieces jerked from their hands as they clamber and yell. Others are motionless, blinking the world back together again. As if they ever could. There's a woman whose trunk is a parquet of blood. There's a man running with a leaden child.

The black map of tarmac has sunk, and cars are running downstream. The buildings gush with shards and hang with water, the alarms pour down your mind. Your car is muzzled, front end knuckleboned. There's a gale of smoke, and a dog barking at it. Your legs go out, an aftershock, and you watch the hotel wall, for a while, turn to powder. Like it always held your ashes.

There is a path home, but your footprints crack it. Your dress is riven. Your baby is an insect buzz. You keep passing people whose houses are quartered. Families squatting in foothills of glass. Aluminium in backfired continents. You walk stop-motion, and people take shape out of smoke, with limbo in their eyes. Everything sounds hydraulic. Someone has skeletoned the world. There's a man dragging along a keyboard, and a woman clutching an arrangement of flowers. Some people wave at you, even try to stop you, but you blunder on. There's an undertow of black where the bridge once lived. A man with a loudspeaker calls to you to halt. But your baby is hot and your feet are in the basement of the world where the liquid is deep and full of ghosts. Your heart is an epicentre. A palette of red sound slides off your tongue. All you can think of to say is *sorry*.

keep bones from moving, do not try to straighten

I think Dad's taking me to visit Mum's grave when he asks me to tag along today. One thing Dad holds on to: my mother's headstone never got a scratch on it, so he can sit there from time to time, prop up a new sprig of flowers, chat with her undented angel. But we pull up instead on a road in a nice suburb. I wonder then if we're lost. But I don't want to push him: he's ashamed of what's happened to his bearings. It's one of the zones that looks almost untouched, still stately, bar the odd crimp in the kerb, a slur in a paling or gatehead here and there.

We come to a stop across the road from a villa nestled in silk trees. Its verandah is iced, and wisteria trails the trim. Dark leaves have been box-cut into globes along its formal front path. Its intactness, right-angled, looks surreal.

Very *Alice in Wonderland*, I tell him. So where in fact are we?

But he can't get past the street number. The cab vinyl echoes his convulsions. My touch doesn't stop it. He's bowed by tears, beyond reaching. He drops his face against the wheel.

We have to sit a long time. Once it slows, he fiddles with the dash, like something's going on in the dials, the mileage, the meter, some tampering he has to get straight.

Then he says, It was my fare yester –

The sobs in his chest pull the sentence up short. He swallows, starts again. People tell me, that's all. They hop in the cab, and they talk. And I know it's what they need.

But you need, too, Dad. Come on, tell me.

It was just a lad. He didn't mean anything by it. Just full of himself. He seemed – excited by everything. Like he was –

Amped up.

Dad nods.

Then he just kept going. Didn't stop –

To think where you might have been.

Never gave it a thought. They made a stretcher out of pipes, used their jackets, he told me, him and his mate. On the day. He was doing his bit, I suppose. He seemed a good kid. Rushing round, the two of them, being heroes. And he just kept on.

Detail you didn't need.

No. I should have . . . just been glad he had life in him. They don't, you know, day after day. My fares. Some get in, and they don't even know where they're heading. Like I'm an ambulance, but they've no idea where they need to be. So I should have been glad he had some spark. But . . . what upset me was the way he said it. He said they'd loaded a girl onto their stretcher. Already gone. She'd been checked and checked. More than once. She was signed off. A sheet pulled up. Everything. But they were walking her away, and she lifted her head. They got such a scare they let her crash down. She's all right. She came around. Just like that, he said. She sat back up. And she was talking away. She got up, and started walking home again. But . . . he told it like – it was a joke. Which it probably is. Cause for laughing. In the right light. I know I need to look for the upside.

He sighs. His hands are still on the dash, working.

It was just . . . because it was a girl. A young lady. I just found myself thinking –

She didn't arise, his fare that day. *I'm busting. Christ who art with me. Please. We lift them to the Lord.* Despite his prayer, he lost her voice.

It's stupid. I know it's pointless. But it seemed – why couldn't she have woken back up.

Then he's sobbing again. Because I was late.

He repeats: I was late. And if I hadn't been, she could have. Been in there.

The house is what he's waving at. The address she'd chanted at him from the backseat, like they could still find their way. There's a bike, vintage, black-spoked, propped on the porch. There's a trellis, staked with deadhead roses. It has lace-lined windows, ivory sashed. It's a dream.

I might have got her home. Or close. I could have gotten her at least –

Dad, no.

I'm not late. I'm never the sort who. But I can't change it. I was. It was me.

In the rubble, he lost her voice behind him. He tried to keep praying through her last vowels. Then he heard a gored sound, liquid and unbreathable. It wasn't even long before the first slabs of stonework were lifted from the cab. But all her talk was over.

Those minutes would not have made a difference.

Yes, they could.

You don't know that. Dad. How can you.

He stares back at the house, as if someone might swoop through the door, cross over to the taxi, take a swing, smash the windscreen. He cowers in the driver's seat like he deserves it.

She would have been your age. It might have been you doing something. And someone had been the one. And what would I think, if they had been. Like me. Made you late. If they took those last minutes off you.

But you didn't lose me, I tell him.

No, he says. I didn't. He's looking at the villa. Sunlit timbers. The dark bell waiting to chime at its door. Then back at me. As if he's not certain.

Dad. You didn't lose me.

I think he's going to pray then. His hands drop from dials he can't turn back. The numbers don't mean anything. Minutes, payment, routes erased.

Then he turns and stares at me. That's what we all have to think of, I suppose, he says.

I reach for his hand.

Of what we didn't have taken, he says. Of what we didn't lose.

I know it is time to wake. To get up and walk.

know the natural warning signs

I'd said I was leaving, and he should do the same. We should meet at the hotel, then just take off, aim somewhere like outlaws, put miles between us and them. I wasn't even planning to break the news about the baby. I'd barely broken it to myself. It was a figment, a glitch of hope I hadn't bought into. I wouldn't tell him until deep into our getaway. I had a horizon in mind, and I must have thought I could lie there in a no-strings dress and sell it to him, smile wide, legs spread, suitcase splayed. Like some juvenile runaway.

But he was late.

I think I knew, waiting on the black chair.

I told myself his lateness meant nothing. He was always running late. Such a paradox, a guy who always moved at top speed, always paced and revved and fidgeted, should also be the one who was always thudding through the door, full-charm, in a tardy skid, a barrage of cute mock-reasons ready to wipe out any mutter of irritation. He was just always late, his energy pulling him in all directions, so he couldn't toe the line, keep his movements timed and straight. Just adorably late, in his DNA, *babe get used to it*. I'd plan the next time to be so damn backward and delayed, no excuses, so I could get back at him. But I couldn't stick to it. The next time a meeting came round I was twitching in the drift of my skirt. I couldn't keep pinned to a seat at home for an instant. I'd be staring at the clock hands bang. I'd be panting at the magnitude of hunger I had to get across town to him.

When they found his body, it was foetal, in his chair. At the arrowhead of an anonymous desk. Intact, all the strands of his building unplaited. Steel cords wrapped him with the tonnage above. There was no way of knowing if he'd ever been conscious, had to wait, or if he'd been blindsided, instant. There was no way of even beginning to think such things. Although I do, when I'm at the white chairs. Sitting in the eerie parade of their stillness, gaunt, unnamed, their bodies in negative. The baby seat stiffened, its scoured fleece cradle. The office chair, aerodynamic, with its tough back, hydraulics on its thick base, weight-distributed. The star of wheels that could take him clear across the room – because I'd seen him do it, I'd called into the office, just to sneak another look, and watched him, the force of him, belting his seat across the lino in long warped joyrides, laughing, as he nearly brought a head-on collision, spinning on his tomfool axis, the life of the office, the bad-news spark of it, the mischief, jazzing up the mundane tasks with his offbeat antics, racing his chair past the cubicles in loony jackass stunts. For my benefit. Catching me side-on, on one rotation, gliding me along for a circuit, the temperature-controlled air rushing into my protest, as he flung us into a spiral, a long wonky spill of us, side-car and gasping, my husband just shaking his sober head across the room. *Stay away from him*, my husband shouted over, laughing. *Stay away from him, he's a disaster.*

How is it possible not to know your world is falling? Because it didn't seem that I could be pulling our home down around his head, that I could be cheating on everything that held us upright, eating away our foundation, and my husband could not feel it coming, couldn't sense the slightest shift.

I think I knew, waiting on the black chair.

Lovers say it breaks us, makes us bleed, leaves scars. Love hurts. We call ourselves crushed.

Today, at the hospital, my husband's wheelchair arrived.

How to be haunted: have no photos. No images of his body in the doorway, the light along his muscles so fine it looks acoustic, or stretched half out of the fishtailed sheets, grinning with misbehaviour. None of him coming towards you, hungry for a takedown, slipknotting your waist, while you give him lip, make little pouty sallies against him, lie back with your thighs in his thumbs' soft garotte. None of his diehard smile, just that, filling the frame. Just that, giving you amnesia. None of his hypermasculine walk, a bareface strut really, too much not to snicker at, until you draw near to the swagger of it, musky and iambic. None of him dreaming – because he can do that, just slump into sleep in an easy instant, his trunk rolled deep, his forearms untethered, his eyelids tweaking like unlucky stars. None of you, hacking into his dreams, messing with him lying there in lazy extremis, because you can't stand to let him slip free of you so smoothly, to shrug aside and drop into a no-worries snore, so you brood and nip and meddle, subtracting him from his doze, until he backfires like you crave and pins you giggling by your wrists. None of his cute domesticated shuffle round the kitchenette, a goofy parody of serving you tea, flicking little sachets and acting like a butler, with his cock still looking half interested. None of his face, close-up, when you ration him, making him beg, giving him a glistening inch. None of it, forlorn, when the time's up, and you can't stand the feel of your clothes, their weight and their fastening, and you pause at the door both wearing a sadness you don't want but have no choice but to take. None of him shivering as you open the throat of his shirt again, like this is an emergency. None of it stop-motion. None of it ever. No messages, no texts. No images. No evidence.

Just a letter, lost in a red zone, that thinks it knows what love is.

protect your head and neck with your arms

I'm coming back from the hospital when I pass a line of people. Their faces are stoic, filing to a wide desk, waiting for their turn. They're queuing to add their names to a register, saying they promise to stay, rebuild the city. I watch a woman turning from the book, peeling a sticker that she lines over the heart of her t-shirt, smooths with a palm. It reads *I have signed the Pledge.*

I've seen her a few times now, different places. She parks up a blue, beaten five-door, panels rippled with quake – just a light brush of death in the metalwork, no big deal, still running. The rear door is too warped to pop, so she has to half-crawl in, drag her easel and supplies out the side, heavy body on a camber. She pants with the strain; she's not such a young woman, the movements aren't easy for her. But she does it. Juts the tripod out, angles her canvas. Squats, to recover for a while, on a low stool. Watches. Then looks down, mixes her pigment. If there was a moment when I would go and speak to her, it wouldn't be this one. The work of grief is just between her and the paint.

She stares a long time at the wreck, as if she plans to enshrine detail, pick out the splintered updraft of hallways, the doorways smothered, the harpooned walls. But she doesn't. She draws what no longer stands. She recreates what's missing. Stroke by stroke, she lifts the stone. Her brush restores and stiffens the framework. The ghost of the structures that used to stretch beyond her she raises back from lengths of paint. Her resurrected buildings are whole and smoothed. And

133

there's always a blue light she pastes round their angles, a bold resistant cloudless shade, a sky that makes the walls thicker, roofs toughened in relief. The colour of hope, a blinded postcard blue. It sets with a determined sheen. I don't know what to make of it: two parts faith, one fake.

People buy them before the paint is dry. I don't think she's in it for the turnover. She takes the cash, hands over the canvas. *I have signed the Pledge.* But I can't read the look on her face.

There are never any people in her frames.

There are some things that won't rise again.

stay low to the floor, stay away from the windows

I can't find a way to get to the letter. But there are buildings that I can get into. Some nights I walk, without aim, where nothing's left to scale, and I break in anywhere I can. When you push through the cartilage of other houses, you find a mausoleum of familiar things: shoes, utensils, rooms anchored by stone. No one has heirlooms to pass down – they have junk to dump, shake off, not worth coming back for. I take risks. One bathroom is a cameo of mould, the sinktop edged in pearls, the shelves baroque with bird shit. The shower drain is eyewitness testimony, silver over a sunlit void. The botched touchdown of a cot lies under the last windowpane. My steps feel high-wire but something has been here with claws: there are pellets on the couch. The curtains experiment with shadows. The walls do balancing acts they were never meant for.

And then I find the entrance to the last hotel.

There are only a handful of tall buildings left in this city. Hardly anywhere left with a high-enough ledge.

134

I start climbing it for no reason.

The columns are a trick, their faux marble tilted, waiting for their colossal moment to capsize. The floor is a rink of leakage, glass and potholes. There's a statue whose Greek face is buried, the bloom of rainwater discolouring her skull. There are doorways that arch and bell, in rows, the sounds of near-night bloated through them. Visitations of spotlight and headwind. It takes a long time for a building to die.

Futile notices are pinned to the wall, banning inhabitation. Someone has fired a stream of missiles at them. *Keep Out* tape is balled up, barring nothing at the base of a stairwell. Graffiti recoils around the oxidised walls, tags slung high on a brazen axis or tinier scribbles of quiet claim or goodbye – not the tenants the place was built for. They like the fact that the quake has let them in, leave initials, hearts and fuckyous.

In one hotel room all the chairs lie on their backs, a queue for a cinema staring skyward. In another some prowlers have played a game of throwing them at the wall: there are three whose black legs have pierced through the plaster and hang suspended there, with the names of the champions. In the next room there's an unaccountable pile of kettles and irons ringed in a corner, a white nest where rodents have journeyed along their cords. Turned to the wall there's a stack of shattered headboards.

In the dining room instalments of cutlery are waxed with filth, still wait around flinted plates. A couple of napkins are shaped like a demi-swan. Headshots of stone are randomised around the tables, dust and pigeon shit icing the feast. The frilled wedge of a pie, the black curl of a sandwich, laced with blight. A milk bottle stands by the coffee machine, swollen to a thick balloon. Something stands caramelised in a glass, the stippling of mould, seal-skinned, a floating umber. The toxic stillness of it, final and aquatic. Cake forks crisscrossed on a fetid serviette. The standalone algae of the fridge.

There's a corridor of tremble, a corridor of seepage. Everywhere the detritus has turned gossamer, gotten a kind of flaking shimmer to it. Nothing's lacklustre, the waste displayed in petals, loose farewells of web. You can't fault the groves of rot, the damp that has honeyed everything. Buds unhook from the couches. Tables ooze, posing for the droves of flies. Bathtubs snake with slime. Everything is veiled and blossoming. And I stand there and remember my delusions: that we'd rise from the wreck that we'd caused all around us to somehow drift up here to a happy ending. The honeymoon suite. The bridal wallpaper has turned forensic, and the luxe wool carpet is branched with light. Big magnolias of mould, thick as jewellery, are the new stars on the vaulted ceiling. The quilt is rewrapped with spored trim, congealed spills. The pillows are dewy, ulcerated. Feathers of rot etch everything.

I walk to a brink. There's a split that's in ascendance through the wall near the king bed, jagged with moonlight and chill. It's wide enough to feed through one of Jack's postcards: I could take the one he's trusted me to post out my pocket, let its delusion spin and drop. *Close your eyes, write my name*, my lover once pencilled on the monographed paper when he left me sleeping at the hotel. I think about waking up, filling the page with the sound of him, the ache of his name in my sternum.

Perhaps I climbed up here for a reason. Perhaps I came up here to meet him.

Once, I lay in the hotel waiting, with the white sheet pulled up over my face.

Storeys of cold call up from the cracks. *Close your eyes, write my name.*

I think of a wedding dress, passed through the gap, wired through the sunlight in pearly plastic, rescued, an angel craned down into rescuing hands.

When my smoke is lit, I lean into the plaster, breathe it out through the hairlined wall.

There's light through the roots of the floor, a series of debased doors. The marshes of the carpet melt and mislead. But I hew past broken and cabled things. Girders laundered by blackening rain. Disappear into the sacked hotel.

stay calm and position yourself in a safe place

How do you pick up a city, a house, a small room? Jack does it piece by handled piece, watching for what's left. Because it's not all rubble to him. It's not all crushed. Sometimes there's an object, still whole, or a shred that's enough to build a memory on. A cold token. And if you can turn it in your palm for long enough, it grows warm.

Tonight he's pulled the chairs close to the house, propped a munted little table out and spread its surface. At first I think it's another jigsaw he's salvaged from the berm – he's taken to carting them into the hospital lately, shaken pieces that are never complete. He lays them out on my husband's wheeled tray-table, chats away to him like its teamwork. And from time to time, I imagine my husband does blink down, watch the fingers sort the sky from the stones, snap together the shattered trim of a fenceline. Jack will even lend him credit for a find, for a join. *Jesus*, he'll say, and give his latest fit a palm-heel whack to cement its linkage, *you're an architect, mate. A bloody architect.*

But what he's scored today is not a jigsaw. It's slides, a whole clear sack clicking with transparencies. So he's on a stepladder to hitch up an old sheet on the back wall of our unit as a makeshift screen. He's loading the cartridge – he's had the projector for weeks now, a plastic wheel he fished out of untold trash in a skip, couldn't believe his luck when it switched on. But he only found the stash of slides this morning. *How's that for meant to be*, he grins at me. He's ringing the carousel with them. He hits the squares he holds up with his torch, so the tiny figures flare, like signatures scratched on the night. He takes a squint, reloads the chamber, fiddling at the order.

So the three of us sit in the backyard. There's a bit of a letdown when the light spits out, goes dud to start, and Jack does a dance round the grass with his set-up of plugs. Dad offers him a weary caution about wet ground and electricals not mixing, but Jack won't hear of it, keeps jigging at his daisy-chain, restless – then acts up a *fizzzzzzzz!* like he's taken a decent jolt. My father is not impressed. He makes to exit – he's jumpy enough with his chair settled here, in proximity to brick. But I shake my head, put a hand out to keep him, grizzling a little, on his stately mahogany. With his sleep roll packed round him, so close to the house, I don't have to tell him what I wish. There've been nights when he's almost drifted off, so close, stretched careful on the couch. Then a twitch takes his spine. And he makes for his shelter, the taped glass ticking as he leaves. Now he huffs, but stays in place on his chair, stagily disgruntled.

And then the sheet turns golden.

Jack looks on, like they're breathing things he's picked from the rubble.

There's a woman, standing with her palms cupped round her globed trunk, cradling a bell of blue cloth. Her face a blush of plenty.

There's a man in overalls, holding aloft the hood of a car in a stream of blown-out smoke.

There's a set of old hands, fanning something they've spaded from soil.

There's a toddler, spot-lit in naps and black sunglasses, giving a milk-teeth shriek behind a steering wheel.

There's a girl, suspended in the backyard blaze of a sky, heels joy-kicked and hair a nimbus. Her squeal is launched from the mat of a tramp – you can feel the chords the springs are playing. Her ribs are bundled, exultant with shout. Beyond her laughter, an unwavering city.

And not a single memory is ours.

But the images rattle. Nothing falls, nothing leans. Nothing gets translated into dust. Nothing is lost, and we sit and watch it. I hear Dad sigh, and we blink in this radiance, where nothing dissolves and nothing drops. More than once Jack has to pat the machine until the next memory jumps. But it doesn't matter if there's a wait. It doesn't matter that nothing belongs to us.

Some nights we look up, surprised the stars are not broken.

some facts about her home town

1. The shoe-store owner finished at five, slid shut the thick copper screen and bolted it, then walked to the station, where he waited for the evening express. He didn't so much leap in front of it as take a last understated step. She watched him from the platform, dropping, in his clean shoes.

2. There wasn't a speck of blood left on her blue uniform, but she dreamed there was – tangelo, collateral.

3. There were three swings at the only park. She could still thread her legs through the scooped black rubber one, meant to balance toddlers. She liked its afterschool heat, and where the buckle jutted.

4. Bananas crated in thick green plastic, and avocados with lizard skin, went softly black as she walked home from maths, calculating their four o'clock drizzle of fruit flies.

5. An older girl at high school with orange hair told her she could use two tampons, demonstrating on fingers cocked like a gun. She had baby-oiled thighs and an eyetooth missing. Her knuckles didn't love or hate anyone.

6. For eight days after they installed her braces, her upper lip would get snagged when she smiled. She had to manually un-grin, picking her cupid's bow off the sharp black equipment.

7. The pub was by the church was by the dump was by the graveyard was by the TAB was by the servo on the route to the station.

8. The sun zig-zagged everything.

9. A younger girl at high school was carrying somebody's baby. Phys Ed broke her water and she stood in the gymnasium, blinking, still in line to scale the climbing net.

10. The station sold the kind of apple pies that turned to a kelpy gel green and got priced down in the afternoon, two for one. She liked to pad her tongue around their syrupy lumps when no one on the platform was watching. It felt especially good if an easterly was blowing up the tracks from the south, just hard enough to wrinkle the sugary paper bag cupped round her chin.

11. The frilled ring of cream was dotted on with such finesse. She liked to comb it with her fine-wire braces. A light artistic nuzzling.

12. From the top of the climbing net she could see the monument, through wide, hinged windows that needed a special appliance to wind them out. She loved the silver pirouette of sound cycling her collarbone when she was window monitor.

13. The monument itemised a white tower of dead men, and if she was lucky a boy-in-a-car would drive her up there later to fingerfuck.

14. The statue on top was a brave rubble youth wearing a bayonet and graffiti.

15. When she was little, she'd bought new shoes from the man in the suicidal shoe store. They were red patent and the clasp was a ladybird whose edges beetled her left arch till it bled. She hopscotched around on the good one, scabbed, but still sort of happy with its brand-new clack.

16. There is not enough sound for what is happening to him.

17. In the TAB the radio was always tuned to brown loneliness. Pens hung on slack abdications of string. The old blokes smoked their wins and losses.

18. The maths test asks her to tally up stories about two trains coming from the west and east, and if she blinks at the right miles-per-hour will they pass before she can stop her pencil braking nowhere in a long graphite drag?

19. The older girl borrows her blue pen, but for the whole test-hour only works it into the asterisks she inks in her knuckles, an architecture of black ants and roadkill hearts.

20. Her piano lessons take place twice weekly through the lace drapes of an old lady's villa. The keys are cold and stick with musty semitones. Wisps of the old lady's thinning hair silver the flip-top stool's damp tapestry.

21. In the graveyard there was a woodcutter clipped to a tombstone. It didn't take much breeze to make his milled axe go whirring.

22. He quits the edge with a metronome click. Her splashed eye pinpoints a grey suit's collision.

23. The vodka the boy at the monument will give her will tip her half unconscious fast. There will be a warm accompaniment, elastic and thumbs. The honey-coloured vinyl, close-up, will be noisy and pucker with topstitched anointing.

24. In the pub toilet stall, the older girl will teach her, two-fingered again, to jukebox her meal up. They've just shared the best battered plate of her life. The bowl will be ringed with Fisherman's Basket.

25. She will rock her head back on the baby swing and think chainlink things about sunlight and blowflies and time.

26. The boy will climb the plinth with a rattle of spray-can to glaze the young soldier with a curse. She will have no choice but to wipe her thighs on the seatbelts. There is nothing else.

27. The tapestry is sturdy but sanded by musical arses. It has maidens in long faded robes, holding apples and leashes with doves on them and harps. She thinks of the pie slush unplucked from her teeth, the sly tune stuck in their sugary guitar-strings.

28. In the eight days she couldn't smile she went to the shoe store to ask for a job. She handed the owner a pink sleeve of wipe-clean reasons why she would be ideally suited to kneeling on the buff carpet fitting shoes over straggles of chopped-off mocha pantyhose. She smiled as she modelled how good she'd be at fondling reptilian heels.

29. It wasn't her fish-hooked lip that stopped him hiring her. It was the look of the older girl outside waiting, with her rep, the bird she flipped passers-by, the maryjane biroed in stipples across her army surplus satchel.

30. There is not enough sound. And then there is a skyful. Engines of screaming, miles of siren. When she hyperventilates someone makes her breathe into the bag, so her panic tastes like apples.

31. The old lady plays piano at his funeral. The town lines up for it out of nosiness. It's not in the church, though, but in the gymnasium, where even a symphony plonks like chopsticks.

32. On the other side of the monument someone has carved the names of girls who got knocked up there.

33. There's a photograph of him, at the service, looking teenage in a jungle of khaki sadness. Behind him, like some prop from M*A*S*H, is the shady complication of a camo net.

34. At the servo, she gets a job filling up wagons, popping hoods, threading in the spiny dipstick. Hoping the cute

boys case out her arse as she funnels down the quarts of oil. Swishing the frothy brush out the bucket, to nudge little insects off the metal frontier.

35. She's not in the wrong swing when the younger girl brings her baby down. She's up on the tall one, watching her feet trail in and out the concave bowl of bark. The baby in the rubber seat is lemon and sulky and wobbly, and his mother can hardly be bothered to push.

36. If there's sunlight coming from east and west, her feet dangle for how many miles? The chain sings a long diesel equation.

37. She thinks of her red shoes, one foot stretched out, burning in air. In the new shoebox he'd packed up her battered ones, so she could carry them home from the shop, like a too-old secret, held just between the two of them.

warpaint

It's your basic pub accommodation – walls pockmarked a candy-mint. Chunk bashed out the blue Formica bedside table, forked on four metal legs. A sagging old sash window that won't lever up, a clapped-out single under it. Bunk beds door-side, low slung aluminium hammocks. I test out both, but they whine like a bitch. Teen bedspreads read *Angel Bait! Don't Cross: Queen of Hearts!* Two towels, green-grey, gone stiff with sun, a stub of plastic-wrapped fern-print soap propped on them. The blonded goddess on the bedspread pattern has thick green satisfied eyelashes and a smirk that looks cuntstruck at herself. *Universal Girl Power! Kiss Command!* Her wink triggers a pink graffiti trail of mini hearts.

I won't even get to bags the single, and rib Bruz all night about his stocky arse squealing the bunks. He asked the owners for separate rooms tonight. He's bringing his new girlfriend.

He tells me I'll like her. I'm prepared to try.

Apricot blanket on a locker, punctuated by moths. Rectangle of nothing-to-see-here mirror glued to pastel wall. Creak of doors up and down the hall, but somehow no footsteps. A navy-blue-and-white-striped bin, plastic-lined for sicking in. Bruz could fill it and then some, after a good binge. Pirouette of hair crimped into floorboard dust. Bolt-on sink with a brown mouth stamped Royal Doulton. Out the sash, an acre of corrugated roof, and off its stretch the town – wharf, red cones, jacaranda, Liquorland, big fucking deal. The fire escape's a joyride over split-level tin, strap-on steel-punched tread and wonky rails like bits of fairground knocked off some old attraction and clipped on at random to the vintage pub. Downstairs in the bar, above our stage, there's a game on the wall called *Chase the Ace!*, the whole fifty-two pack framed with loser cards purple-dotted, mostly bad picks of diamonds. And a cartoon strip of three wise men bringing gifts of hard grog to a Mary who's no damn virgin.

His guitar gets your blood up. All these years and that's still true.

Fuck gently weeping. Bruz gets going on a solo and it can make you moan from where you're frozen, right down into old pain.

And who wouldn't want that?

But I doubt his new girlfriend has any. Bruz backs the van up on the kerb, ready to unload gear, and she climbs out the cab. Little sugarcane bleat of laugh. Patent heels that should come with a warning. And what's worse, she tries to help unload, stabbing about in the lethal things, humping stands and amps. Up on the shonky stage she teeters way too close, unstacks bins, tries fishing out cables and mics. I'm in my rights to give her a stormy look. One false step, her stilettos could skewer me.

At least Bruz picks up on it. 'Babe, we've got kind of a system. How 'bout you just go get us some drinks, eh.'

To her credit, she totters off. Her hair is a palette of over-dyes, jet to blue to astronomical blonde, and her bralet is a fierce piece of scaffolding. Flag of black silk sketched into a see-through shrug. Bullet hole of lipstick, dark clouds of blush. If Bruz and I had ever had a daughter, she'd be this age. *Warning: Pout Power!*

Her epic fingernails make shouting us a drink difficult –
she can hardly grip one glass, let alone weave back with three
of them. But she pulls the trick off. 'There you go,' Bruz grins
at me from where he's crouched onstage, daisy-chaining the
monitors. 'Get some of that into you. Bit of the old waipiro.' I
can't resist the old shithead's wink.

I've never been able to.

So I go over to down a drop.

'Fun fact,' she says. 'It's the first time I've even heard him
play.' Bruz is just soundchecking the first few scratches of
chord, an easy jangle. Sampled from a setlist that would have
been written before this girl was even born.

'Well, you're in for a ride, kid.'

Bruz glides into a lick that shimmies all the hairs on your
spine.

A little femme snicker. 'Yeah, I've already had that.'

He coasts off the edge of a riff, lets a chime of harmonics
glint from the fingertapped bridge.

'Oh I'll bet.'

Which is as good as it gets, before there's a big belt of
feedback warping from stage left, and something terminal
cuts through Bruz's amp.

He yelps, kneels down, tries resuscitation, checks leads and
knobs. Stomps pedals. Pleads. But it's a goner.

'Holy fuck. Oh bubs, no. Don't tell me. Ah Jesus, bubs.'

'You'll just have to use the backup,' chirps the new
girlfriend. I have to fucking pity her. Because she's right, we
always cart a spare with us. But Bruz has never once had to
hook it up. And it's a B-grade fail-safe – he may as well be
playing handicapped. His regular amp is an altar. There's
ceremony that goes into tweaking its settings, microtuning its
galaxy of sounds. Days go into invoking the right shine on his

treble, the right crunch and gain on his lead. Bruz is prostrate at its black case now, looking like he lost a kid.

'Lucky you've got it covered,' she follows up breezily. I watch Bruz double over with a pang.

I should put her out of her misery. 'He's superstitious. Like most musicians.' I remember the soundcheck where the wah-wah pedal started picking up AM stations, and a vengeful Christian preacher came pouring out the amp. Howling about punishment. It put the churchy shits up both of us, froze us to the ugly pub carpet. It was too damn close. Until we clicked. This one's not so easy solved.

'Ohhhh,' she says, eye-rolling. Hooks her gaze on to me. 'So what are you superstitious of?'

Bruz leans back on his heels, one fist round his ponytail, shaking his bandana. The amp head is toasted. He knows it. He glares at me. 'New fucking girlfriends.'

'Yeah,' I say to him, risking a smile. He deserves it. 'Feels like déjà vu all over again.'

Fire hose reel located opposite Room 8. The view down the fire escape is into a tower of white plastic buckets, off-kilter with scraps. Wasps round the pulp, a-shimmy in the vegetable peelings. Three tin storeys of kegs stacked on blue stencilled pallets. Mops hinged onto outbuilding walls to bake dry, grey-rope rot-flecked heads. Patchwork of sheds, lean-to with cracked slat windows, pink dregs of blind and chinks into dark wood shelves: potato sacks, yellow biohazard tubs of fat. A kitchen hand is hosing out PVC buckets and watches me clambering down, a cellulite sight for sore eyes in my leopard mini. He wipes his apron with a thick grin and tries to entertain me with yarns of all the drunks who've tumbled down. A fair old tally, including his young self, when he was good and unco pissed. The concrete is a maze of cracks beneath – he tries to convince me it's all the bad bloody dismounts. But he reminds me I don't want to take the route in through the kitchen – I took it when I first got here, through the swing doors, zipped my kit and pillows in past the cookers and white coats, until the chef spotted me and had a proper go. He's a prime cunt, the kitchen hand confirms. So my best bet down to the bar is this sheer drop. His come on is a glint of yellow canines, a scrub of palms where apron dampens cock. If Bruz were here he'd be rolling his eyes, and I'd be hating the fact that he gave zero shits who I hook up with. Tonight I give the guy's attempt an as-if eyebrow, but not too harsh – might pay to keep him in play. Who knows? Could turn out to be that kind of gig.

Across from the shed-maze a chain of fairylights starts, and climbs into a rising cross, bursts in a web overhead of the outdoor diners. It's twelve bucks for a cheese toastie here. Family menu for now, until the late-night cranks. The kids are all sawn-off with sunburn and boredom, pulling pissed-off dances round the garden bar tables. Blend of punters, from a team of nanas sipping something naughty in their polyester tunics to homies trying to look point-blank dangerous, basketball sheen on their tees and caps tipped back, biceps a street scene of tatts. When I was the age of Bruz's girlfriend I wasn't even cool enough to glance in here from the door – couldn't have trod four steps across the boards, let alone stood here and eyeballed the barman, who's a young hulk kissed by the rugby gods, a nose scrummed flat but a jaw you could worship at, logo tee stretched broad over arrogant pecs. I'm more than twice his age – it's the invisible era for me now. And I missed the visible one – too stunted with scripture to ever doll up and get messy here. Those types are flocking in now, trimmed with chem-straightened hair and jeans you couldn't crowbar off. We're due a feed on the bar tab, but I know Bruz and the new girl won't be down. And if they were they'd probably be squeezed in a booth, swapping lovetalk I couldn't stomach. So I order a burger with the works from the laminated list, and wait for it to arrive and disappoint me. Over the leaner where I sit is a black-and-white photo commemorating a record catch. Unbeaten, hooked in '35 aboard the *Lady Clare*, two stoked cobbers fondling the big silver body. Its landed eye looks beyond sad. And something makes me skip most of the burger, a few mouthfuls of tomato pips and beef fat in, mixed with my own lipstick. Retrace the fire escape one crabbed step at a time. Sit on an old school chair that's waiting at the top, inhale my way to an empty pack. Keep my hands busy, and my mouth ashed, though it's no good for my voice. But there's no Bruz to hound me about that. And it's not like it's a habit I'm alone in. An overturned Steiny bottle, fag-ends and days-old rainwater brim in a metal bucket.

I can't be bothered stripping off the day's makeup so I just bog tonight's on over top. Besides, there's no tissues in the room, and the rolls of loo-paper on the sill in the bathroom look like they're tinted with a century of dust – they're bunged in a pyramid, crimped and thinned with heat, fly wings sprinkling their base. No fucking thanks. The bathroom louvres are not-so-frosted and barely holding on. Around the lightbulb in the shower, the mould has turned a kind of pink-brown beautiful. It's possible to blink at it a long while and not see a pattern, just a loose moist weave of freckled stain. The curtain is lime green, rigged with rings ready to shatter. I strip to my cami – I know my pits are rank from the 29-degree drive down here – but then I just can't find the will. There's a bath instead, but sitting in its tub there's a cracked television with what looks to be a CB radio piled on top, plus a dud single bedhead. A slash through a lit one on a poster reminds us all this is a smoke-free area. I scrub through the basics at the sink, a scratch of flannel that the chugging tap can't hardly change. Don't even dress, just head back to number 8. I kept my kit light, but there's a bottle or two in it. I drink my chardonnay warm in my room, spiked with toothpaste.

When the thump comes I recognise its tenor. The whole muscled pace. Gone twenty-five years of me and Bruz playing, I know him throat to fingertips. The thin pub walls don't help, clap along with his efforts. I don't hear a peep out of her. That'd be right – these nights, girlfriend-free, he'd be ready to open my hand and put his limp dick in. A tradition. *Warm up your vocals baby.* I'd just smile, croon a few bars and spit. Work him harder for our big duet. He took some priming, then came easily. Sometimes, if I whined a bit, he'd thumbnail my clit. But if I really wanted the favour back I'd have to help out. You can love a man that hardly makes you come, though. Beats me how that fact is true. But all too plain, it is.

The cream topcoat in the shitter has bubbled and got chips kicked out, the same mint as my bunkroom. I went to the loo before playing tonight – or tried to – and there was a guy behind the Ladies' door. The dumbfuck thing opens directly onto the sinks, a varnished balsawood swing like something from a classroom you had in Standard 3, and the guy gave a big surprising male *Ugh!* when it hit him, buck-towelled and shaving in the girls' manky sink. And I said *sorry* and backed away – because that was how I was brought up, sorry – and had to pull the door off his trunk where the thump had half-stuck it, and he said *no worries*, although I should have said, *what the*

152

fuck are you playing at mate, what is your lonely dick doing in here, we hardly need competition for these scody stalls, and there's a goddamn TV in the biggest one complete with a widescreen of custom-crushed dreams and a radio to say over and over and over and over and a bedhead slushed with stickers, not stars, just junk, just slogans gummed over your head and to get the fuckers off you would have to scratch down to the paste, to the bone, to blood's adhesive screeching. So it's hard to find a reason not to fuck the guy – who's really pretty portly in his budget blue towel, and not much to speak of, and doesn't even smell clean, though the fern-print wrapper reading *Natural Body* is shucked by his knobbly toes on the lino, and clearly he's tried to rub its little wafer on his guts, give his sour bulk a scrub – but just the word wafer makes you think of that thin disc of plasticised Jesus they used to feed you weekly as you kneeled in a white dress with frizzy hair bow-tied to God, and his taste in your mouth, backing up with it, given for you, given, given, and the towel shed for you, and the cup of the sink with its hot-cold faucets staking your buttocks, and nothing is porcelain, there is a gruff blue flannel you can dab yourself up with, and the guy pulls on a basketball hoodie like he belongs to a winning team, and you try to think up lyrics for him, so downstairs you can sing like this is beautiful, half as beautiful as mould in a halo round the fixtures or a merry-go-round of dead flies or a broken TV with a bootprint of glass like a long-running life that couldn't even shatter properly.

So now I'm sitting tight, for a breather, in the mint-chipped stall. Counting down to the gig.

Fun fact: it was a room like number 8 where I told Bruz years ago about the baby. And he drew the line and said the music was everything. So I did what I had to, to keep the band. And I had a procedure, and it was simple, and they

153

sent me home with a timeline to bleed. But I ran past a gig date. So it was a bathroom like this where I washed off what I needed. The final parts tacky, clinging to me. In the grouting like putty, my spread quads rattling. Then I yanked down my skirt. And went back to Bruz, onstage.

Downstairs in the bar the Ladies' is packed with girls but none of them are pissing. They're mostly clicking at phones – and a group by the handblowers have skirts hiked or low-riders cocked. Of all things, they're comparing their styled vajayjays. Fritzes of dark fuzz carved into hearts they prod at with squeals and lacquered fingers. Full plucked peaches, all glitter and sting. Little bitches glare at me. I don't take shit. I'm about to front them when the new girlfriend sweeps in.

Her makeup is architecture, but what's really holding it up is a kid's face. Hair raked high and sectioned into colours. Another skinny tank on, geometric bra in bold view. The paint on her mouth is a self-inflicted bruise. Eyelids powdered with violet prisms. She's here to check it's all staying in place. I grub a lipstick out my leathers and go to recoat too. But she grabs for it, laughs at its flattened tip, the muck round its edges.

'What the fuck you been doing with this? Deepthroating it?'

I think of all the stayovers I've sunk to my knees and sucked Bruz into fondling me. Half-hearted, but something.

'Just the dregs I guess. An old fave. Hard to let go of, eh.'

What she gives me is not a token smile. There's a wiliness in it, and something tight-wound. Like the general state of me is not news to her. She hands back the tube of mongrelised colour.

I think of the teen etched on the bedspread upstairs with her logo reading *Angel Bait!*

'You got to know when it's time, eh.' She reinforces it with a steady voice, girlish but gritty. 'When its day is done.'

If Bruz and I'd had our daughter, she could have been this blend of lovely and lethal. I think of the sign in a field I passed on my solo trip here: *Deceased Estate*.

Out in the bar, I hear Bruz warming up, a mundane strum, but it gets me pining.

She's back in the mirror, busy with her blindfold of eyeshadow, blending it with a thumb, and double-exposing her teeth to patrol for plum smudges. Rejigging her bra under buckshot sequins, dark C cups not short of cargo. The group waylaid over their decorated crotches are still giggling wholesale in the corner. I want to deck the girlfriend. Punch her low, where it's clear she's never been hurt. But Bruz is only pissing around on his lead out there, and it still breaks chains in me. So I can't go for her. Just stand while she's gloating at her spot-lit beauty.

And hate my motley heart.

I shove my way past the vajazzled and hit the stall hard. The door is a joke. It comes back at my shoulder more than once before I get to bolt it.

I've always known our day was done. Held on through all the girlfriends, but have no clue why. Just this: it's Bruz. Have you been in that kind of love? If not, go fuck yourself. And fuck you too if you don't feel the music the way I do. If a leadbreak doesn't lure out all your ghosts. If distortion doesn't make your chest-wall feel like a dog kennel. Twenty-plus years and his playing sidekicks me in the gut. What have I got to replace that with? All those girls on the dancefloor tonight think the supply is endless. But I'll tell you what. Town after small town is dry. I should know. I've toured round most of them.

And Bruz is hitting the frets a little harder now to wake me up. It's long past our kickoff. But I don't budge until I hear a voice over my mic. Trying a melody, wannabe. She's fucking lost it if she thinks I'm gonna hand her that. I topple the stand when I get there, and it sickles through the lights, nearly shorts the spare amp. But Bruz lets me handle her offstage, doesn't even put down his gat. He's professional. And at least the scuffle comes here, and not later, on the fire escape. I grin for a moment at the thought of that. My brain zooms out on the easy ballet of it, the *oops* it would take to disconnect her pretty grip, to stage a stealthy trip on the croc-skin, a tweak of stiletto. The slither of peelings waiting as her mattress. The kerb of concrete jutting for her spine. Wouldn't rule it out.

'Fun fact,' I say through the mic when I've got a good grip. Eyeballing her. 'This is not my first rodeo.'

Did we miss our turn? was the most like love he ever said to me, lazy one night, played long past closing, too late. I think there was a time when he almost considered me. I've held on hard to nights when his hand might have slid my face for just a second, picking up the sweat I build singing, the bronzer turned to paste. When we've had to pull the shitbox van over, loaded with rig, pop the hood while the radiator sizzles, spend roadside time playing cards in the cab, a splatter of fates along the vinyl. Once he fanned my overheated cheek with his deal, leaned in for a full kiss that wiped off my warpaint, and we clawed quick to the backseat, made the van our mechanical bull. But I've never had any luck. *Chase the Ace!* Out in the audience there's always been fresh stock for him: I watch them scoping him while he plugs in, then centrestage, his acidwash jeans akimbo, his eyes closed, priestly and horny. His playing glazes them. Good as it does me. It takes. It lasts. Not such a fun fact: I'm in no position to blame them.

The setlist is full of songs about it. I lay into them tonight, and Bruz is proud of me. I can see it in his stance, the thrum of his hands. His head drops back like gods are listening. When the backing track cuts out on one tune his riff shrills on, and he glides off on a long shred, stalking round the stage in his Docs, creating a glistening racket that fills the room with gooseflesh. And by the end my throat is going. But a bit of rough is okay. I've never had a clean voice, zero grace. I've always had to reach for the note, give it a bit of torque. It's not the right note, it's the real note, as some old rocker says. I work the ground either side, with an ache, delay. A dose of gravel comes natural. And even when I back off, breathe a line sweet and right, there's some tougher tint there, lying just under it. It always comes out collarboned, tarnished. Worm in the tequila. That's my voice, if you ask Bruz.

And what would I have been if it wasn't for him, taking smoko from band practice out in our garage all those years ago, just knocking round tunes with my bro, then catching the sound of me, keening some hymn out by the washline. Striding outside to stand there like something I had in my voice was making him thirsty. A holy-ghost stare. Grabbing the wet slump of sheet from my fluttering hands and turfing it, muddied, not even in the basket. Kicking over the wickerwork of pegs, and crunching clean through them, his boots spurting colour. And pulling me into the centre of the practice, unquestionable, with his eyes lightning-charged. Dead set, all commands. So the choirgirl was gone. Standing me by the mic, and plummeting a riff that drove right into my loins. And came out my song.

The best bit of the night is: the new girlfriend is not a good dancer. She can't get her bearings with the beat. She tries to groove her hips around, do snaky things with her hands. But unhitched from the music the routine looks half-baked. And frankly, a little special needs. And of course there's a cast of chicks schooled in how to twerk, and they fix Bruz with stares while they're pumping and dipping. And the new girl gets awkward. She hadn't factored this in. She stops dancing. And she's not a good sport.

So Bruz and me, later, get to share a few minutes out on the roof. I give him the school chair and crank off his boots, hauling them backward clamped to my guts.

'Fucken' watch it,' he says. 'You'll arse up. Off the edge.'

Their tread outlined on my halter, I hug them for a while. Their warm alpha doublestitched stink.

'Yeah, then where would you be?'

He lights up and doesn't answer. Bruz can be a cagey cunt like that.

'That pig amp lasted the distance, but.' Sometimes I just don't give up.

'Yeah, well. Second best is all there is. Tonight.' But he's not looking at me.

'Sounds you got out of it though . . . Fully beaut. For a substandard unit, you had it really singing.'

The weatherboards of the old pub creak where he rubs his head back, school chair on a lean. He's got a dangerous smile.

'Yeah, she gave it up. Like she had much of a choice.'

He's still got that infected toenail he's had for the last handful of gigs – bashed it on the amp when we were packing-in a few pubs back. Could be what rooted the head. The nail's well cracked now, so he has a pick, and lifts off a chunk of it while we smoke. Passes it to me like a trophy tipped with pus.

Which I cheers him for, and flick into the burnt-out bucket. The rails run over the tin like a bad chart of something. And that's it. Just the two of us in leftover moonlight. Same as always. Last of the punters out on the street, bouncing on the hood of a ute, a clumsy hellraising. The bouncer, offering to waste them, had it with their antics to his back teeth, no comedy in his bloodthirsty yells. Me chatting, Bruz yawning. I get the CB from the bath, and Bruz pops the back, takes a quick jack, reckons its circuits should be passable. I trail a cord from the socket in my room, and fiddle with the thing, but nothing comes through. No over and over and over and over. Just the sound of some lonely bastard down the street still going, full throttle, at another pub.

I feel there's a young girl out there suffering

She has to shade her eyes at the faith-healer's house – it's glass all round the outside. Too much pool and not enough palm trees. He takes her to his office, shelves of bibles in a glossy saved glare. She wonders if he dunks people out there, if his suit wades in and he bobs their souls like holy buoys. If they splash up rinsed and bright, with chlorinated hallelujahs. Her mother has dressed her in her best ugly clothes, and she's sweating up the seams, trying not to smell teenage – she wouldn't mind if salvation meant getting in the deep end. But the preacher would need to keep his layers on. He's thick-set with tortoiseshell eyes, greasy dome between ears. His socks are Fair Isle, tugged to mosquito-bite shins. But he's supposed to know his business. The night he came to town she missed redemption, but her mother's friends told her of the miracles he struck, the bargains on the stage that the demons couldn't back out of, bucked out of hosanna chests, hurled off shackled legs. So her mother praised the Lord and gave her bus fare. And now she's sitting just about in the faith-healer's lap. He'd called to the audience for her: *I feel there's a sick girl who needs to come forward*. Her mother paid extra for the kick of the whole town gossiping that girl was hers. *The Lord has called me to lift this girl's pain*. But the Lord has a strange way of moving through an old man's hands, their hairy sunlit knuckles. The Lord has a bad taste in dirty words. The Lord doesn't care about all the open windows. He has her by the scalp, glinting nothing like glory.

extraction

Remember those buzzy bees the dental nurse would make for you, cotton-wool swabs she'd leash with floss, and tie-on white wings she'd snip off the bibs that would paper your collar to soak all the dribble, remember how you'd loll in the whirring chair, bare legs sticking to its aqua slope, headlit with sting from the long-neck swivel of the lights, their terrible probing silver, and the mouth of you broke open, numbed, just blinking till she passes you the string, fuzzy eyes and smile she's felt-tipped on? Remember?

They should give them out after your abortion.

ladybirds

At the last minute, we had to take her little sister: pigtail
silhouette, left knee always cobwebbed with scab, rusty and
pickable. Ladybirds dawdled round her sundress – not the
look we were going for. There could be boys – me and Marty'd
snuck on something slutty, baby-oiled our legs so we shone
from the shinbones. We kept our walk drowsy and so-what-
about-it through the hips. But Lolly didn't walk so much as
hopscotch, heels coming down on a skinny four-five. Me and
Marty were bitches all the way to the bus stop – by the time
we were finished, Lolly had zero bounce.

On the bus, me and Marty got busy rejigging each other's
braids. I leant back on the metal seat and let the gear-changes
tug my nape, while she snagged up a pattern of blonde that
looked like fishnet. Seriously, you would not believe her
fingers – high-speed and fineprint, strand by strand. We liked
it tight as real tears at the eye corners. I stuck my toes in the
stirrup of the seat in front and let Marty crisscross away. On
the outskirts of my head I sometimes still feel it, the swish
of her pinky nails. I didn't get hers right, so I handed over
the plait, three black leashes from around midway, a trade of
slippy fingers, and then she took it home, top-speed down her
skull, showing off.

So of course then Lolly wanted a lookalike. Marty suckered
her in real mean. Over the kid's head she slid the design into

place but at the neck she flicked out a long feed and lashed it round the bolt on the seat back, hissing sweet the whole time at her little sis *keep still, keep super still okay.* When she finished she tapped Lolly's shoulder – Lolly's head pinged forward then ricocheted back, taking a tough whump on the rail. She sang out a squeak like air fannied out a balloon. *Teach her,* said Marty. But someone had to reverse the hair from where it was screwed round the bolt. In the end, I busted a fingernail.

Lolly wanted to push the bell, so the least we could do was let her after that. Or that's what I reckoned. Marty just shrugged, and rigged her eyebrows when it was the right stop. When the kid didn't click too quick, she punched her shoulder, hurry up. We slid past the driver but he looked like we left a nasty taste. We'd hardly unloaded all six legs before he swung the door shut.

I don't remember what we talked about while we walked to Marty's dad's. What do girls chat about? Are you expecting two dead girls to talk any different? What I remember is having to backtrack a lot because Marty was hazy on the route. She didn't have a map, just a vague hunch on street corners, so we spent a lot of time hanging round where roads forked while Marty scuffed her jandal and narrowed her eyes. She'd only been there a couple of times – her guesswork was wired to bits of ground-memory, like derro cars in the front lawn on blocks, a pair of sneakers lassoed from a powerline, the All Blacks flag some hardout fan had strung up. She remembered the dairy with its red roller door, its *Fresh Bait* sign. We turned right in the end. And then we got to her dad's park: thirteen hectares of dropout heaven with a playground through the gate on a bed of old bark and black tyres.

Her dad had one of the hillside chalets – Marty liked that word and would say it with a lick – dotted round the panorama of clapped-out caravans. When we got up there he was in a deckchair in his jockeys, and the plastic awning picked up tree-fern fuzz and mixed it with corrugated sun. He finished his smoke before he cranked himself out the seat to give Marty a hello that was more like a mugging. Me and Lolly hung back: he wasn't her dad, and I got the feeling I'd be levering him off my sternum. He just nodded, and led us through the munted French door into his crib. There was a sunbaked nugget of shit turning chalky on his welcome mat.

It was mostly just one crass room, with random lean-tos for a dunny and a bunk. Marty, being Marty, had built it up but you could clock it in a couple of blinks. It smelt septic. The laminate on everything wasn't retro, just queasy. The over-sink cupboards looked ready to drop, but not through overstocking – you could just see the odd bung tin and mangy baggie stuffed back on the ply. On the bench there was a shoebox of sachets from takeout joints, little crimpy slugs of tear-off sauce – and beer caps pinged round the lino you couldn't tally. The sink was deep, unshining and fishy. The bed was a wiry yellow seen through an unhinged door – he was dragging some jeans on at least. To start with I squatted by Marty on the couch, but when he came and sat with us I thought about the rubbery things you'd find if you rammed your fingers down, which got me goosebumpy. So mostly then I stood out on the front deck and pretended like the sea view was worth squinting at. In the salty offshore light the chairs looked bandy and the blinds unravelled.

He must have known it was a comedown from Marty's stories, her big talk on the holiday park. He told us the mess was mainly the fault of a gull who'd got itself trapped when he was out of town. Must have jimmied through a window he'd left cracked then gone mental in the blinds, couldn't find an exit. It properly trashed the place he said. Days out he was still finding the splashdown of shit. He picked a feather out the couch-back while he said it. It even managed to knock out the power to the freezer while it was freaking off the walls – he waved us over to take a jack while he propped up the jellied lid. In the bottom was a slump of plastic he hadn't got round to spading out. I think about it sometimes now, that clammy oblong view down. He said it wasn't meat but it may as well have been. The stench pumped the back of your tongue, and made your gut wall buckle. He dropped the lid with such gusto the stink hit your eyelashes.

How does a girl catchup with a dad she hardly ever sees? What do they have to say? He fished out a pack of budget biscuits and we chewed that into vanilla dust. I didn't want the Raro stuff he fork-whisked in a glass for each of us, so Lolly sculled mine in big gulps that left her a temp moustache, goofy and neon. Then she let her tongue out, and got busy lifting the chequers of scab off her crusty knee: when she finished, her tweezing left a pattern of pink snakeskin. He mostly tinkered with his lighter, while Marty prattled basics, home and school details. He nodded along like her smalltime kid shit was of minor interest: when he wanted to look like he really cared a trail of B&H would trumpet out his nose. Up his forearms he had the kind of homemade tattoos that have fogged over, a furry blend of barbed ink and hair – I looked at those when I went through the ranchslider with Lolly and closed it while Marty kept talking. That's all I knew about the visit: at some point she needed to get her dad alone. So I helped. I pinched little Lolly, like I might have a good game, and led her out.

The front deck balanced on brown-stained stilts and a bottlebrush was pulling in bees the ranchslider end, in jittery hopped-up orbits. Lolly backed off to crossleg as far as she could get, but I stood and looked at those bees, fizzing like atoms round the ugly bars of red bloom. Through the glass I could still hear Marty talking gibberish. It was 75 percent hum, and it's not like there was subtitles. Like I told the cops later, you can't exactly pinpoint the words when it's like that, weird and offstage. But I picked up enough. I expected his tattoos to flinch when she told him what her stepdad was up to, but all those green blurs of flame never gave an inch. The skulls lay there in limbo, useless spells looping from their sockets. Later of course, when she told again – a teacher at school, a friend's mother – then she took it straight back, cried off and said she'd lied, nothing ever got done. Everyone assumed that was her pattern: make some shit up, then panic and retract. But I know she looked at her dad that day head-on. In the beginning, she didn't take back a thing. She just waited, and I looked on, and the hellfire stamped round his wrists brought no reckoning. The death wishes trickled to his fingers, but I know he didn't even flex his knuckles.

At the joint of my ribs I felt the sizzling sound of bees.

Lolly's favourite trick was to sit there thumbing her milkteeth, testing for a suspect one – she narrowed down enough that her dumb smile was always black-notched. She was at it now, crouched on the deck, with drool dewing out while she counted down holes. At some point I went and sat with her. When she grinned it was really too dorky to be true. She always looked grubby, coloured outside the lines, and her dim face was scattershot with freckles. *Sun kisses*, she'd correct you, if you teased. I told her I'd rehash her hair. I suckered the stretchy ties out and it gave like silk. As I restrung it she puffed out little sighs of happiness her sister would have slapped her for.

At some point the dad slid out the door and lit up, leaning on the fall-apart rails. Bees vied past him for a sip of the raggedy flowers, but he just waved, gave them a rev up. Lolly's hair had come to an end in my hands long before but I kept tweaking it, doing clockwise wisps, for somewhere else to look. I wish I could have made her a dreamcatcher. Round the side of the shack I heard garbage bags fluttering.

We left not so long after that. Lolly was still chirpy when we walked down through the park grounds. Side to side, she kept whizzing her head as if she might catch a glimpse of how sweet her plait was. When she skipped ahead, I tried asking Marty what she'd told her dad. But she said nothing at first. And I didn't push – she knew how to fix you with this dead-end stare. Instead we scuffed around for a bit, in the bark playground by the park gate. Lolly mounted the seesaw goggling with please, so me and Marty worked the metal T bar to lever her up and down on the whining slat. She peeped while her cushiony ass boinged up, then slapped back down, astraddle – you could hear her thighs grating slivers out the paint. The joints of the seesaw played bad unoiled chords. She giggled with whiplash, and kicked her minnow toes. Then Marty let her drop to the black-tyre buffer hard and bossed her back out to the road. Lolly begged to jump real quick on the wood submarine thing that was beached on the bark – Marty hissed a major no, so she knew not to cross her. It had a steel-pipe periscope so you could pretend to scan horizons – anyway, the view was only thick black leagues of dirt.

I did try asking Marty again, once Lolly fidgeted off, out of earshot. But she was all excuses dealt out in a who-cares voice, said she'd just been joking, said she'd just been looking to get her asshole stepdad messed up. And I could understand that: her stepdad was a cliché. You've seen footage by now I guess.

On late news clips, sitting in the docks, he looks no different to how he did at their place, a mix of high-handed and can't-be-fucked, waiting in the same old chair just daring you to front him. She shrugged: big whoop, so much for that. All her dad had given her was an ice-cream tub she was carrying now, its lid bird-shit frosted. Inside were marbles, a glass nest of rolls and clicks. At its core each globe had a tinted fin of light. Later, on the bus home, when the driver wasn't looking, Marty poked them one by one through the window and we watched them craze and spit on the tar seal, a pinball of blind eyes.

What do dead girls talk about? They don't ever talk to me. Marty just looks at me and shrugs again, like there's fuck-all point ever telling. Why would you? In the end what he stuck into her, body or blade, didn't much matter – he'd been jamming in so much pain for so long there was no space left for her. She reaches up her arms and tightropes her hair down her skull as close-knit as a scar. Ladybird, ladybird, Lolly comes tagging along, her painful cute coming too, so you can't help smirking at her kaleidoscope of freckles, her uprooted grin. It's always Lolly, Lolly at the last minute, waking, waking to see what she shouldn't: they say she wandered their room in bloody footfalls an hour before she lay down by her sis. No one came. Marty's lies were truth the whole time – but leaving the park I think she already knew I was starting to listen less. On the way home instead she told me the rest of the story of her father and the bird, so I could see it belting the walls of her dad's cabin, its black-and-white panic, its eye a red pin. He came home and found it, Marty told me, washed up and stupid in its feathers and soil, and he beckoned it out of its splinters – then he took it outside and finished it.

devil's trumpet

There was a rumour about the boys who smoked the wrong flowers. Hiked into the bush with a legend and a scheme to get high, and picked the wrong vine (a white flower, tricky and forked at the stamen, spiked and purpling at the petal-tip). Three of them, crippled that night round the campfire, only able to roll the parched terror of their eyes. There was a rumour about the girl who could manoeuvre a whole Coke can up there. Who made cash taking small gangs of guys round the back of the Metalwork block, and demonstrating the technique (a cotton hitch, a hushed crouch, a bow-legged swallowing). There was the rumour about the boy from Special class who'd lurk by the gully on Cross Country, leap out and maul your bra (the skidding of pine-needled sneakers, gurgled *I love yous*). There was a rumour about the Phys Ed teacher, who'd wander the changing rooms with a beer-soaked smile, gold-tooth-third-from-the-right glinting at the scurry of half-checked girls (blue checks, regulation, like shrunken maths grids, a timid trigonometry of thighs). There was a rumour about the boy the Physics teacher bawled out as thick as bricks: the next time the teacher walked into the class there was a pile of bricks stacked, dumb, on his chair. And a rumour that once, the Deputy had sat with his spit-shined shoes so deliberately akimbo a student caught a clear view up his walkshorts to unencumbered cock. And a rumour that you'd bragged you could fuck every one of my friends before we were finished.

When I was nuzzling your collarbone I couldn't hear the rumours. When I was tucked into the musk of your neck, and busy licking the body salt there. When I was out of my seatbelt, cock-teasing you driver-side, begging you to get me spreadeagled. When you were thumb-deep in my opaque school tights and I'd arch and coo on their 70-denier pucker. When the stars were rhinestones. When your car was a blue Holden god. When kisses spread to your back teeth, marathons of sucking, and jaws clicked from laughing so long into their wet. When we pashed through jokes, through tunes, through homework, through the leftovers we shovelled out our schoolbags, warm clingwrapped afternoons of kiss. Sticky third-base sunsets. When you let me tattoo you with talk, whispered onto your chest-wall, while an image of sea slid the windshield like a distant rumour.

And the one about the perv who collected antlers and pelts, house stuffed with creepy arcana (animals posed in downy flight, detail stiffened to the fetlocks and eyelashes). And the one about the kids who broke into the millionaire's beach house, the concrete joint we nicknamed the Castle, and found a spray-can you could aim at your dick if you needed to keep it rock-hard, or your nipples if the measly pink let-downs should have been plumper (a blouseful of ozone, a flysprayed breath, the crinkle of skin under chemical spackle). And the one about the boys who went rogue on the homo's house, pasting his windows with centrefolds, so when he woke up he was trapped in a kaleidoscope of lace splitting open at the airbrushed lip. And the one about the guy at the service station who had a collection of pregnant stick-mags, frame after frame of hairy men hammering at the moon. And the one about the boys who took the stray down to the rockpools and took turns aiming at it with the crossbow. And the boys who took the shotgun to the dump to pitch the noisy seagulls wide. And the boys who were with you in the wagon when you bet you could each pick up a fresh girl and drive the mainstreet getting simultaneous blowjobs (silhouette of stallions on a silver five-seater, a fistful of hooped earrings and hair gel, ponytails' mea culpa. Difficult elbows, novice tongues. The Doors on the stereo, light my rubber-burnt knees. Applause. A sob of monoxide).

There was a rumour that if you turned left on Highway 6 and followed the black-bodied pines and the black-bodied pines and the black-bodied pines until sudden phantoms of white stock started appearing in the moonlit fields and the fenceposts whirred along the glitter of the gouged-out industrial lake you'd reach another small town. And maybe you could live there, once you drove past the freezing works and headstones and quarries and smelter and boarded-up Four Squares and piers. Or in other small towns beyond that. Beyond even that. But that was just a rumour.

The one about the girl whose lunchbox got done over on the school bus so a tampon string trailed from her sandwich and she got photographed at interval taking a big unthinking fluffy bite. The one about the boys who wank into the vats at Kentucky Fried, crispy coated spermatozoa in the foam, so the poultry gets a genital crunch. The one about the retarded kid who the boys train to lizard the aisles of the school bus peering in oblivious blinks up the squeaking girls' skirts. The one about the Mr Whippy man, who gets girls to blow him to the Greensleeves jingle in exchange for unlimited snowfreeze (taste buds demolished with icy sediment). The one about the girl who hung herself from chains in the corner of her stepfather's workshop. The one about the baby who was found looped inside her. The one about the girl who got cells inside her cheek scraped out for a slide in biology class and when the teacher projected the microscope up onto the pull-down screen everyone could make out the flicker of semen, tadpoles travelling in neon squiggles. The rumour it was yours.

There is a rumour that the stray lasted seven arrows, circling circling circling. The seagulls think they are prize fighters, but there is a rumour that the dump got sundered, a buzzing requiem of feathers. When you are told these rumours, it's the boys who tell you. It's boys who hold the title. And you are expected to laugh. Go on, cough it up.

None of my friends tell me any rumours. I try to stay close to their bony congregation. I try to monitor their giggly amnesia. I try to smell the truth in the mellow arrangements of their hair. The symbolism of their earrings and ankle-socks. There is a rumour that the guy with the glass eye who runs the pub likes to pop it out and slide it up inside his women. I would like to do that too. Guide that gaze up through the dark slip of their misdeeds, find out where you've been. But there's just the daily cellophane sound of them talking. Unwrapping nothing. They don't have a word to say about you.

There is a rumour about the girl whose body got snagged in the swollen creek. She was snared for a week in the rickety debris, still trying to signal with the limbs' black click. Face in residence under the surface. Fingernails miscarried in the crooked trap of wood. There is a rumour of her branched and everlasting beckoning. If anyone is listening.

The one about the party I go to, once I believe the rumours. The one where I'm on my back on the stone-cold beach. The one where I skull, inhale, spin. Thorn-apple, witches' weeds, moonflowers, hell's-bells. It hardly matters. The party after that. And the party after that one. The one where my dress is crippled (past the black pines). The one where the cassette deck crows (on the cusp of manmade lake). The one where I'm lying denuded on a ute bed while catcalls root for the strokes I've lost count of (fenceposts knocked into blankness, one after another). The one where your name is the wound that runs the centre of my voice. The one where the future without you is gooseflesh. The one where I stumble back up from the gravel to the barn, missing a clutch of hair, the sight from my right eye, a small town and a shoe, and mutter to somebody, 'I think I've just been raped.' But everyone laughs. Because they've all heard the rumours about me.

god taught me to give up on people

She walks in wearing this dirty, heaven-sent dress, and stops to sway a few seconds by the jukebox, although it isn't playing any surprises. Turning all see-through on her thighs, the skirt is a calico of scrubbed-out flowers. One of God's leftovers, seventh day. Trust a smalltown Man of God to have a line of pale, fuckable daughters – she was the last in the aisle, where their blond group trailed to the Lord, itty-bitty to tallest. Muttering, head down, I always used to long to reach out, twitch her white bow open so I could see something worth all that throat-clearing praise. Back then they would have brushed out her hair, but you could see the buckled blonde where pigtails had dented it. She bobbed around with the velvet sock for the offering smelling like popcorn and patent maryjanes. I never sucked in her father's words like that whiff. Straight hymn of hopscotch and purity.

I was with her three days ago, but she's got no recall. Up at the counter she smacks down a glass and says, *the Lord is my let down. He maketh me walk to the bar.* There's something grisly at the base of her voice, and her eyes look repainted without stripping yesterday's off. She tines her nails back on her scalp – there's no holy water to rinse those dark roots. In the hotel room she'd crosslegged on the green quilt, repeated what I wanted, a bad act testing a microphone, check, breathe, check. Her bra, with its grey mechanics of lace, smelt like turpentine.

She still has teenage knees, but a store-bought blink she aims at me limpid with liquor. I listen to another black hit click into the jukebox, a hoop she starts crooning to – litany of smoke and real old news.

dorm

He'd turn up at my dorm room, having woken in the next strange bed. He'd still be too drunk to be subtle about it – he'd blunder our corridor, slurring for me, before his palm belted the door, and I kicked from bed, flicked the latch, and let his body tip in. He'd land on the carpet, muttering, prop himself back so the story could spill, his skull a dozy topple against my desk, knocking my essays slithering. He wouldn't know the man. He'd just have come around, in a clinch, piled with limbs, off his face in some gully of bed. He wouldn't stay. It still shocked him, to wake up nowhere, fucked and stripped. He'd bolt to me instead, break in the way I'd shown him, make a racket on the stairs with his wasted cartoon stealth. He'd talk me through the lead-in, pieces of street sign, dialogue, skin shots that all the drink had blitzed. He was so dazed with happy shame, dumbstruck with being touched, using my pages to clean out the blood that was gluey at his nostrils, or stuck once, going blacker, along the hem of his shirt. Sometimes the clothes that he'd grappled off the floor, half-lit, weren't even his, yanked on, smelling backwards. And I tried not to want to load him on a bus out, as if there were a fare we could pay to go home to the high school where we'd held hands three years solid in smalltown boy–girl love. The bruise of smile on his split lip shone and shone. When he could stagger straight, he'd take me out to breakfast, we'd shovel something homely out a bakery warmer, and then passers-by would watch us on a park bench, trading alternate nuzzles of pastry out the soft mess in each other's hands.

What You Don't Know

We went to a hotel. You'd earned a deal through work – wife included, not the usual corporate bonus plan. You showed me the brochure, a gatefold of wide-angle rooms with models relaxed in them, couples on hourly hire reclined in a mock-up of love by the endless pool. We packed simply, didn't say what we hoped to save by this glossy visit. Why would we need a retreat? The grounds were so clean the horizon left a chemical aftertaste. Nothing in the lobby was allowed to wilt and the staff were apparelled in seamless neutrals. I felt followed by their 360-degree smiles. The kind of sex expected by the suite didn't come to us, but we tried, made do. Part-way through it didn't seem workable, our two bodies jointed in the cream rental room, but we kept it up, handled each other to a low-key habit of come. I couldn't close my eyes. They were still open when you scuffed my cheek with an afterthought of kiss that felt air-conditioned, got up half-mast to pat yourself down. Then you sat on the edge of the too-beige bed to read me the in-house menu. This is how you save a marriage. The booths for dinner were deodorised as coffins, and globes lit our meal with retro orange.

I was so long gone. We'd left the boys alone in the house, so I thought of him there: drool trickling into the rough brocade of our guest pillows, leaning sideways into our spare bathroom mirror to thumbnail a dark pore, jaw dissolved in strokes of heavy breath. Mapping our hallway with his palms as he shuffled, blinking, for a predawn piss, the cup of his marl jocks warmed and stiffened. (I could smell the cotton, front soured, I could feel the nudge of that half-dozing cock.) I'd left the rooms so straight all the angles ached. The whole place was rigged to catch his steps. When I got back I imagined it would be forensic, how I'd trace him, through the spaces I'd primed to catch his prints. All night the nerves between my thighs were shrill under the pastel quilt. If you had woken and rolled to me, the way the man in the brochure did, you would have been surprised I was so wet.

*

Sometimes it seems he's in every picture of our son. I can't turn pages without him recurring, a stowaway, a twin. They are drag-racing sleeping bags in silvery bashes up the hall, they are winching themselves from a roped-up pine to somersault the creek. They are small haloes of faces padded in parkas grinning at the spazz of sparklers, their fists zig-zagged with burn-time. They are crossdressed as chicks for a mufti-day stunt, their tough calves shredding my second-best pantyhose, my leftover eyeliner glued round their lids. I remember the twitch of his gun-shy lashes as I leaned in. My Revlon reversed around the liquid of his mouth – there was still Weetbix at the roots of his teeth. I know he was once a bed-wetter. I know his blood type. I once stood at a school camp holding a clipboard that listed him as a strong swimmer. I once beached him, recovery position, nursed his lips free of a black-sand belch. I know the password his family uses in case someone else needs to pick him up from school. Only two years ago I spoke it: he was shaky on the sick-bay bench, grey to the eardrums with shame and chuck. He'd capsized in science, hadn't been able to scalpel the mouse, tweeze out its listed innards, its tiny paws spreadeagled on the ice tray with pins. He was the same the next year with the sheep's heart, the aorta's dark bubble – a sick classmate had put his finger in, wobbled it, gory, puppet-like. That was the end. I shouldered him across the carpark, steered him at my wagon, and gave him the code. He said, 'I'm too old for that now, Irene.' My first name, used by his mouth, the first time. 'I'm way too old for that.'

By the time we reached the hotel I knew that if I didn't stop, my son would have to slice his childhood album through its ringbound spine. But I didn't know the safety word.

*

The couple from the brochure were on the television, too. At the hotel, they had their own channel, beaming through a programme of local activities. The words had been removed from their mouths but everything mimed satisfaction, the kind of sleazy bliss that couples project when they've fogged their room successfully with eau de fuck and are heading out into the promo-ed landscape they've earned. They tampered with each other's fingers while they ticked off the itinerary sheet. The long-shots tracked them through the complex wearing compatible outfits in a post-coital dusk. The voiceover, listing the highlights of the area, was a tenor croon I recalled from an eighties blind-date show. As a teen I'd had a crush on him, his come-on-downs issued through sponsored teeth, his crow's feet neon in his faux lifesaving tan.

We'd done the expected. We'd been down through the anodyne foyer to order a taxi for our first sightseeing outing. Perhaps it's optical, the effect the lodge plans on a marriage – grounds to reception, everything looked so maintained and parallel. The staff stood sentry with their eco smiles. The lobby played a soundtrack of ringtones. We sipped something sedative, waiting in an alcove for our top-end lift. But the driver in his cockpit wasn't tipped enough to narrate landmarks where we were headed. His indifference was constant in the rear-view, the tariff ticked past subsidised vistas. I could feel you tightening your lips, making a mental note of his substandard service.

There is a hotel for everything. Back in our room your thumbs on my buttons tried out the positions of rehab. You tasted like your appetizer, a marinated kiss, overpriced, that couldn't hope to fill me up.

When we were out I'd sent the boys a dual postcard, although you'd tutted and told me off (and you were proved right: we did in fact make it home before the mail had a hope). The spiral racks were loaded with mandatory mountains and sheep in lush paddocks: I thought about their dark handfuls of heart under photo-bleached fleece. I chose the adrenaline shots, 3 for $2 – lean tourists in bodycon brights taking leaps into canyons, hog-tied to elastic. There was no room to write anything quotable. I said something mumsy and practical (check the elements, don't forget to lock up) and watched the pen weaken where it signed off love. I couldn't let myself X a kiss: my hand shook and looked too bareknuckled.

We sat outside at a table for a while. We can afford to sit, not talking, in diverse settings of manufactured green. It's something the advertised couple took frequently, drafts of al fresco quality time. An atrium of groomed leaves latticed the breeze and your cufflinks tapped the marble tabletop. You'd gathered brochures from the tiers in the foyer, and sampled a boutique ale, speculating on a golf course. I thought about overturning another card, inking it with unforgiveable things. I thought about the column of feathers at his navel, the crosshairs broken with inlets of skin, how I'd seen it unzipped, just before we departed, and I'd been grounded, stranded in the hall at the chance glimpse, shaking at the cove of a button, the indent of stud, how the roof of my mouth turned liquid, answering it. He'd gotten a fright when he spotted me hovering, then tried to man back up, grin it off. 'Woah. Jump scare,' he'd joshed, flustered. And I'd pretended I was sorting out dirties for the wash – such a good carer, always on the lookout. He granted me his top-mum nod. Oh, you know, just part of my job. He stood in his daks and packed my palms with shucked gear that was still warm-blooded.

Back in the room your touch proceeded. I said it had been a long day, I didn't mind, we could take a break. But you had an agenda. You'd made an investment in this suite. It was not sex but a takeover. This is a place where money changes perspective – and you'd paid a premium to love me again.

We switched on the TV so we didn't hear the sound of our less-than-half-bothered hands on skin. The eighties host guided his models through a softly lit grove for a multi-choice meal. There was the sequel of an intimate sunset they were directed to nuzzle in. So when we were finished there was somewhere else to look.

*

It was last summer that started it – the sun-flooded lounge flanked with boys. Lowriding boardies, bare brown trunks. The scuffle of limbs on the leather, sweat on the controllers, as they bucked in time to their games. They were fucking up, gunning down everything, laughter so loud it jarred the windows as they watched each other lose. Their hardout thumbs worked the X in a spasm, with dog sounds, and teeth sunk into their lips. They yanked the blinds, pissed off at the set-up of light. Our cat flopped in their shade, rolled sluttishly against their shins.

It was the evenness of all the surfaces I was learning to hate. I wiped everything down and re-wiped it. The sink shone its hole at me. The oven offered a clean place to lay my head, racks of silver hygiene. The boys were blowing whole torsos into pixels, loud coronas of meat. When they left, their sweat would be on my couches, spinal, evaporating. I wasn't even background noise.

But I still made them sandwiches. That's what mothers do. He wandered to the island wanting more, handed me the warm dark oval of his plate. He said sorry for its brackets of leftover crust. He was sheepish and cheesy, like he was starting to guess his charm. Horizontal, as he leant, there were tiny clefts in his abdomen, the shade of dirty honey, and as he chatted he itched them, slow, with his trigger finger. I laid out a board of white bread. The harness above his velcro had frayed into black fuzz. I fell in love right through my sternum. I could feel it coming like a muscle cramp.

I wrote that, later, on the back of a postcard. On the front a woman had paid to plunge headfirst through miles of terminal sky.

*

The real couple was down in the aqua plaza that afternoon. The pool slid nowhere in its infinite chemicals and they didn't look like they'd had a matinee. I'd seen her earlier in the morning spa, where we lay on our designer gurneys being groomed. She'd asked if I'd recognised the muzak chiming: it was the theme from *The Young and the Restless*. For a while, as attendants paddled us with cream, we'd chatted through our memory of soap names, Brooke and Storm caught in blond storylines of high-class pain. Now she dithered by the shallow end and the nether line of her suit looked stubbed. She wore her bikini like apologetic underwear. I knew I'd look no different.

You took up a posture that indicated you didn't want to talk. And I knew better than to fuss on the topic of what the boys might get up to in our absence. You'd never had patience with my neurotic forecasting, my automatic parental fear of the worst case. But I thought of them, prowling our rooms, colliding with heirlooms, bass line cranked to full, hosting a gang of their mates with your hijacked whisky. I hoped they were raising hell. If they'd been here by the vacant lot of the pool they would have been ambushing each other, they'd never be able to resist the leg-sweep, they'd scrag each other into the water with acrobatic thumps. The place would be booming with their mongrel shouts. I hoped back home they were playing up. I imagined bathtubs boozy with ice and oak-cracking battles on our bespoke furniture. Maybe girls. They were due to start fucking the same rough-house way. Back when we'd let them hold an early party, I'd sprung him in torchlight stuck into his first kiss, ramming a girl, whose suck was just as rugged, against our garage door. His hands were frank on her skittish arse and I could hear the tack of their mouths, crude with hunger. I'd thought it was a cheap laugh then, the teenage ruck of it, all traction and moisture. Now I'd do anything to get pulled into such a roughneck kiss. The woman at the pool's edge didn't know where to climb into the engineered water, so she wandered back to where her husband was reading, something spiralbound branded with work. She toyed with the SPF in its complimentary tube, then presented him with her tinted spine, cupping the middle-age nape of her tasteful hairstyle. Everything about the passage of his hands said boredom. With his task dispatched he slapped his palms, one, two, but it wasn't enough for his documents – he followed up with a serviette, sighing in brisk inconvenienced scrubs.

I remembered taking both boys with us once to one of your conferences – a vast concession, letting our son take a mate, letting kids attend at all. But I'd begged – I was always at odds with the corporate circuit, the women who weren't wives but operatives. So I dodged the Machiavellian teambuilding and cocktails, and spent my days herding the boys through revolving doors, to hit laser-tag or climbing walls, to chug budget burgers. The whole time they were a riot. One night they even staged penalty shots in the hall: you lined us up like crims on the couch and issued a red-card threat to ship us home. Right to the end they'd gone on causing havoc. They'd coveted the cellophaned loot of the room, banked their pockets at checkout time, edged past the desk in goofy eight-year-old stealth, their cargo pants crammed with crinkly contraband, stupid Earl Grey and useless slugs of gel. And then I thought of how, before we left for this trip, you'd ushered them into our son's bedroom, pointed out the precautionary condoms you'd stocked up in his undies drawer, no questions asked, just patting the foiled squares with an informative nod. I thought of the brief you'd given them, brisk and man to man, a summary of what you expected in our absence, basic standards, an airtight don't-cross-me look. Then you'd grappled them both close for a second, laughed the ultimatum off. I watched the stamp of your trust on his shoulderblade, tousling his t-shirt with its delta of sweat. How I envied the ease, the gruff allowance of that touch – your hand, permitted, deep on his trapezius, resting there in benign massage. And then all I wanted was to lie back down in our room with its made-to-measure blackness, formulating how I'd undress him, how his spine could bump like the links of a rosary through my open mouth.

*

Once I lived in a scody villa flat and I knew how to fuck. I fucked at shin level on a legless grey bed we'd tag-teamed home from the Salvation Army, a scuffle of flatmates humping its bulge uphill, tripping on its padded satin scallops. I fucked boys I'd blundered into at parties, long brainless snogs to the boom of the right indie tunes – A-side LPs, B-side boys, that's who I was in those days. I comfort-fucked the relay of boys who hunched on our front step mooning over my flatmate, a D-cup princess who was always out exercising her right to be cruel and untouchable and blond. I perfected the art of the consolation fuck, no-repeat, string-free, cooperative and warm, a fuck like a glum favour – after six dates (her average for dumping them), I would simply leave the door to my room ajar. I learnt from them that I was middling, I learnt to observe my limits, stick to them – on the perimeter of student raves I learnt to spot my match in boys, to love the meek, to love their sinews and band tees and hair-parts and ill-fitting elbows and bleak smirks as they waited on the outskirts of the cool throng for a cue that wouldn't come. I knew my level – I knew I was strictly temp – but irrelevance just made it easier: the mattress was stippled with earlier lives and somehow smelt like waiting rooms, and it was a cinch to climb on it naked and give a performance, limber, animal, more than a little bit stoned. Because it wouldn't last, because I wouldn't take, I clowned and choreographed. I was a more-than-passable lay – I just got demoted when they opened their eyes. But I didn't really mind. I got used to them sloping the walls on their furtive predawn exits, used to their fumbled bashful sounds as they tried to regain their clothes. I didn't mind not counting. So I could not comprehend what to do when I woke with you – and you had stayed. Mid-morning, even though my face was flood-lit, its special effects smudged off on the pillow, you stayed and stared down, companionably, at my plain shape. I feigned a yawn, lay there in stalemate. You looked resolved and leaned down to give me a steady, focused kiss. I remember turning inside out with gratefulness. You breathed a hangover into my mouth that has lasted an obligated lifetime.

*

You liked to spend time with the handbills, get our next day's itinerary mapped. Ruminative and topped up with supper, you muttered off to a nap on the beige king bed. I lifted the swipe card and padded barefoot to the foyer. I took the postcards you'd tried to prohibit and wrote the last one in the minimal lobby. My printing no longer looked sane, but I handed them across the counter for the next day's post. I don't think we'd been married for long before I started to think about it: checking into a hotel room and leaving a sign out saying *DISTURB*.

*

The hotel didn't have everything. Bad weather wasn't in any of the brochures, and on our fourth luxury night when a cold front came in there wasn't a library. The woman at reception didn't look pleased when I inquired, but led me to a cubicle with a few colour-coordinated spines. Most were new-age business manuals, that blend of pop-psych and quasi-spiritual capitalism you've always liked, seven stations of guaranteed prosperity. The rest were titled in blousy metallics, heroines swooning on mutinous decks with windswept men brooding over their décolletage. The kind of books I was brought up wanking over, rigid on my teenage bedspread, cast up on one hand, fingertips working along to swashbuckling detail. I'd always plundered myself to pure fantasy. I sat in the cubby and laughed until staff came to check on me.

When I got back to our room you'd given up and powered down the lights. My memory of the floor plan was useless and it had been therapy to unplug the clock. I went for the bathroom but couldn't get it lit. The door buckled on its frosted slide and made sounds of big dollars coming unwelded. By the time I got the three-way mirror into focus I was faced with seven of me. They moved in pieces either side of my twin, a triplicate of jawbones and elbows. I leaned and crawled to see what he would see. I knew of course that she'd never have the courage, that cornered woman, to take off her clothes. Why would she take out her four lax breasts, their nipples inexact and low, why would she think he'd run the pouch of her downgraded abdomen with his tongue. What could he see in us but give and hang, the skin tone of long-term apathy. I talked sense but that didn't stop her. Into the fork of her slackened thighs she still wanted to misplace his mouth. I watched her laughter wet five faces, shake a trio of wasted obliques. Only two of us could look each other in the eye, equilateral, sobbing with jazz hands. I tried to choke her, but the cistern just fizzed discreetly, in sanitary eddies. She swore, almost, on the body of our son that she would stop. She almost meant it.

*

We were paired in the ark of the restaurant when I asked you what aftershave you wore. All through that last meal, with its tinted tease of meats pinned onto panoramic plates, I'd leant into the scent and felt accused. You completed your mouthful of eye fillet before you proffered the name – Swagger – and you kept your glance on your cutlery, edging it surgically through the silky steak. The brand of that woody spray-on vapour with its low notes of diesel and twist of coarse spice was not news to me. I'd been gulping it for weeks. I'd lifted a can he'd let slip from his gym bag, coveted it in the quiet of the laundry, running its cylinder for dents, thumbing the nozzle, and huffing its discount spurt of sex. It was the reek that would be patterned on his ribcage, primed with saltwater and resins and glands and scrum and I snorted it, like I'd upend the last blue slurp of his Powerade when tidying up, hoping a shiver of saliva survived in that last chug. I was gone, and I can't begin to say how far gone. There's no point telling you now. You severed the fibres of your next course and reported the model of his cheapo smell – such a dumb bombastic word – and I thought it was your way of issuing a warning. So subtle: gaze still averted, you separated strands of morsel and savoured. You didn't reproach or gnash. The blood under my hips ran cold. I said I wanted to leave the table. But you'd prepaid for the degustation so we stayed for another unpalatable hour, supping from dish after ugly signature dish.

*

The scale of my wrong made me fear that our plane home would be struck from the horizon. The kindergarten God I still half believed in was the kind who smote and did not joke. But then I recovered – I dreamt of his suited lats sobbing at our burial service. Still, for a long time in flight I found the 'Domestic Safety Instructions' in my hand – the line-drawn couple, transplanted from the hotel, braced in their storyboards for a modest oblivion.

When we pulled into our driveway nothing was strange except for a spasm of birds, a sudden pixelation of wings twitching up from the verge away from our grille. I'd not seen them before: more thinboned than sparrows, with yellow belly feathers. They wouldn't flit clear of the car, kept highdiving back to spritz the grass between our oncoming wheels. Inside, we learnt where they'd surfaced from: the cat had clearly started dying, though she was doing it quietly, showing her tiny incisors in a soundless bleat. The boys weren't to blame: she hadn't been eating, though her plastic plate showed they'd tried to tempt her with steak. It sat there in dried grey snippets. She wouldn't be cradled. She looked bored with her own pain.

The boys were on kill cam, the lounge rewired, as much sun as they could get hotboxed out. They couldn't drop out of the gameplay to update us, so they barked details while they slaughtered, in league, long-range. You pulled the blinds on their gutted heaps of hologram but they went on gunning their way, giving one-word answers, spluttering in graphic slalom. I expected you to object, to order them to shut it down, get his gear packed into the car. But you didn't intervene, went to the bedroom and unzipped your suitcase, stowed your possessions back in their appointed place. I stood in the doorway for a while and blinked at the vigilance of your refolding.

They had ploughed through the provisions we'd left them so we ordered a pizza. We made them unplug and sit to the table, stretching their slices from the pepperoni disc. They leant their heads back and lowered the meatlover's into their smiles, the topping slithering in. Grease drizzled onto his t-shirt and you didn't meet my eyes. I couldn't offer to drive him home. I waited for you to clear your throat, pick up the keys. But you did nothing I anticipated. And I went on believing that this was my punishment, this cold, methodical divergence from the norm. I believed it when I got out of bed at 4am to try to find our ailing cat, queasy with guilt that I hadn't soothed her more, hadn't petted her down on some soft cardboard deathbed, tried answering her stricken miniature yawns. I believed it when I went to the garage and you were by the freezer in the kiss that I wanted, driving him back on the hood of the whiteware with a shiver I could not remember seeing. I watched you handle the curls at his nape to lever his skull, slide your palm under drawcord. I watched him freeze, like he was posed in another of our family photos waiting for the flash. What you don't know can hurt you.

For the next few days I let you clear the mail.

compact

It's a junkshop find that brings back the smell of them – a kind of sweetened pinky-beige topsoil my aunts would carry everywhere with them, gilded flip-open discs of powder, hard-caked, that still puffed traces over everything. A push-in metal tooth worked the clasp, then they'd unhinge it, anywhere they needed to, perched on a bus seat, queueing at the cinema, blotting off steam and suds over the sink. Inside lived another face. A swipe of coating for the wrinkles and pitting, a swab of glamour for the sweat and the soot, and they'd dab and polish with their onion-skin hands, and re-emerge, their smiles resurfaced, to take themselves off to a matinee or square off their seats in the cafeteria for a good old session of sip, hiss and gossip. Friends met them there, equally floral and bloodyminded. But it took my aunts to preside. And I pick the bronze disc out of the litter of the shop, and I fiddle with the rust of its scalloped fastening, and a gust of them wafts out, the sound of them cackling, the squeak of their complicated undergarments, the musk of their costumes, all dance-hall and armpit, the cumbersome tamped-down plenty of their blue-silk busts. Always jolly, until you crossed them. Thick as thieves, a formidable old-maid front, glossy and tough as they come. Mouths akin to fruit in their tropical acrylic, over a crooked assortment of teeth. Battlers. Hard nuts. And I used to be able to see myself in the circle of light when I rifled their handbags, I used to take a peek and think I could rub in their tint, could repaint myself robust, could frost my little face with a swish of their moxie, be brazen, bold-as-you-please. But I've disappeared in the mirror. It's like dusting for fingerprints.

the deal

When the do-it-yourself coffin arrives, Dad calls me over. She picked it out, but he doesn't want her to hear the hammering. So I tuck her chair with blankets. 'Some anniversary. Too many years for plywood!' she laughs. I wheel her out.

We head for shoreline, a sea that hisses louder than her oxygen. A breeze we can let stroke her balded skull.

Black-sand fingertips.

Thin boats shine on out-tide.

Hours blinking gulls.

When we get back, there are two caskets, pollen-coloured, propped on twin beds. 'Two for one,' he nods at her. 'Got myself a good deal.'

if found please return to

She will forget the house. It will leave her one window at a
time, breaking off in pieces of pine and lace and quartered
glass. She will forget the feel of the rooms on her skin, the
stir of their smell when she walked them. The cool of the hall,
which held the scent of sour fruit and locked mahogany, so her
footprints couldn't help but slow in its long polished gloom.
The sharp kitchen sunlight striking the steel bench with its
rack of illuminated drips. The froth of the laundry, the soapy
fluff churned from the tub, her forearms chugging in their
glisten. She'll forget she could never get through the weekly
scrub without a cheeky song. Something sudsy, because she
felt springtime, bubbly with showtune and get-go and sweat.
The bugger of a wringer with its rubber cogs squealing, the
slithery feed of shirts gushing into her bucket. She'll forget
him, scragging boots off at the backdoor, a stompy, gruff dance
on concrete steps, shovelling his coat pockets for tobacco and
stray tools. She'll forget him saying *hey up missus. Smoko.*
She'll forget his dip, down into the pursed hair of her nape,
her collar flustered, *ooh leave off you.* Forget his leathery sip.
The roof of her mouth will forget their bedroom's simmer of
late afternoon dust.

*

She'll forget the words. She'll forget the name for the things her son stands in a jar by her bedside, ruffles of red that flag and bruise on their sticks. This new room is easily forgotten. It's never sunk in. It's only the smudge of linoleum, a yard of grey flecks, wipe-clean with loneliness. It's only the grizzle of trolleys wheeled in to tip her head and rattle in pills. She'll forget the use of the black balloon they strap and pump to her pulse-rate. She will forget the numbers on the glass stem they slot in the woozy vowels of her dentures. She'll forget why they lever her over, a tutting struggle on the steel-bridged bed, why she's sandbagged with white. She'll forget how to work herself upright, except for wild starts in the night, when 3am seems to tug her wires, and she rumbles from her monitors, escapes a few muddled steps. Of course she'll forget where she is, and the names of the people she meets in the nowheres she wanders to. Of course she will falter and two-step and turn and the loneliness will just stretch down new corridors, a grey route that empties in numberless doors through which she still remembers no one.

*

She's forgotten her baby. She left him at the shops. Didn't she? Had him swaddled, had him snug in his pram of peachy wool, had him drowsy with pavement-roll and dopey milk, had his snowflake bonnet on, had his plump chin shining in pleats of ribbon, the cleanest, chubbiest face of snuffled content you'd ever be likely to see, and she parked him in the shade, and she nuzzled at his thick vanilla sleep and she murmured *Mumsie's back in a trice my bub*, and then she just popped into the butcher's, just popped in a tick, it was honestly only three shakes of a lamb's tail, and then somehow, somehow she propped up her parcel like always in her astrakhan coat, cool with blood in its corded wrappings, and spongy with the comforting slouch of meat, and she marched with it all the way home, and her next-best heels on the pavement clapped a stout little singalong. She hummed, just in musing over putting the kettle on, just in portioning the pot with its few black feathers of tea. And then her nipple buzzed. The drizzle of what she'd forgotten burst out on her breast. And she dashed, she bolted, she raced back, a blat down the bricks, until the lane brought her up against the braked pram, its dark trunk hooded, its wide wheels glinting, and she stared down and down, slopping big tears into his snooze. She was the worst mother. Ever. But it was all right. The baby forgot.

*

One foot. What's next? She will have forgotten. She'll sway in her slippers in the ultraviolet. She will have forgotten her mouth is open, and oxygen and words spill down. Her neck is a tremor. Her voice comes out of it nothing like a hymn. Is it help or hello? Her tongue has forgotten. It blinks in and out of her pleading. The corridor throbs and splits four sealed grey ways and she shakes on its cross of clean roads. All she will want is to make her way back to her blue cell, to her crocheted crawlspace. But she'll have forgotten which side of the world it is on.

*

She will forget the clock. It is lines on the moon. It is stones in a pool. She will remember, somewhere, a pool, for a second, and she will see herself, trailing a tide of pale hair, all slipped from its pins, which she knows is like silk to the boy she teases, which she knows is as good as a lure, which is golden and sultry and tugging at her scalp, with her toying and flouncing and leading him on, with whinnies of bad, so she takes him, on a dance at the end of her mane, takes him off on a shimmery goose chase, through slashes of birch and stumble of fence, through breezy laughter and muddy romp, and they come to a pool, and she lets him brace her, his shivery length along her frock, at the water's edge, she lets him cup her cool palm with the tilt of a good flat stone, and he teaches her to skim, and she remembers the scud of the pebble, its grazing rebound off the gleam. They forget the time. The hands they know about are under their seams, are urging at cloth. The hands they'll remember are clammy, and paddling with heartbeats of want under heavy serge. The hands are making her dip and rise again, arc and lap and rise. She'll forget the clock. She'll forget what time her father wants her home.

*

It's the music that doesn't forget her. Where do they play it? Is she in church? She will forget she never liked the carry-on of scripture, couldn't stomach all its uppity fuss. She's never liked the vicar who warbled and strutted round his pulpit, a finicky font of shalt nots. She's never liked the disc she had to suck from his index, doesn't like the goblet with its plasma slurp, his gown's musty swish. She doesn't like his crouch-down to bless her, breath as bad as his flowery twaddle about sin. She doesn't like the mortified picture of Christ tacked up in his loincloth, chicken-skin white. She's got no time for pomp. But she can't fault the music. Against her better judgement, against her grudges, those notes press in, make her chest swell. Her breathing rears. Her wristbones hallelujah. And she'll forget she's an oldie in velour, forget she's been tucked in with crochet squares. She'll forget that the tune is being henpecked out on a keyboard of corny plastic watts by a troop of God-botherers the likes of which she once used to dodge on her street with merry snorts of scorn. The bones in her feet know the tempo and bob in their pumps. The bridge nods her balding head. Her eyelids fill: *Jesu*.

*

Down at the base of her skull the siren has picked out the crossings of terror in her blood. The shelter, the shelter – she's forgotten the way. And now the road hairpins, there's billows of brick, the buildings making jagged shifts, the chapel coming at her in floes of stone. Out of its white side she watches the next hit blowing the blueprints of stained-glass God.

Where is the shelter? Where is it? Where? She should know – her father walked her, chanting, mapped it, over and over and over. But now there's nothing where she should turn left, the landmarks crushed to haze. The shops are chalk. She calls his name, but her teeth are liquid. She takes unwieldy steps, fresh alleys scraped by fire, black girders, her shoes blunted with blood. Windows she recognises stretch their last gleam, then ignite. The pavement fishtails, breaks the grip of her feet, tips her face-first into dust.

The bombs go off until all the world feels bloodshot.

When her father finds her, much later, there's no talk between them. Their mouths brim with silt, their hearing numbed. Atoms still hang in the air in spasms trying to find the shapes they were blasted from. She stumbles with him home. She doesn't question. They slip and blink. They pass what they have to. A man whose sleeves unspool into nothingness. A child tugging at the tongue of a boot, above the ankle his parent a load of smoke. She follows her father's trudge.

She will forget they're the lucky ones. Because her father never recovers. He gets her home then he lies down and does not get up. He stays put, woundless and whole. He lies in his bed, what they've seen like a stone on his chest, his name carved cold. He dies of it. She watches him die of it. He dies of not being able to forget.

*

At night the walls of her room will be a bare screen for small things being forgotten. Willows over a plate, in blue shivers. Cockles dropped with soft clacks in a bucket. Pine needles picked from the staves of his boot. The scallop shell where he tapped his ash. The school gate swinging on its crisp hinge of lichen. The tongue of a scrabbling lamb, its warm ribbed suckle. White shirts breaching on the shrill back line. An east wind chiselling light through trees. Never enough to keep the film running, never enough to still a scene. She blinks and they're watercolour. Tries to speak and they pass like dreams or breath. Her lids are a vanishing point.

All forgotten.

*

The boat will move in her mind like forgetfulness. She won't remember the sway of it there. She will forget the ache of its rolling, days lost to salt in the lurch of its tread. She's left one world, split off from the wharf, and has no pictures to bring her the next one. What will the next world look like, and who will she be, standing fatherless in its fields? She seems to forget anything but the ocean – ocean rising in iron lines of swell, or sleek as glass in the wide landless glare. For nights she latches herself in her cabin, bolts herself away still dressed, her heels in their buckles, the sweat streaking into her coat – she won't meet the alarm (which she knows must come, as sirens do, they always do) with indecent skin in the moonlight, a spectacle of bare limbs sunk. She lies down terrified, groomed and buttoned, waiting for the sure SOS. But the rock of the ocean speaks to her, enters her clothes, the blackwater rhythm of smooth and shock. She slips to the deck, a graceless stagger on boards. And finds that she loves it. The water moves like whiplash. The wind laughs in her throat. Her hair blurs with stars. She raises her arms in the silky overhang of cloud, says the word *starboard* like it is beautiful.

*

She will forget the photographs he pins to the wall beside her bed. The faces in them will go out like lights, the trees and streets standing in the wash of past, nameless. Some days he will lift them from their thumbtacks, he'll float them in figure eights above her gaze, *remember Mum, eh Mum, look, you remember.* But she will forget the girl by the birdbath, her bulldog huddled to her gingham dress. She will forget the low stone wall with its slurry of muck, its gaggle of piglets, the child in giant galoshes who gives squealing chase. She'll forget the man by the gangplank, holding out the woven tropic nonsense of a hat, mock bandito, his grin in its tequila glaze, his fool shins sunburnt. She will forget the same man, stooping, to mortar the base bricks of their house, shirt a white straggle poking from his back pocket, the sun working north along the bones of his spine, against the grain of his sweat (she'll forget how much she loves each seam that liquid runs). She'll forget the roly-poly woman with her Xmas tipple in her crêpe-paper hat, laughing at the chit of the cracker joke until she topples off her chair, takes a rush of tinsel with her. She will forget the joke. She will forget the stitch on the blanket that the woman is rocking – shell, chain or crocodile? – forget the lullaby she's humming down into the bundle's drowsy face. Is it 'Danny

Boy'? He can't remember either, as he pins the dark snuffed squares back to the wall.

*

She'll forget the white rabbit. She'll be out by the washline and flick up the catch to let the little thing out. She'll be strapping out the heavy slumps of sheets to set their wet loads cracking in the northerly, and she'll let the baby jumble round on his bum on the dewy grass to get to the lemons, scattered from the tree in dimpled thuds. She'll let him suckle on their pocked yellow balls. She'll shoo the rabbit closer to him just to make him gurgle, clapping his podgy hands at its flops. It's the sheets, it's the sheets that conceal it, the black-and-white bullet of the next-door's dog. It comes in and out the sheets, their wet white banners, the bloody lightspeed launch of the dog, which hits the creature, flings it up, figure eight, in a grisly snarling jolt. And the sheets will bluster her outstretched hands and coat her mouth and blanket her calls. And it won't be until she beats to the end of their terrible flapping corridors that she'll know what it is that runs wet in the dog's manic growls, that she'll know what is pinned and barbed in its muzzle. She'll forget to bring the washing in. But in two days' time she will refill the coop with a small bright bunny, a twin of born-again fuzz. The baby forgets. The baby will never know the difference.

Did she forget? She must have left the cage open again. The dogs have got to her memory.

*

She will forget her teeth. She will watch them in their blue cup of soak and not know they were ever hers, their pearly stained curve, their arches of caramel. What did she say with them? Who did she use to open them for, clicking through the puzzle of sounds, her tongue swishing the glyphs. She watches the bubbles, which lift off the molars like syllables. The half-moon palate fizzed with translucence. A beaded vocabulary sizzling, and lost. Anyway it will be easier to let go the words now she's forgotten them. She can let them go soft. They can run off the edges. If her mouth can't make them neither can her mind.

*

She'll forget that he's already gone. He was always getting ahead of her – into the bookies for a flutter, the pub for a pint and a yarn, down the wharf to see a man about a dog. She could never keep up. And is that him now, hooting down the hall, with talk full of blarney, all smiles and tall stories, roping everyone in with the scheme of his grin? She'll forget supper, be dragging the kid by the hand to hunt him down, to smarten him up, talk sense, get him on the straight track home. But you can't knock that grin, how he'll nod *fair enough*, fall in step, turn his racket of charm on her and the boy, and he'll canter them home, all cheek and malarkey, the kid a fool for his chuckles, smitten. And her no better: how can a woman be expected to fend that off, the wow of it. How can she store up the scores against him, the list of sore points and fibs and flaws – she'd dare any red-blooded woman to do it, faced with the dimpled no-good of that grin. She knows the moment she'll give in – he'll pledge to clean up, and he'll hand her the razor. Kitchen chair straddled, he'll cantilever back – into her fingers he'll stretch his dark throat. He'll say nothing, but hum as she grazes, philtrum, shadows, Adam's apple, the blade in the soap a bristled hiss. She'll forget it all. She'll willingly forget.

*

The nurses are a side effect of forgetting. The face of one nurse slides into another. Their blue zip tunics and tough white shoes fill with ghost after efficient ghost. Even her son will forget their names. But he'll say to the last one, as he's hunched by the bed, *there must be a word for this*. And she'll pause behind him, place a palm on his shoulder. *No*, she'll say. *Without a word for it, you can let it go*. He won't believe her but he'll drop his head, let her voice in. Repeating: *in time, you'll forget*.

*

Kisses in the threshed barn, the itchy glow of hay. Catching her breath in his laboured clothes, his musk of pine and turpentine and honey. A picnic table at the foot of a gorge. The deep-fried rustle of fish and chips. Playtime, zipping her boy into his parka, the plastic crunch of old rain. Flax moving to the creek in fibrous whispers. Bathing the baby in the late afternoon, laying him out on his shawl to babble, her face above him teasing up squeals and kicks, his fingers waggling for ends of her stray hair – just let her remember this – wordless gurgles of love.

point of view

(for L.B.)

I'm giving my character a drinking habit. Or drugs. I haven't decided yet. Part of me thinks her apartment won't be real unless there's the sound of bottles – the cold at her back door, its late-night mesh-screen squeal (I don't know, I could maybe cut this?) might need the bottles' secretive clink, her spine feeling the teeth of her zip as she works to huddle those bottles down in the bin, under the layers of other tenants' rubbish, plastics, a nest pulled from hairbrush quills (ash blond), frills of rare steak and citrus. Paper showing amounts owed and personal stains. That scene's not real without the bottles.

But maybe she (Gabriella?) brews tea. Maybe she looks up on the internet how to boil leaf, only leaf, so it's not so illegal, or doesn't feel it anyway, feels culinary, herbal, strictly medicinal, kind of wise-woman to be standing in her galley, in her dressing gown of scarlet fleece, with its fat waist sash, the pale sag of her belly bisected by its decent felty knot, stewing up a broth, a brown-green decoction (check colour details) that looks wholesomely slimy and seemly. She's an older woman, fifty or so, slipper-wearing, with grey roots, leached of oestrogen – it's not an addiction (she tells herself, prodding the seepage with a silver spoon, one of a fancy set inherited from her mother – might the mother be useful later?), she just needs a nightcap to sleep. No one knows the madness that sets in if you don't sleep. And don't sleep. And don't sleep. And don't sleep. And Gabriella has been laid straight on the sheets for weeks, her eyes jammed tight on the frontal lobe of her brain, which buzzes with hot black lonely weight.

But it's hard to give up the sound of the bottles. I'm thinking it might prove too hard. Because: Gabriella could remember a day where she once took a trip on a miniature train, and it ground through toetoe and sunlight and tunnels and often when it jerked out the dark there would be a bright bank built of bottles, blue and green, or clear and amber, a spangling slope of domed glass light, and the light on it, trapped and flickering and swollen, made the DTs look beautiful. It felt like being in a cathedral. Except it was a cathedral glued into clay with glass leftover from her own emptiness.

Don't worry. I'm giving her a reason for her drinking. Or her weed. It's not what you're thinking. She's the strong one.

I wanted to write about being the strong one because I'm not. That's where Gabriella came in.

As you were leaving, you paused at the slider and said, *Don't you have anything else to say for yourself?* Behind you the trees were stickering the window with crunched gold leaves. I didn't. You left. And that's when I felt Gabriella, on the back of my neck, answering.

Answering.

I'm thinking the ash-blond hair in the bin could be tugged from the brush of a beautiful sunbathing neighbour, one who spreads out the tropical tones of a towel meant for oceans, or no, a padded Li-Lo that is see-through metallic with vertical seams and blown up through a squeezy clear nipple. Gabriella could remember how, towards the end, she used to wheel her husband out onto the balcony to let him ogle because it no longer mattered. The roof where the neighbour stretches out should be black (that fibro topping, what's that called, that gritty seal?) and spiked with aerials like post-modern Xmas trees, and the neighbour should slowly tweak parts of her bikini, just straps off at first, then nudge down pants, and glisten. Once they would have fought if she'd found him staring. She would have stomped and batted closed the blinds, so the fight would have had the sound of blinds clattering out light, the corny tap of them swinging and plinking. The neighbour could have been seen face-down (slow pan into an ash-blond close-up) with a laugh puffed knowingly onto the back of hands that smelt of coconut oil and engagement ring – but that would depend on point of view.

You're the strong one. I want Gabriella to have your strength. I want her to lift her husband in and out of the chair (in memory, because in the now of her story, in the bottles glancing light round her apartment, her husband is gone, and the bottles make the echo gone, gone – or maybe that's too much), and be able to take the stale feel of his skin, the clamminess of his deadweight. The spindly hair between his nipples. The blueness of his elbows. The given-up smudge of his bellybutton. I want her to hate and love his torso as she washes it. A slow awkward swab. With a lime-green flannel she dabs into a tin bowl of tepid water laced with antiseptic, a chemical splotch she tips in, 5 ml, and stares at, frilling out into the fluid, holding solid in a small pale clot at first, like a foetus, then tremoring out, dissolving into ripples. He's hard to roll. He's hard to clean. He's hard to talk to. It's a bowl from a set of nesting bowls that she once used to mix him a pancake breakfast, after he'd first stayed the night, and she sees herself humming half-dressed in the after-sex kitchen, barefoot and skittish with getting loved-up, whisking the batter with whimsical flicks, checking the notches on the edge of the small tin dish to dust in the perfect ingredients, all the time thinking of his body, a-sprawl in her bed, which she would feed, teasing him with the spoon (oh, that smutty syrup all over Mother's silver), snatching kisses through his carefree chomps, then tote the tray off to the kitchen, tiptoe back and straddle. I want her to spend a long time pushing the lime-green flannel into the solution. Watching it billow. Wringing it. I want her to spend hours refusing to sob.

You'll say the wheelchair is too much. But he needs to really be broken, the husband. He can't just be in pain for nothing. Like me.

There's no 'I' in pain. It looks like there is. But that's a trick. You can't use it. There's no narrator. You can't say 'I'm in pain'. It doesn't work. It all comes out sounding like teenage self-pity. *You're talking like a teenage girl*, you said to me last night, when I said I was done with it, the pain had finally won, I wanted out. And all I could think of was to drink my way out, drink myself gone. You were right. You see? First-person pain always sounds like such a teenage girl.

That's why I need Gabriella. I need her to be the strong one, fifty-something. But also, she can drink.

Or maybe she gets the weed from a student. Maybe she teaches writing, like you, and one of her students slips her the weed, or not even slips it, because it's not like it's a big deal to them. They laugh at her, camouflaging it, ramming its baggie down in a used envelope black-block-lettered *INTERNAL MAIL*, and zipping and flipping compartments in her satchel so it's stashed with an old bike padlock and half-squashed tampons. I can see this student – she's an acid waif, ultra-thin, with a blasé swathe of hair she trims herself, in chic deconstructionist chops. She's got more talent in her little finger than Gabrielle could ever muster – she writes loud mean beautiful poems with timebomb images and shitty doubletakes on manifestos, and every stanza ends in a luminous bored-with-her-own-entitlement sneer. She's a genius. And Gabrielle's embarrassed to have to pretend to be teaching her – in workshops she doesn't mutter the astonishment that is the real reaction that detonates her sternum when she reads the latest of this girl's poems. She feels it would be too harsh on the other students, who work very hard on their pedestrian imagery, who strain to tidy their quotidian stanzas, pushing round flecks of punctuation and nodding at Gabriella earnestly, *yep, cut out adverbs, check.* She's so jealous of the lines she can't breathe – they float on the page in offhand sophistication, their self-reflexive floweriness glinting with bite, and once, on her bus home, while the driver brakes at lights, she sees the student reflected in a bar, and her tiny expostulating pose at the table with a beer bottle ticking in just two fingers is as bulletproof as her poems, as slender and high-IQ and impossible to wound. A bitter girl that's come from a very good home. But she doesn't smirk at Gabrielle. She calls her Gabe like she respects her, when she could have just coined the easy jibe of Gab. Lobbed across the classroom, *yo, Gab.* She acts fond of her. She slips her a little sleeve of weed to fend off her sleeplessness.

Motor-neuron. Motor-neuron. That's the machinery she listens to at night. (Gabriella, of course. Who's going to make that mistake?) The neon dashboard of his breathing. Gabriella blinking along to the cardiac twitch. The trail of meds shunting. Catheters on snaky release. That's when she starts the drinking. She starts one night, sitting out on the balcony, sitting in the sixth month unable to sleep, motor-neuron, motor-neuron, with the sky a polluted powder-blue, and the gritty seal on the rooftops ticking, and a faint fine-boned shrill lifting up off the aerials, crookedly, in the built-up apartment-block breeze, or coming from her, from the spot where her spine meets her mind and the bad join keeps beating and beating. Everything juts to that point. Everything juts there, gets stuck, keeps beating. She drinks to black out that. But first, she stands on the balcony and takes off her robe, unbuttons her nightie at its thick homely yoke, then does a clumsy hop out her underpants, which are serviceable but still silky, cupping her abdomen like a deep satin bucket. Elasticated, but sloppy. She thinks of the long blond hair with its coating of tan lotion, oily and desired in the light. Of the pert gloss of caramel thighs untied from their tiny flicker of lycra. Her sorrow such a joke. The lime-green cloth she weaves around her husband's anus. The muslin she trades to smooth along his eyelid (silver bowl inside a bowl). The pinprick sheen where his lashes are fastened to the rim. She used to lie awake to watch them tremoring, the sheets kicked dreamy in the aftermath of sweat, one pillowcase wisped with come. Her sorrow such a bottle-worthy joke.

I'm getting that wrong. I know. The timeline's off. I'll go back and fix it later.

There are other bits that might not fit in. Like: I see the student picking up a photo of Gabriella's husband from the desk in her office, and holding it like she held that beer at the bar, a cynical dangle, and it would matter here if the husband is gone or not yet, you would think, but maybe it doesn't, maybe Gabriella can watch the girl with the photo fluttering in her brilliant pinch, and can listen to her say something clipped and jaunty, some cutting send-up of married love, while her sardonic fingertips work the frame in that dangle (you'd tell me, in the margin, if you graded this piece, *time to find another word*) that looks tantalising, and does it have to matter if the man in the frame is here or gone, because isn't the whole thing one long blur of dying, and even the strong one can't get out the end of that corridor of dying unscathed, and no one could blame them, even the strong one, for catching a breath as the brilliant girl – because she experiments with people as easy as she does with words – leans closer so the silvery critique of her earrings snarls in Gabriella's hair, and the devastating wit of her lipstick comes down, tangy and elegant and fresh and slick, and practised, so practised, and ending with a chichi little nip. It's like eating a line from one of her poems. Urbane, tart-cherry and unapologetic. Who could ever blame Gabriella? So the husband in the (photo in the) girl's grip is dead and alive, for now. Just another thing to fix.

I'll get there.

I'll drink there. There's nothing like drink to smudge images.

The pearly click of chicken bones winging in slithers down the bin. Papers measled with gravy, A-neg. Clear ribbed plastics, popping as the bottles drop. (The ampules she snaps out their grid and squeezes into his mask, his drip.) Gone. Gone. The ventricles of liquid ribboning away from that slow-motion tin-bowl heart.

She's still the strong one. The strong need something.

The strong need some nights out on the balcony, wasted into off-key song, like the full moon was just laid as bait for solo tunes, sloshed show croons of half-cut self-pity. *Don't write a letter when you want to leave.* She gets blasted and performs them with alleycat steps. *I know the way we should spend that day.* Gabriella's neighbours give her leeway, as she bangs around the planters on her Juliet balcony, as she cabarets the scrolled metal chairs and pulls medleys between slutty nuzzles of vodka. She slugs deep. Her soprano is not strong. And also on the balcony I think she has a canary, a small freckled pet in a scuffle of feathers, which doesn't even peck at its bell or bother to set its mirror spinning, just sits there in its cage of shit-sequins, but is otherwise no company, zero help, which doesn't learn to talk when she squashes her face to the bars to interrogate *who's-a-pretty-girl-then-who*, just pings blankly around its newsprint base in tiny bickerings of seed. And sometimes she thumbs at the hinge, and fumbles in, and watches her giant fingers cup it, so the swivel of its pastel skull is delicate with panic in her too-hard hands, and the pad of her palm is tapped with a threnody of heartrate that is sickening. Just sickening. She would like to crush things. This could be one. This could be one. Surely they deserve to, the strong? She feels entitled to want to stop something. To feel it end. Because it has to end, doesn't it, sometime? Even for the strong. The neighbours will let her serenade for long boozed hours, tugging their curtains on her breeze-blown love songs. She licks, mic'd up, in heat, some nights, along the lonely neck of the bottle. So beloved. Three sheets gone.

I didn't know what I'd done last night. When you got up this morning you asked, *do you remember what you said?* I looked at you, because now you're the only place left to look. *Do you remember I had to carry you to bed? Are you trying to finish yourself off? Yes*, I said. I know that. I said *yes*. And watched you leave for work. The trees behind you were gluing leaves all over the glass in fine-veined gusts. You walked out their wet crackling. You had a job to do.

Pain is not a job.

I don't know how you teach writing. I could never finish. I remember that about your class – that I'd start each exercise you set with a rush. You'd say *freewrite*, and my pen would slip away across the page, tripping over its own images. The whole time I'd blink at you through dizzy agitations of ink. All I really wanted was to get to your body. Words that would get me inside your clothes. That's what I needed, not sentences, but a way to get through seams, into clefts, to get clambering and handling – when you dictated *active verbs* that's all I heard. How to write my way to you. Which was all right in poems. Not prose. There was no ending. Until I stood on a balcony with you, on a night when my tied hair was pinned with summer insects, and through our chatter you kept shooing off their dustmotes of glitz, and you moved your hand to smudge one off my temple, but you didn't know how deep I itched, and I leant up and bit you, and I had to teeter, so I tripped out my sandal with my stoned right foot, and you bent down and caught it by the straps, and let its leathery spangle just hang there, waiting in your fist, while you watched me recover and climb back up the buttons of your shirt, one-two, and sip, and sip.

There is a hill where the train drones out the holes they've burrowed through the ranges, and it's built of bottles and the light makes you thirsty for all the love you never got to swallow, all the beauty brushed by blue fern and birdsong and cirrus you almost got to taste. But now there's only pain and booze and only one of them you can drink to the bottom.

Which means nothing to the girl. As she flaps round the photo in the office, of the husband (who's dead or alive), and tells Gabriella she's banning that stale old exercise, *write from a family photo concentrating on concrete detail*, she's outlawing it, it's had its dull old day, so it doesn't matter whether the man in the photo is stripped to the waist, and shot on black sand, with the dappled wax on a longboard and the chapped rim of his lips a thin zinc echo of the coastline, or if he's taken throwing a child high in the air, so the baby is a creamy star of giggles, hanging in the safe void that lives above his hands, shocked into squeals at the launch (which he counts down, five, four, three, two, with the child already wriggling and shrilling) but trusting in the big wide grab of the palms, just waiting for the quick pluck back from sky into cuddles. Which means nothing to the girl – has Gabriella ever had a child? How could she have? She left it too late. (A clot in a silver bowl shimmers, disperses.) It was too late, then there were only bottles. And on one too many, one night, she could slip to his room, and try to mount his hospital bed, half-clad, and at least press skin, push warmth through the tug of seams and wires, hold a dog pose, which doesn't wake him out of his deep glaze of meds, which they both forget. A brief face-down prayer into loneliness.

Which means even less.

I had too much to drink last night. Or I had nowhere near enough.

Some of your images are luminous, you used to write, *but the narrative line is too unclear. Your transition to prose will mean less poetic texture, more stress on a linked sequence of events, portrayed with clarity and forward movement. Point of view needs thinking through too.* I'd retrace the loops of your ballpoint with a fingernail. It only mattered that you'd touched my page. That something of you, eyelash, brainwave, had brushed past my paragraphs, if only to subtract marks.

There were once insects clipped into my hair, a small dazzle of mites that kept simmering our dusk, so we'd do laughing semaphore arms on the terrace, or wave off their bloodthirsty dives with our glass, or sudden claps when we thought they hovered still enough to ambush, and then you shooed one from my temple, a stray flick, as if you were tucking a flower in my hair, so gentle, I'd feel the stem travel my scalp like a silk scratch that caught on a synapse, because everything you did, every move, travelled in from the surface of me, and stuck so deep, and you caught it, its body a black smear on your palms, its thorax detached like a memory, its clear jointed wings just a twitch of light, blood-tinted, unpicked from living with one swift crush, so I had to drive up into a kiss and tipped out of my shoe, which you tied back on, stumbling, lacewing, later. To the pulse of my ankle. Like a promise.

Pain has no events. I've told you. There's nothing left to write about. No narrative to move forward with. Last night you had to carry me to bed. When I'd drunk through the bottle that would black my body quiet. Which was not enough.

It's enough for this story that Gabriella is the strong one. I think her husband is called Martin. Now Gabriella has to watch Martin die. But I'm not going to watch. He can't even watch himself. I can give him a name, but not a real story. And never a point of view. You think there is an 'I' in Martin, you think there's an 'I' in pain, in sick, in terminal. There's not. There's nowhere here to narrate from. I know the last scene now, but Martin and I, we can't look on.

So I need Gabriella. I need her to get the call while she's at work, while she's in the office, with a light coat of gloss from the girl's kiss still smudged along her smile, acerbic and distantly saccharine, the call that he's bad, that he's turned, the signs are not vital, so she's shaken, and she dithers with her keys, she flounders and gulps in the door of the office and doesn't know if she can balance on her heels, or not like a fifty-something sensible brown-shoed woman whose husband might be dying, who's the strong one, who knows not to hope it will be quick, who knows that dying lasts for nights, who has already watched those nights stretch away from the balcony into a city of shadows and wires, a vast horizon that no one else is awake for except the person dying, who is doing all the hard work, the hard hard work of dying among tubes and silence and vials, so the girl does a swoop across the office to the rescue, self-conscious, and commandeers Gabriella's keys (*I'm not silly, Gabe, I know you're still loaded from last night*) and insists on driving her, though the route to the hospital (yes, it's the hospital this time, that final place) is clogged with one-way roads, and the girl is comically shonky in a manual, racking the gearbox so they get there in a goofy chain of hops and stalls and waving out the rear screen at backed-up traffic fuming and honking, which doesn't faze the girl, who is still so chic she can giggle it off in one-liners and elegant scoffs, but who doesn't do hospitals, she says when they get there, when she bunny-jumps the hatchback into a park, who frankly doesn't *do* anything more ickily medical ever than a *band-aid*, so Gabriella has to go in alone, the strong one, through the sliding doors, where the leaves are plastered in a shimmering golden overlap. No, I have nothing else to say for myself, just watch Gabriella take the lift, although a place in her abdomen doesn't, it trails behind for floors and dark floors, but she gets there, follows her sturdy tan shoes along the lino, checks along the numbered doors, with the relay of faces turning too slow from their steel beds to watch her passing, their blinks too weighted, their wrists too tired on the leash of their needles to lift hello, their lashes too colour-blind, and the bottles on their lockers always topped with nothing strong enough, nothing to the clear plastic brim, and it happens, what happens, the thing that has been her-life-his-death, the doing of it, the daily events that link her to his infinite going, so it doesn't matter which stage it is at, this narrative, when she wanders from the bed, for an instant, just an instant, and there is the girl. Seen down through a fourth-storey window. Across the carpark where there's workmen repainting a church. And they're stripping off the old paint, so it's awash on the autumn like a series of ghosts. And the girl is laughing as they graze the old sacrosanct boards and the lead-based haze lifts off in filmy riffs, she's laughing and ruffling her hair in its transparent grit, scurrying the pile-up of leaves that punctuate its veil, and Gabriella can watch, as one of the workmen halts in his sanding, and slides a grin sideways out his white mask, and walks over to the girl and scuffs around his overalls, a four-square pat (two pockets down, two up top) for a lighter, and he and the girl withdraw a short distance, and there in the carpark, while headlights edge in and out of the allotted slots, she sees them sharing a joint, their heads together on the intake like it's the easiest thing in the world, okay, a little shady, but still blasé in their instant smoky intimacy, like four storeys up there's no need to worry where to tell a story from, you've said everything you need to say, you just lever the latch and hang over the edge and gaze at the afterlives of white paint drifting off the girl's mouth and God's walls.

list of addictions in no special order

1.

My mother's makeup. Palettes hijacked from her ivory dresser when she was out. Flip-top oblongs of flaky aqua. Lilac highlights, scraped with a wand. The traction of microscopic sponge on the glitter. Powdered stink of blush on my breath. Shock in the mirrored cabinet of my eyes, tipping at the nape to stretch an O mouth. Crimson heads, swivelled in their gold-plated cylinders. When I smile: my canines' magenta.

2.

The French metal handles to silkiness. The cloudy opal in its 12-carat cleat. Hinges of satin, and jewellery that smelt like slut. My mother's dresser: the great unhappiness behind the glass.

3.

That page in my hardback copy of *Pinocchio* where all the real boys start to turn. They're supposed to be turning into donkeys; it just looks like they're becoming men. Jawbones thickening, flanks meaning business. Cloven hunks of darkening hair. I've still got that dog-eared picture-book. Smudges the size of my long-ago fingers.

All the men I've loved have looked like picture-book animals.

4.

Cream at the top of the morning bottle, a cold blue plug of it in the glass neck. Sneaking it first from the grill by the letterbox. Using a thumb to pick off the foil. A tongue in the chamber to dislodge silky gulps.

5.

Cock, let's be honest. Its girth and pump. The pulse at its base, the pearl at its tip. The liquid bang of it so deep up in your body it can get to your memories.

6.

My mother's books. *Forever Amber.* Hollywood everything: men, stars, wives. Long, slow soft-back historical fucks. Whalebone foreplay. Highrise treachery. Dusk with a stalk of cut-throat cowboys. Flutter of so many skirts to get a finger inside you. Jerking yourself through the fineprint. Sessions of moonlit clitoris so hard you break the stories at their spine.

7.

Things left over from my snakeskin father. Spider amp with a splintered head. Samples of misted paraphernalia. Double-jointed cigarette case. Bulldog buckle of a belt. Leathers you could zip the sleeves off. Long ride through the hanging stash at the back of the cupboard to get to any of it. A battle with the boxed-in shadows that took days.

8.

Anything my brother owned. Clicking baggie of lizard-eyed marbles. Wheel of death with its pink-eyed mouse. Double happies, their palm-sized racks. Backyard sizzle of contraband gunpowder. The chucks on his Godproof skateboard, oiled with blood. His scabbed knees, bronze-capped, cracking heroically.

9.
Sick days off school, watching soap opera. Wiping snot on the velvet couch. Screen full of episodic blondes; stand-offs with fake-tanned Italian rivals. Dozing to *Days of Our Lives* violins, while my mother filed her nails. Homework, punctuated with pills.

10.
One decent nurse to hold your ribs while you puke. One decent nurse who talks like an overdose is something that's visited, legitimate as cancer. One decent nurse who uses her breaktime to plait your hair. Her pinkies in your cold sweat. A tight French weave that pulls at your scalp like cleanliness. The kind of nurse who's next to mercy.

11.
Anywhere, needle dig. Alley, stall, backroom. Brother's house, his three kids with Disney laughter out in the lounge. Let it go. Anywhere. The beauty of the tied-off vein.

12.
Swings of the girl next door. Oat cookies her mother gave us, tutting, still hot. Sky high, levering up with our piston-shins, trying to be the first one to wind full circle. Legs of the metal frame lifting with our screams. Letting the chains drop, with slackening ankles. Damp grass brush of gathering dusk. Pulse on the plastic seat where your lips long to piss.

13.
Relief of it coming, that thin beloved flood. Rise of longed-for spinal oblivion. A tourniquet round your consciousness.

14.
Tingle of medicine, hitched from your mother's dresser, tipped from its vial. Peach screw-tops. Pearly bracelet whose plastic band seals with a clip. The hospital type of her maiden name. Dosage of secrets. Arranged on your lifeline. Countable. Loveline. Each blue seed, with its fineprint stamped in an ideogram. Keep out of delicate reach.

15.
That moment when they're turning. Turning into tunnels, turning into lies, turning into animals.

16.
Deathwish pashing, way past curfew. Parked up with any boy, just for the grip and sweat. The feel of your fresh cunt under school uniform. So wet and hungry in its pleats. The not-yet dates, the brinks you bring each other to. Risky edges of shoreline and zip. Headlit wavebreak and leverage on vinyl. Taste of your first saltwater hard-on. Or just kissing clothed till your tongue felt bloodshot. Necking under streetlight till your vertebrae ached. Murmurs of chapstick, and lovebites glowing for days.

17.
Boy that first hooked you. Room above the servo. Forecourt of citizens in dirty light. Mint-flannelette-and-camo sleeping-bag on his single. He pumps you to a petrol soundtrack. Pizza boxes under the wire-wove, kisses composted with capsicum.

Bedside louvres winched open to blow out B&H. Late-night mutters of secrets and grease. Nutty crewcut smell of his pillows, feathers browned and bruised by his scalp. Minutes the gear has dumped his head there. Helpless Elysium in his blink. Beg.

Because he's got something money can buy.

18.
Pink cash register I had as a kid. Tinkerbell ping of its plastic tray. Play money fished from the Lucky Dip: head down into the mysteries of sawdust. High-rolling ragdolls shopping with courtesy. Hairclips and knucklebones for small change.

19.
Other ways you can earn what you need. Reliable. Skin to pimp, not yet too pitted. Easy, quick jobs up your secondhand skirt. Hallways with fingers, face-down in hatchbacks. Small-change convenience fucks in neon. Bargain on all fours, sweet moans optional. *Oh yeah baby, give it to me.* Budget pussy. Wipe-clean mind.

20.
The way, if you sleep on his pillow, your hair will slipknot the smell of him for the next day. You stand at the bus stop, stroking your face with a tail of fermented loneliness. Oatmeal, Zippo, rancid fragrance.

21.
Teaching elastics to your brother's kids. Trading giggles, lashed at the ankles. Cola in tumblers and unicorn t-shirts. Little titties about to start. Patterns of diamond leap and snap. Jingle, jangle, cradle, bangle.

Until he finds your stash, and draws the line.

Pigtails' ricochet. Laughter cancelled. Backlash to the street, half-dressed, with your bag of no-good.

Let it go.

22.

Bubble in the level of my grandad's garage. Peephole in the metal with a neon bead. Testing every surface he nailed into sequence. Staring at the window for the slippery balance.

Scent of his lathed wood, spilling to the concrete in spirals.

Smoko: my grandmother calling. Squatting on their backsteps by the sweetpeas. Too-hot tea with a blue taste of her false teeth. Cupcakes levered from the tin that you can suck the crinkles off.

23.

See-through vinyl of the next IV. Any decent nurse to rig you to its trickling. Watching it rock like the only moon you want in the night ward. Monologue of metered silver drips.

24.

Room in the care home where your mother's forgotten. Forgotten you proved such a dead-loss girl. Days you can slouch on her corduroy cushions, breathing in her polaroids. Cold scent of Earl Grey and woollen rainbows. Every sixth blink a new *hello sweetheart*. Fresh, like her iris only just found you. Days she will grin and let you dose her, one for me, one for . . . Days you can rake her purse.

25.

Sanctuary of board-lined dives. Anonymous voices, good as graffiti. Blackbox hovels to lie in and spike.

Breaks in the rain. Weight of soaked clothes in the hush. Tar seal slid to black velvet. Plastic speckled in your pocket, and traffic in your iris – full of your next fix.

26.
Names I thought, as a kid, were beautiful. But proved deadly: Pearl Harbour. Watergate. Enola Gay. Orange Crush.
  Joy flakes. Heaven dust.

27.
Chapel we once drove to, on some beach. So stoned, I don't remember. Disused shed of God in tussock. Shell path to doors a good wind would unbolt. Standing, swaying, in the weathered aisle – where a bride would, if she wasn't a junkie. Love of my life shooting up in a pew. Gulls and veins on hallelujah. Chorus of scavengers outside chanting *him hymn him.*

28.
Circus tents. Their big blue and yellow, in crescents, like some kid crayoned them into place. Sawdust dimpled with scat and candyfloss. Lining up to force-feed clowns. Oil-drum mirrors that play with the bubble of your brain. Girls that dangle from the roof like death-defying birds. Their swoop and pivot into rhinestone cross-hairs. Silence for the next stunt, spot-lit, net-less. Bridled creatures pacing the glitter of their cages.

29.
Laundrette nights with no one to fucking judge. Lean back on the bald slat bench. Bleached world spilling through the ordered portals. Perpetual cycle of rinse, repeat. Powdery tokens that can't kill you. Automated whir of comfort. Scorch of super-dried sheets that crackle your eyelashes.

30.

Image you can't scrape away from your back-brain. The tankers on the forecourt are filling up the huge black vats that live beneath the concrete. He's in his jockeys, round back, inverted on the stairs, whose tread speaks the vowel sounds: alone. T-shirt half off, collaring one shoulder. His beautiful jailbird ribs are bared. Face upended in a chute of light. The last time you see him, he's gilt with diesel. Tankers are churning out their black load of sound. A breeze scans your hair but it's not his soul leaving: that bailed, hours back. The needle's intact; he's chambered it so good you can watch it give a quizzical bounce. You don't even flinch. There's foam in his final kiss.

ministry

The night feels amphetamine.

Top-speed laugh, razorcut hair. Her quicksilver way with a shot glass. Not an inkling of where she'll lead you next.

Past the long blue bandage of posters on a club wall, bassline strobe, alleyed blur. The ministry of vodka. Dancefloor wakening under the hounding of heels. Ions of her perfume, her irises. The beat doth magnify her pearly hair. Equivocal pixels of her face, under a glass marquee of sound.

In the stall, her touch comes like predestination. Her juice along your shirttails. Ceaseless, vagrant fingers. You want to bark with joy, nailing her. The happening of skin, so fast you feel your load-bearing heart.

Morning, you catch sight of her scars.

Her apartment is a slice of dirty city, a petrochemical smell. She's an unexpected child in sleep, tinted streetlight blue. Her hair lies flat, doesn't look CGI anymore. Flies on the sill, shift of her breath in faint decibels.

Wrists a pale slipway. Yesterdays thickening.

You can see through the vanished sutures to real throats of pain.

What else can you do. But dress.

And leave.

the best reasons

They make the very best decision, standing under the trees. They come to it together, trading the words in sad, rational sentences. It is a hot day, and while he is speaking she watches the neck of his blue shirt convert the words to sweat. He undoes two buttons to clear the right things from his throat. They list the givens, the necessities, so later they can't pick out whose final decision it is. Her heartbeat feels uphill. Her guilt agrees, mutual. He stares at the sandals that quarter her feet. She can't make her hands do anything definitive, but he can't reach out to take one – it's a touch he won't be able to stop. He tests a quick joke – they can catchup next at one of their funerals – but it's bitter, and their eyes can't meet, their skin on the brink. And when she writes about it later, she will think about putting in a scene where they can watch X or Y – the detail of a child howling at the topple of their ice cream to the concrete, the leftover cone poised stupidly near their scream like a fragile tooth-marked megaphone. A lone gull limping round a black mesh rubbish bin, dragging the gouge of a fishing-lined wing. An old couple spreading a moss-coloured blanket over the spongy park-bench slats, the doddery ritual of their stainless-steel thermos, so tepid and requited. But she won't be able to. She won't be able to take her eyes from the two of them, withheld, under all those trees. The leaves underfoot are a dark trance. She will listen to the names of his children. Recite the good points of her husband. Then they will turn and walk apart. They are reaching the best decision. The birds vote from the branches.

postcards are a thing of the past

#

This morning I squatted in the showerbox and shaved my snatch for my husband, the way I would have done for you.

So you can't say I'm not trying.

It would have seemed like redemption, except that my lips swelled. Like they were moaning at the contours of you. Remember, you once did the job for me, demanded to, pinned me back, and left me sleek and nicked. Then bent to kiss a tiny slip-up, hauling at my slathery hips, to get your laugh into the blood. I remember. I was tempted to reload my fist with complimentary soap and crouch in the memory for hours. Watch my ugly needs in stainless steel. Such a hot-blooded cowering. But when I travel with my husband, we've always got a timetable.

#

On the flight here, I didn't sit with my husband. Some booking glitch got us an in-flight divorce. The first thing I did was pick up my phone: but then I remembered, you didn't want to hear from me. I sat beside a little girl selected by the hostess to hand around the sweets, the ones you suckle for descent so the altitude doesn't get stuck in your eardrums. She wore a pink tiger t-shirt, with blond curls ponytailed, but a jackal face. She had a touchscreen baby PC, with games that ran on pink tracks, and her fingers triggered flowers and stars. Across the aisle, the rest of her family were strapped: dumber little sis, mother half-bothered to love the loud swaddled demands of a babe in arms, and father, sexily greying with long-haul exhaustion. The hostess made a special trip to brief them in the fitting of infant life-jackets, the recommended brace positions. Neither parent could muster more than a blink. The man who got the window seat by me was wild: he'd been stuck near the kid on his incoming flight too, and felt unable to make violent movie picks. The sound of the little girl winning over and over was glittery. I refused her stock of rainbow sweets when she skipped round. I thought about your reason, your daughter. I wished I could programme a bloody zoo to screen on the headrest in front of my seat, a reel of R18s. The attendant didn't like me, made a point of checking that I'd fastened my silver-buckled crotch for landing. We could hear the quarantined dogs barking from the hold, stress soiling their cages.

#

No one told me of the drone of marital fucking, the habitual understated rut of it.

The bedside lights here are like black trombones. They pull out from the headboard on steel concertinas, pitched low, as if ready to conduct a gynaecological exam. I could imagine what you'd get up to with them. Angle my hips back on the plush basin of the quilt, search me for sulky details.

But my husband, post a kind of dull coitus, is watching men hunt on the backblocks of TV. 'Well we went out and we found something,' one guy says, scratching back his plaid cap. 'Now we just got to shoot it.'

I lie here, breathing the vanished scent of your shirt.

No one told me the brace position for this.

#

We had a fried pile of fish today, bite-size, dumped on shells, a platter of withered scallops. It tasted like the estuary I used to swim as a kid, like seaweed, vinegar, chilled togs and snot. I had my first kiss there, under a bridge, and it tasted like that, with bubblegum mixed in, with a faint itch of the coconut that used to spritz the white cream of the school-issue Sally Lunns. I remember my pigtails catching on the sharp frills of shell that clung to the concrete, and a pincher coming at my demi-nipple until it hurt through my rubbery suit. I didn't like the boy. I just needed to be kissed. It was time. There was a troop of kids watching from the rails of the bridge, yelling us on. I rotated my head the way I'd seen on telly, and tried not to gag on the complicated seafood of his tongue.

I've been doing this a long time, it seems.

Subtext: I've only ever loved you.

#

Tonight the wet skin between my thighs only knows profanity. I've used all the sachets in the bathroom, leached out all the single-use tubes. I'm a slippery cocktail. My skin sounds gluttonous. Ylang ylang stroked into cavities, wheatgrass massaged over wide-open bone. Bergamot and neroli get me blossoming.

All this toxicology makes me miss you.

When I lie down the sheets will be foxed with me. There was an anti-theft notice slid into the pocket of the lush white bathrobe (a pair in bleached towelling with their arms tucked into each other like a cute origami hug): *I love it here. Please buy my twin in reception.* So I know everyone wants to steal a skin.

Come back. I've forgotten the terms of the standoff.

It would only take a short-lived kiss to flip me over and fuck me to the marrow.

#

I've never seen hills with such secret velvety creases, all this high-country pasture combed and moist. Clouds easing over them, into their mellow smoothness, glazing their curves with sky. In declivities, the unmoving slick of a lake: a single black swan, stillness. The slope and roll of everything golden green, like earth brushed into slow waves.

Or maybe that's just me.

#

I look like a slice of motel hell this morning. You wouldn't even recognise me. My vision is equal parts gin and mascara. There's hotel soap in my wedding ring. There's a married taste worn into the back of my mouth. The window of our last room had no vantage point. But this one is high-rise, a vast pan of glass over town. Late night, an epic stretch of lights changed the alleys, dressed all their grime in an optical shivering. I downed a whole bottle in front of it. My husband sat around for a while, in indecisive underwear, then opted to snooze. I wandered over once, held my face close to his snores: he smelled like yesterday. Then I just sat and stared at the glass in my grip, like there was a lot there to swallow. And out at the view, hoping something was zoned for demolition.

#

He's been enjoying the driving. Though we can only tune our rental car into shitty stations, retro radio that spits up lyrics where love 'cuts like a knife / but feels so right'. 'I hear the secrets that you keep / when you're talking in your sleep.'

That was today's pop offering. And somehow its corniness put him in a playful mood. He crooned along, with toots of cheesy sendup, underlining it in full disco delivery. 'Don't you know you're sleeping in the spotlight,' all jazz hands and loony tongue. But I didn't sing the harmony.

It's not like him to let his sombre outlook go on holiday. He even got an on-road semi. 'Touch it. Oh go on, just touch it.' But that particular traveller didn't last long. We got stuck behind a truck that read *Waste Management*, crawling the range with a streak of black leaking from its tail plate. Our windshield went gauzy with its hissing trail of filth. Pinned in its wake, he dropped gears, raked the wipers, yanked the steering wheel in a spasm of rage. 'They shouldn't be allowed to get away with it. Who the hell knows what the slime is belching out of that thing.'

But I was face-down, unzipping memory. Forgetting white lines, in your oncoming thrusts. Laughing at the brake jerks, filling my squeals with come.

There was a number on the waste truck to report it. I imagined it was mine. Or yours.

#

Let me tell you exactly how I wish you were here. Since you tell me that you're not jealous.

I wish you were here on the refit seventies carpet that is chic again, an asphalt pile with accents of tangelo and teal.

I wish you were here on the balcony that floats over tussock.

I wish you were here to tell the neighbours' kids to shut the fuck up with their jandals and Coke and happiness. I wish you were here to snarl harder when they gave you sass.

I wish you were here, exactly, on the long back zip that bisects my dress, your knuckles slipping and unco on the top hook and eye, always tricky since it washed kinky. I wish for the scent of your whispered cursewords at the base of my cervical spine. I wish when you finally mastered its teeth you breathed in, prolonging its metal reversal. I wish that shudder that comes from the graze of your thumb could never stop travelling me, scalp to tailbone.

I wish I could strip you back, here, where this green light is planetary, bare you in the sway of its globe, and get you to kiss me, my whole face, smearing off its legacy of lies and eyeshadow.

Then I wish you take me fast, wish your grip on my hips, a soundless monopoly so hard it blackens me.

But I guess: if you can't be with the one you love . . . then get on all-fours on the room-serviced bed.

#

Sun so sharp the mountains are cubist, black geometries cut from light.

We stop at a café boasting a kissing gate. Turns out that's nothing to do with valentines. It's just a basic contraption in rough board, hinged so it doesn't let in the animals.

The café's a crinkled villa set in a garden unruly with frilled and salty herbs. I take a Ladies' break in an old shearer's hut, gussied up with green gingham drapes. Antique washhouse utensils on the wall, copper cistern, oak toilet seat. Wood ironing board for a baby change-table, and calendar of carthorses hitched to a post. So all in all it's like taking a yesteryear piss.

The hut is big enough for us to bang around in. That's what I'd be doing with you. Wrangling you into the calico, while bumblebees doze into the weatherboards bombed with rosemary.

Every small town we drive through has a Coronation Hall. And at least one place where I would fuck you.

\#

Mountains thinking prehistoric thoughts. Sunlight all over their soft switchbacks. How does their altitude look so gentle? We, more than anyone, know they're not asleep.

The rub of sun on grass tips, windows open to pale gusts of heat.

My husband says, 'Just think of how far away we are from our lives.'

And then he says, 'I love you.'

\#

I'm going to the restaurant smelling like my own come, as the light in this hotel room is my five-star witness.

So it's fitting that the waitress in the backstreet joint I pick wears a t-shirt that reads *Hot Secret Shame*.

I chose it because it was the only place in town I could find that was promising (kind of) live music. The entertainment turns out to be a balding hippy, man of blues riffs and long cedar beads. All the songs are jangling synonyms for each other, one giddy-up verse, one lonelier chorus (because somewhere on his journey, peace and love got a little hurt by one ole California gal). After the bridge, he gives his braced harmonica a spurt, a growled choo-choo of irony. I clap because I love him. I clap more, and knock back Chardonnay. My husband has started counting.

And it's fine until the cover he plays that is just a muddy stomp and a chord progression aimed at your roots and the lyrics 'Come back baby, come back, come back to me'. I'm fine until he down-tunes for dirtier frets, and the howling starts in a minor key that makes you know that your soul is sitting in your gut just below where you shovelled your dinner, just above where your lover has been, a place he can't reach. And doesn't want to. Though the words won't ever change, 'Come back baby, come back to me.'

\#

Tonight at dinner, I must look encouraging because a man comes over to our table and bends down to me. He's pasty, kitted out in smart-casual, cosy tones I can see his wife packing for him. 'Tell me,' he says, 'where do the dancers go?' A gesture at the town, with a travelling salesman's hand. He wants the music of moving bodies: he blinks at me with a balding kind of hope. But I just shrug: 'Oh I'm a stranger.' And my husband heads back with my top-up, gives him a glare. This guy's not up to fighting territory.

It's a good question, though, don't you think. Tell me, where do the dancers go?

Back to their wives, in your case.

\#

Do you get road rage? Today, at the servo, my husband was steaming over two young dykes playing on the forecourt with the windscreen brush, as if they had all the time in the world. One flicked the other with foam while she was pumping the gas, and then had to fend the brush from a tackle. The reprise was cute, and not at all butch: they squealed and fondled in the counter attack, splashing suds up their camos. Their windscreen bubbled. They had matching black beads round their wrists and their biceps were glazed and beloved. I couldn't help smiling at the struggle (would that have been the same if one of them had a cock?). But my husband went straight to boiling point. Was about to thump the horn, when they panted to a final fizzy kiss, and slapped the brush back into the bucket.

I can't imagine road rage getting you. Taking the miles with a boner the way you do. The way you once let me watch you. Cruising the plains with your strokes on lazy repeat, highways ideal for in-car handling. You didn't even ask me to touch it. Just brought yourself to a hazy finish, dabbed with a rag that doubled for the windscreen, and sent me a self-sufficient pleasured grin.

Oh, my grubby unstoppable love.

#

There's a blue mine, suddenly, steppes of it, gouged in like an amphitheatre where nothing but death's showing. It's ruled out the ground in such rigid lines, each grey level scored so straight, descending to a brilliant azure trough. A pattern of orderly wounding. It forces a vast kind of silence upon you.

Did we cut to the plates, and really think they wouldn't twitch?

#

The bed is a lonely plateau. We are its only guests.

#

We book into another room that's been hoovered, semi-glossed a soporific shade. I'm so tired of what I'm here to mimic staring back at me from the practical furniture. But I still flip through the plastic-coated highlights, a swatch of prosaic reasons to stay and 'things to do' while in this stunted metropolis. Shortcuts to companionable fucking.

#

There was this island we always used to pass as kids, from the motorway, a fern-tangled hump. By the time we saw it we were deep into grizzling at the journey, the long vinyl miles filled with our whining, the backseat airless and crammed with shins and sweated out with peppermint singing. (The two things my mother always had in the car were a packet of Oddfellows and a list of jolly pass-the-time tunes. She'll be coming round the fucking mountain.) The island was a black dome in the mangroves, just a chunk of offcut clay topped with bush. But we imagined someone was living there. Made up stories as the island passed, pretended we could see the glint of a hut, a stab of tell-tale lamplight. Some runaway was in residence. Someone had stumbled out there, through the shallows, hid out, staked their claim to unauthorised twilight. Or two people, living rough on each other, wild skins sleeping out.

So: are we there yet?

#

Café today with zoo bars so you sit and feed up against the railings. (The dogs are barking in their cages at a cruising altitude of 10,000 feet.) There is snakeskin everywhere, the roar of plaster creatures, and bar leaners mottled with leopard print. A sticky buildup on the knowingly carnivorous menu, the tropics of plastic foliage. I chew and look at the people in a wall mural, bodies broken into bone and hide, so you can't tell them from animals as they fork and bend, beasts gliding through the edges of each other. Your eye thinks it's picked out a figure, but it's lost the scent.

Subtext: I want you. And I can't change my spots.

#

The pisser in this place looks like a wedding cake. Cushioned wallpaper of faux white leather, stamped with fat buttons, and stencilled with gold fleur-de-lis. Meringue of white nets gathered at the louvres. And a pull-chain toilet, porcelain handle still damp and swinging from the last in the cubicle.

Inside the stall, there's a full-length mirror where you can watch yourself urinating. I think about sending you a spread, white span of my flanks on the china, wet pink interruption. I've never even thought of taking photos before – I'm a collection of impulses that never crossed my mind. I shuck my jeans right off, line myself up in the gilt frame, tilting the cold of my pelvis. Swipe until the focus is a white square round my gash. It's turning purple under the spotlight. The nets above the cistern ruche with radiance, trim me like a dirty bride.

Then I just squat and cry.

#

Last night we stayed at a B&B, each room named after the iron flowers in the ceiling, roses, tulips, orchids torqued into colonial tin. We got Lily. My husband was unsettled by the high weathered storeys of the place, its latticing of cobwebs, its parched boards and spire. He hated Lily on sight, its cornflower quilt, its periwinkle window seat. The doll on the scotch chest, with her antique deathstare and chilled enamel limbs, made him expect a ghost. So I christened her Lily, teased him. (It was nearly like old times.) Every draught that whistled through the keyhole was her calling. She was lonely. She was jilted. Her ceramic nails were signalling. Supernatural drips oozed the jet lashes anchored to her eyes.

In the morning, he grunted from a good sleep, saying, 'Well Lily didn't come to visit.'

But I'm not so sure.

#

Then a dam settlement, vertical acres of concrete bolting back the water. Everything vacant, the bare range of worker's stone huts.

I want to stay in one of them. Teach you how we can't control this. Over me the dark eaves of your ribs.

#

We pull over at a junk store today. It's not even a town we stop in, just a fork in the road, clustered with a few shops – or hunches of building that used to trade, signs now snuffed and windows boarded up. Everything's mangy. In the store we step into – through the flak of insect blinds – the woman looks taken aback. She pats the beige tines of her spiral perm and blinks at us, as if she wasn't ready to receive. The tattoo that slithers down into her cleavage reads *Davey*.

Everything inside crawled here to die. Trinkets, doilies, taxidermy. Ice skates, swastikas.

I scratch at the odd vinyl, poster, souvenir, try not to release dust.

Then the woman springs to life, wags her hand over at me.

'I don't s'pose youse could let me use a cellphone. Mine's munted. And I need to call my man urgent.'

I know, of course, that my husband won't be budging. I can feel him stiffening instantly. But there's something about the woman's fried hair. I hand mine over. Her crimped tan grins at me. She's missing canines and her eyes are rolled with yesterday's kohl.

The conversation she has isn't long. But it isn't with a husband. My own has gone out to wait in the car, clipping the driver's door to mark his huff. I glide round the dim stands, feign speculation on brooches and tools. The woman's voice is greasy. She mutters at her cash box, hushed suppliant things. A whine of bargaining that tries to be sexy, plea and purr. Her fingers worry at the bra line of her stretch-lace top. He cuts the call off for her. The wattle of her throat keeps swallowing. She's too unglued to say thank you as she passes me my phone.

I buy a burnout top that reeks of BO, a civet acidity leeched into its velvet. And a black deathrock t-shirt, tattooed with cannibals, headed *Everything Up Louder*.

When I get back in the car, my husband's silent. He passes me the sanitizer, suggests I wipe 'that crackwhore' off the screen.

#

'That movie sounds terrible,' said the old bird at an adjacent café table today. 'It's about a concentration camp.' She tutted, like dirty historical laundry was the last thing she'd part with good money to see. They'd been on a peony talk, sat nibbling at their lamingtons and chattering about deadheading and fair climate. Now their shrilling had switched to the flicks they'd like to see. 'No,' the other one sucked on her dentures. 'Apparently there's quite a nice love story with it.'

This is how sick I am. If you loved me, I would take the apocalypse.

#

Someone else's waterline lingers round the bath, grey silt where another body sank. The spare blankets harbour the smell of flaking skin. The unconditioned air feels inhabited. Fingerprinted dust runs the tongues of the blinds. The lamps have given out, gooseneck.

My husband is calling reception, dressing them down about the lapse in hygiene. I don't know what he expects. This whole town has a chickenwire, plywood feel, a place of harsh luck, smelling of kerosene and one crammed schoolroom. We're privileged the door has a latch. But he's not wearing it: the stains of others. He booked a room for two only, he tells them, not three.

I stroke the tideline, feeling for the soot.

It's like you've been here before me.

#

Since it's silence you want between us, let me tell you what the silence is like here. You can taste the ice age in it. I'm standing in a piercing wind and letting myself be gusted by it. The cold is trying to howl me to my knees. There's a roadside of frozen light and a fleet of stripped trees, a long black arcadia. I don't know if I'm breathing. I don't want to love you. It's bleeding me out. But I can't find the tourniquet.

Clouds like spilt milk. Nothing to cry over.

#

A woman on television is telling us about her kilos of weight-loss. A woman on television is telling us about a miracle bleaching agent. A woman on television is describing the outfit her loved one was last seen in. A woman on television is having her face reset along deep butchered lines.

When we finally pick a channel it's a doco on long-distance romances that are getting to meet. It doesn't matter that their ages are way out of synch, that the brides are dialled from third-world cultures. Or that's what the stagey theme music wants us to think, stringing us along with flares of saccharine. Planes land, and there's a gate to bring flowers to, to bring the desperate bouncy logos on silver balloons, to bring handmade signs from ghetto cardboard that read *Welcome Home*. They clasp each other, and you feel that word *clasp*. 'I'm just happy he's not a ghost,' beams one woman.

How many kilos are there in a heart?

#

There's part of the lake where you can walk out on a tiny peninsula to a picnic table. The kind of lake where nothing's moving. The water and the sky one reflection of staleness.

We met at a river once, but you were so afraid of being seen you would barely talk to me. I remember there were flowers floating on the current, no doubt the victims of some dreamy kid. Frilly pink decapitations, spinning in the flow. I think we could hear the faint giggle of the girl who was drowning them, rippled by the trees.

They weren't marigolds, so not set adrift for a grief.

There should be marigolds here. You should die now. Set me free.

Just die, why don't you?

#

I've been sightseeing with my eyes closed. Until we get to the stone church. Then in the window of the Good Shepherd I'm an atrocity. There's an angel on a plinth wearing carved arcs of feather or petal or claw or armour. There's a rope across the altar, thick knots like a mooring, or a noose. Then just a window.

These mountains are enough for any Messiah.

On my left there's an old white woman trembling. On my right there's an Asian family. The man takes off his navy bandana and drives it, with thumb joints, round the salt of his eyes. His wife lays one hand on his crewcut, one finger tapping on his fontanel, like a bird's beak. When he doesn't stop, she fumbles at a baby, packed in her lap in a fat Antarctic pouch. She wobbles it onto his knees, and yanks off its bonnet, so his sobs thrum its fine black pigtails.

I think of your little girl.

And then I cry too. I don't know how – just my chest gets full of the glare and the landscape, and the stale gentleness of the hymn they're playing on a tape deck that says things like 'oh redeemer' and sings of wanting to be worthy, and the woman who puts down the mauve mohair purl of her knitting to pass me a psalm card as I'm leaving fans them like we're facing off over a hand of poker, and I see her faith and raise her the sound of the south wind shrieking, I see her sympathy and raise her my deranged heart, which won't give up your blasphemy in my life, and outside there's a thorn bush, black and spiked, like the barbarous alleys my blood goes down, cunt, scalp, thorax, every time I think of you.

My husband is touched by my sentimentality. Takes a photo of me on the stone steps. Still holding my little ticket to heaven.

\#

White lime town with black steel ornaments. We go to a phantasmagorical foundry, walk through working beasts of industrial dream. Spined dresses and shattered machines, the sound effects of nightmare piped. Metal arcana welded into creatures, shadows that clank with uncivilised promises. Steampunk headquarters aren't to my husband's taste. He stalks through the weird black garden ahead of me.

So he misses the door that invites you in, like Alice. *Open Me.* And I do. And it's not me that stretches or comes apart

245

inside. It is the entire cosmos. I'm standing on a thin silver walkway. And it hangs on an abyss that is mirrored blackness. Below, it plunges down, streaming to infinity; above, it races up into a nothingness that shrinks you to a quivering speck. And all is lit with the hover of stars that echo in endless panes of forever, radiant strands of grenade that set obliteration sparkling. It takes a while for the trick to sink in. Of course, it's just a mirror-lined room, narrow, a slightly outsized coffin, glinting surfaces warping the watching mind. The awe turns my gut over, almost makes me cling to the rail for the moments I believe my gangplank reels over sheer drop. Then my heartrate starts to get a kind of focus. I begin to see the cords on the stars, their calculated dangling.

I'm not on a brink. But then I see the bird. It's a fantail. And I know what it means to have one enter a room. I know that it brings death flicking, its tiny claws pinching at the ropes of the stars. It cannot be still. Its flitting is relentless. It tries to beat itself against the edges of the light. It can feel the black box, but its universe keeps vanishing beyond the borders where the mirrors meet and part. And I open the door, so a piece of the world can come back in to the frame, a thin window of the real enter the circuit. But of course, it's twinned, picked up in the infinity, and even if the bird can see it, there is only an endless corridor of false doors opened in its night.

So I seal the door closed on our panic again. And watch the bird circle in its beautiful insanity. Trapped forever inside the bars of its fall.

And I know I still love you.

Acknowledgements

Heartfelt thanks and infinite aroha to Michael Steven, Jack Ross, Bronwyn Lloyd and Catherine Chidgey, who gave their own precious writing time to be the first readers of this book. I can't say how much it means to have the love and friendship of such gifted writers.

Deepest thanks too, to those who generously gave me retreat time during the writing of this book: to Steve Braunias and *The Spinoff* for a Surrey Hotel residency; to the University of Waikato for time in the Michael King House; to Phillida Perry for an editing summer in the Bay of Plenty; and again, to my dear friends Bronwyn and Jack, for a backyard haven where the words always come home.

Many of these stories have received awards and been previously published in journals and anthologies; grateful acknowledgment is given to the judges and editors who made the following possible:

'25–13' won the Fish Short Story Prize 2020 and was published in *Fish Anthology 2020*.

if there is no shelter was runner up in the Bath Novella-in-Flash 2020 Award and was published by Ad Hoc Fiction.

'holding the torch' was commended in the *ABR* Elizabeth Jolley Short Story Prize 2019.

'three rides with my sister' was shortlisted for the Bath Flash Fiction Award 2019 and was published in *with one eye on the cows: Bath Flash Fiction Volume Four*.

'postcards are a thing of the past' won second place in *The Moth* Short Story Award 2018 and was published in *The Moth* and *The Irish Times*.

'stations of the end' was a finalist for the *Mslexia* Short Story Competition 2018 and was published in *Mslexia*.

'compact' was highly commended and 'the best reasons' and 'Never Tell Your Lover That His Wife Could Be Having an Affair' were longlisted in the Bath Flash Fiction Award 2018 and published in *things left and found by the side of the road: Bath Flash Fiction Volume Three*.

'I still hoped the photos would come out well' was shortlisted and 'I feel there's a young girl out there suffering' was longlisted in the Bath Flash Fiction Award 2017 and published in *The Lobsters Run Free: Bath Flash Fiction Volume Two*.

'some facts about her home town' was highly commended in the Manchester Fiction Prize 2017.

'dorm' was longlisted in the National Flash Fiction Day competition 2017 and published in *Flash Frontier* 2017.

'the receiver' was shortlisted in the Fish Short Story Prize 2016 and published in *The Radiance of the Short Story*, edited by Maurice A. Lee and Aaron Penn (University of Lisbon, 2019).

'god taught me to give up on people' was longlisted in the Fish Flash Fiction Prize 2016.

'Stage Three' was shortlisted for the Manchester Fiction Prize 2015 and published in *Influence and Confluence: East & West* and translated into German for *Lichtungen: Journal of Literature, Art and Criticism*.

'if found please return to' was published in *Landfall 240* and in *The Spinoff*.

'warpaint' was published by *ReadingRoom* in 2020.

'What You Don't Know' was the featured fiction in *Takahē 97*.

'fisheye' was published in *Bonsai: Best Small Stories from Aotearoa*, edited by Michelle Elvy, Frankie McMillan and James Norcliffe (Canterbury University Press, 2018).

'ladybirds' was published in *Landfall 233*.

'Cicada Motel' was published in *Sport 45*.